THE PURPOSE BREAKS

A Two Roads Home Novel

James G. Brown

COPYRIGHT © 2023 James G. Brown
ALL RIGHTS RESERVED
Paperback ISBN: 978-1-954481-06-0

Cover Art ©Tom Clark
http://tomclarkportraits.com

Cover graphics by Jackie Clark

Published by Bair Ink Books
Farmville, Virginia, USA
www.BairInk.com

This book is a work of fiction from the imagination of the author. Names, characters, locations, events and historical references are coincidental or used fictitiously.

Dedicated to Dr. Raymond A. Bailey (1921 – 1980).
My colleague and my friend.

PRAISE FOR
THE PURPOSE BREAKS

"I swallowed this book in one gulp – started in the morning and finished in the evening."

—Inesis Kiskis Vilnium, Lithuania

A pleasure to read. Well crafted with historical context and sense of place. I loved the astute observations of nature, the cycles of life in the Shenandoah, the vernacular of its people.

—Brian Levy, Washington D.C.

PRAISE FOR
TWO ROADS HOME

"I loved the book! I can't wait until the next installment!"

—Suzanne Talbot, New Hampshire

"Narrative rhythm is quick with good descriptions... Daily life details that allow us to quickly become immersed in local life."

—Lucia Frick, Ontario, Canada

ACKNOWLEDGMENTS

It's a far cry from experience and imagination to a tale well told. The extent to which I have succeeded in this endeavor is due in no small measure to the support and thoughtful comments of colleagues, friends and family members. Thank you.

"And what you thought you came for
Is only a shell, a husk of meaning
From which the purpose breaks only when it is fulfilled"

—T.S. Eliot, "Little Gidding"

CHAPTER 1

JULY 1977

UNITED STATES ARMY DISCIPLINARY BARRACKS
FORT LEAVENWORTH KANSAS

For ten years, the cadence of prison routine had been the only real measure of time for Private Gerald Fletcher. Three thousand six hundred and fifty days, each lived one clanging door, one breath of stale air, one tray of nondescript sustenance at a time. But one day his incarceration came to an end. The keeper gave his discharge papers a final once-over, nodded to the soldier guarding the South Gate, and Jerry stepped out into the morning sunlight.

When Gerald Fletcher Sr. recognized his son, the struggle between excitement and apprehension became evident in faltering footsteps as he moved toward him. Their anxious faces searched older versions of each other for clues with which to bridge the past and the present.

"Hey, young fella. You look pretty good."

"And you're looking alright yourself, for an old guy."

Their usual handshake didn't seem to be quite enough so, with some awkwardness, they managed a hug.

"Is there anything else you have to do now, or can we just leave?"

A shadow of uncertainty crossed Jerry's face, and he stood silent for a moment. The idea of doing something beyond the routine that had governed his life for so long was briefly overwhelming and he stared past his father toward the prison. The Army of his buddies in Second Squad, in Vietnam's central highlands, was a distant memory. The Army of these walls, these numbing routines, was a chronic illness for which the cure was at hand.

"No," he said finally. "Let's go."

He took a last look at the stone walls and walked away.

They had never been much for small talk. He and his father had always talked easily when there was something interesting to say but never just to break the silence. There was no need. Jerry had learned from their time hiking and camping together around the old home place on the Blue Ridge that silence could bond as well as any conversation. So, while nervousness triggered the occasional bit of idle commentary in the first hours of the drive, Gerald didn't ask questions in a show of concern for his son, and Jerry didn't feel obliged to entertain his father with a string of anecdotes from behind bars. It was enough that they were once again sharing the same space. Conversation was a privilege of that space, not a requirement.

"Does this have the new electronic ignition?" he asked at one point, nodding toward the engine compartment of Gerald's almost-new GMC pickup.

"Yeah. I guess you heard that Ford and GM made the switch this year. They let Chrysler work out the bugs and then jumped on board."

"That was one of the things we worked on in the automotive program. Big changes in disc brakes, too." The Certificate of Excellence he'd earned in the automotive service program lay crumpled somewhere in his kitbag. Jerry didn't place any value on the piece of paper, but the time he'd spent in the repair shop was as important to his survival in prison as his time in the yard.

Gerald nodded. "Sounds like you won't have any trouble getting up to speed with the new models."

They had agreed before Jerry's release that he would work in the family's auto repair shop in Flint Hill, at least until he decided what he wanted to do.

"No, I guess I'll do OK. At least I'm not worried about that."

The comment tailed off as though he had started to say something else, so Gerald waited.

"Not sure how the guys will take to having an ex-con in the shop, though."

The real question was how anyone would take to having an ex-con anywhere, but that was too much to lay on his old man.

"That won't be a problem," Gerald said bluntly, "and if anybody does have a problem with it, he's damn well gone."

He seldom swore and when Jerry glanced toward him his eyes were riveted on the road.

"You know, as fathers go, you'll do."

They stopped the first night at a motel just off I-70, somewhere east of St. Louis. The first thing they did was call home. With the long-distance charges and the motel surcharge, it was a short call, but that suited Jerry. There were tears and laughter enough to hold everyone until he got home. Gerald suggested they go out for a steak, but Jerry chose to have pizza delivered to their room instead.

"Extra cheese," he said, "and put some anchovies on it." It pleased him to be able to decide what he ate.

Gerald was tired from all the driving, and he turned in after a beer and three slices of the pizza. When he awoke the next morning, the bed next to his hadn't been slept in, and Jerry was not in the room. Trying not to worry, he dressed quickly and went outside.

On the far side of the parking area, his son was sitting in a lawn chair, turned so he could watch the sunrise.

"Good morning," he said. "It's going to be a good day."

Jerry did some of the driving on that second day. He'd have to renew his license when he got home but he wanted to at least get the feel of being behind the wheel again. Things happened faster than he remembered, but his instincts were still good and after an hour or so Gerald could relax enough to doze off. He woke up as they started to hit the traffic around Indianapolis. As casually as Gerald could, he asked, "Do you want me to take over now?"

"No. I got this," Jerry answered. But, by the time they had cleared the city he was more than ready to pull off at a rest stop and let his father take over.

The snack machines in a shelter next to the main building caught his attention. These units even accepted paper money. *What will they think of next?* He wondered. He bought them each a Snickers bar and a Coke and checked his change just to be sure.

Back on the road, the candy and the drink disappeared in the course of casual conversation, but then at one point Jerry said, "I guess this whole thing has been hard on Mom."

"Yeah, she worried about you a lot, that's true."

"That's the one part that I regret. The problems it caused you and her. But, you know, it wasn't something I did on a whim."

"I have to admit, I wondered about that. But about a year after you went to Leavenworth a letter arrived at the house from some church organization in North Carolina. When I saw the logo on the envelope, I figured they were just looking for money and nearly threw it out. But it was addressed by hand and had a real stamp on it, so I decided to at least open it first. Inside there was a note from some guy named Paul Anderson. Apparently, he knew you in Vietnam."

"That's right. He was a missionary in the village where I was assigned in the highlands. An OK sort."

"Well, he said some good things. But mostly he introduced another note that was enclosed, a hen-scratchy thing, hard to read, from some guy with a funny name."

"Was it Kpa?"

"Yeah, something like that."

"I'll be damned. He was the village chief, and we did OK together. In fact, he came to Bien Hua to testify at my court martial."

Jerry stared out the window in silence for a few moments, thinking about the man who had gone out of his way to introduce him to life in the central highlands.

"How come you never told me about the letter?" he asked.

"We figured your mail was intercepted and your phone calls were monitored, and we were afraid that there might be some fallout, either for you or for him, because he talked about that day."

Jerry didn't say anything so his father continued.

"Of course, we kept the letter for you, but I'm telling you about it now because it was a big help to your mother and me in understanding why you shot that guy. Yeah, we worried about you but, after we got that letter, it was about how you'd survive in prison, not what you did in Vietnam. That turned out to be just another reason to be proud of you."

When Jerry eventually turned to face his father, a tear had escaped and was tracking down his cheek.

"Thanks. I guess I owe you for those mountain genes."

It was looking like they'd make it home in good time on the third day but, as the hours and the miles slipped by, Jerry started to worry about the next round of greetings. All the stares, all the unasked questions, all the well-intentioned people who'd encourage him to just pick up where he left off. *What a joke.*

When they stopped for gas in Breezewood, he wandered up and down the aisles of the convenience store until his father grew tired of waiting. "Come on," he said. "We've got to hit the road."

Crossing the Potomac on I-81, Jerry said he needed to stop at the West Virginia Welcome Center to use the bathroom. An hour later, as they neared Front Royal, he said, "Listen, I'm going to need a decent pair of work boots. Can we stop at Stokes's on the way through Front Royal so I can pick up a pair before we head home? That'll save a trip later in the week."

Gerald was tired. Five days on the road to Kansas and back was enough and he was ready to be home. "Keep dragging your feet like this and no boots in the world will do you any good," he grumbled. After a moment, he said, "Sorry. What's going on?"

"It would suit me if we got home after dark," Jerry answered hesitantly.

That's all it took.

*****

The first couple of days on the job went better than Jerry had hoped. People didn't crowd around or push him for conversation as hard as he'd expected. Somebody must have given them the primer on ex-cons needing their space. *Wonder what else they talked about,* he thought and then remembered the briefing before his prison release.

"There's no way around you being a curiosity for everybody," the counsellor had said, "But most people will get back to their own lives in no time. The thing you have to watch out for is thinking that they are still focused on you, talking about you. That's called paranoia and it keeps a lot of guys from settling into perfectly healthy situations after they get out."

Of course, there was always somebody who was a dick about the whole thing. Like the gangly kid hired as a general gofer in the shop, who kept wanting to hear about shivs and bitches. But most of the guys had been with his father since before Jerry went to Vietnam and they were glad to have him back.

In the hall between the work bays and the lunchroom, there was an MIA/POW poster. Under POW someone had scrawled Jerry's name—a long time back, judging from the blurred and faded writing. One evening after everyone else had left for the day, he paused by the poster to take a closer look. When he saw the pattern of passing smudges around his name, he was glad no one else was around.

CHAPTER 2

JULY 1977

UNIVERSITY OF VIRGINIA
CHARLOTTESVILLE VIRGINIA

The man sitting on a bench in front of Monroe Hall that morning seemed out of place. David Williams was neither well-preserved, like the classical structures of Mr. Jefferson's university, nor young and purposeful like the students who hurried past. His veneer of respectability told of recent efforts to overcome a period of neglect. His straw-blond hair was uncombed but recently trimmed. His flannel shirt and wool slacks, thoughtfully chosen, complemented the tweed jacket resting over the back of the bench beside him.

"Mr. Williams?"

David looked up to see his former economics professor standing on the sidewalk in front of him.

"Yes, sir." He blinked and shook his head as he stood, bringing himself back into focus. "Good morning, Dr. MacFarlane! So nice to see you, sir! How are you?"

"I'm well, thank you. I thought that might be you sitting there."

David was grateful for the vagueness in Professor MacFarlane's remark. His appearance could have elicited a much more pointed observation. The battle with bourbon had finally started to go his way, but not without leaving damage that was going to take time to repair.

"I'm surprised you recognized me," he said. "It's been three years already, hasn't it?"

"Well, it's not every day I attend an out of state conference with one of my students and send him to work at the World Bank."

"No, and I must thank you once again. Your recommendation was a key factor in my being offered that position."

"And how is it going at that venerable institution? Are you traveling a lot?"

"Well, it went very well until a few months ago, sir, with lots of travel. But then I decided to, shall I say, retire."

"You're a little young to be retiring, Mr. Williams, even in the rarified atmosphere of high finance." MacFarlane's feigned subtlety invited an explanation.

"It's a long story, sir."

"I happen to like long stories. Would you care to join me at the faculty club for a cup of coffee?"

David hesitated for a moment and then decided to accept the invitation.

"That would be a pleasure," he replied, retrieving his jacket from the back of the bench.

"Tell me, what brings you to Charlottesville?"

"Well, my wife has moved back here, and we had some paperwork to take care of."

"That sounds like another piece of the story," MacFarlane observed. "And what brings you to Monroe Hall?"

"I guess in many ways it all started here. I was just reminiscing."

He didn't tell MacFarlane that the paperwork was a separation agreement, that he had been walking the streets most of the night, or that reminiscing meant trying to understand where things had gone wrong.

"Ah, the scene of the crime," MacFarlane sighed. "Many a tale begins in graduate school, Mr. Williams."

"It was a special time for me," David said, wistfully.

The older man's casual banter was working, and David felt at ease as they arrived at the faculty club and were shown to a couple of leather chairs by the windows in the main lounge.

"This is charming, isn't it?" David said as he took in the comfortable elegance of the room.

"Pavilion VII is the oldest of the original university buildings," MacFarlane replied.

"And to think that Jefferson also wrote a constitution and ran a country on the side."

"He did set the bar rather high, that's true," MacFarlane answered. "But lest we get carried away in our admiration, you'll recall that his life also included slaves and illicit love affairs."

With David's recently acquired ambivalence toward adultery, he wasn't pleased that MacFarlane put it in the same moral pigeonhole as slavery. His mind stumbled briefly over an intruding thought of the woman he had fallen in love with, and the stock list of accompanying questions: How was she? Where was she? Did she ever think of him?

David studied a portrait of the university's founder hanging nearby.

"There were some big contradictions in his life," he agreed, "He owned slaves even though his draft of the Declaration of Independence included the abolition of slavery. He promised his dying wife he'd never remarry but went on to have intimate affairs. Makes you wonder about the line between compromise and hypocrisy, doesn't it? And looking at the Declaration now it's hard to tell what reflects his own ambivalence and what had to be agreed to get thirteen signatures."

MacFarlane chuckled. "That's one of the reasons I recommended you to the Bank," he said. "You always asked the tough questions. Where did that come from anyhow?"

"I have no idea, other than making up for a late start, perhaps. Questions were out of the question when I was growing up."

"Ah, a churchgoing man, were you?"

"Yes, and my father's church at that."

"Hmm, double jeopardy. And did we manage to disavow you of the notion that there's always a right answer?"

"I guess not, although you and Dr. Dreyfus did your best. I did learn to peel back more layers than I used to. I learned to expect surprises under some of them, but I still have the idea that, at the end of the day, there's a right way and a wrong way."

"Somehow I suspect that brings us to your story," MacFarlane said as the coffee arrived.

David smiled without saying anything and watched as the waiter set the service items on a low table between them, together with a selection of pastries, and poured the first cups of coffee before withdrawing.

"So, tell me, what sort of questions would lead a man of your tender years to retire from the World Bank?"

MacFarlane poured cream into his coffee as he spoke, set the creamer back on the table and turned its handle toward David.

"I can tell you that the 'what' and the 'how' questions were really exciting at the Bank," David began. "Talk about a steep learning curve! And what an amazing setting to learn in—the people, the circumstances. I loved the challenge and the sense of discovery of the whole thing. And the purpose was something I could really buy into. Economic development, poverty reduction, international cooperation—meaningful, right? A hundred and fifteen countries working together for a common cause."

MacFarlane smiled at the excitement in David's voice as he described the project he had worked on in rural India and some of the men he'd worked with. His friendship with another project analyst, Ray Baker, came up for special mention.

"I met Dr. Baker at a conference at Ohio State several years ago," MacFarlane said. "He seemed to be a good sort, very highly regarded."

David decided there was no need to share the most recent chapter of his friendship with Ray, no need to admit how Ray had virtually carried him out of Blackie's bar and then seen him through the days of initial recovery from a serious bout of depression and alcohol. How he stayed nearby in the weeks and months that followed as David gradually got his feet under him again and learned to keep them there without his wife or his lover or a bottle.

He took a drink of his coffee and continued, "I felt like I was on the cutting edge of something important at the Bank. What's more, I seemed to fit in. They gave me more and more responsibility. I thought I had found my calling."

He paused again, and when he continued it was with some hesitation.

"Looking back now I'm embarrassed at how naïve I was. Nothing could be that simple, that straight forward. But honestly, Dr. MacFarlane, even when I started to realize that the answers to the 'who' and the 'why' questions weren't what I might have hoped, I still expected something that would be consistent with the Bank's objectives."

"You mean its stated objectives, I assume."

"Yes. And, of course, there's the rub. The closer I got to things, the more I realized that different players were using the Bank for different purposes. Six billion dollars a year. A honey pot like that draws a lot of bears."

MacFarlane gave him a knowing smile.

"The decision to cut the India project brought things into focus for me."

"But surely the management offered some rationale for that kind of a change. The Bank has been around too long to be considered fickle."

"I suppose. They kept talking about rationing limited resources, about using the money to support policy change. They said I needed to see the big picture. But, behind it all, what I smelled was career enhancement and big business, and I was left holding an almost-empty bag for the people who needed us. I kept thinking about the farmers we'd met in the districts, the kids with their flocks of sheep and goats, the women carrying water for hours every day. Those people needed our help."

David realized that he was leaning forward in his seat, his hands gripping the arms. He sat back and exhaled.

"Here's a topic for one of your seminars," he continued. "When is the Big Picture a legitimate consideration and when is it a diversion from what's really important?"

"There you go again with the $64,000 question."

"It's embarrassing to admit it, but I'm thirty years old and only now starting to see what I guess is reality."

"Santa Claus, the Easter Bunny, and now the World Bank. What's next?"

David winced, "That's a bit hard, but I guess I deserve it."

"Disillusionment is like the chicken pox, Mr. Williams. It hurts less when you're young. The issue isn't any particular symbol or paradigm. It's believing in something–anything–without taking a careful look at it. You're less inclined to that than most people, as I recall, but your experience at the Bank just illustrates that that kind of mental short-cut is dangerous anytime."

As he spoke, MacFarlane poured more coffee into David's cup and refilled his own.

"And as for you being late to catch on, don't kid yourself, my friend. Most Homo sapiens never escape the temptation to believe rather than think. It's just too easy to accept some prepackaged version of reality. And, if others share it, there's comfort and security in it, too."

After a pause, MacFarlane added, "But if you want to take the route of prepackaged reality, you'll have to kick this habit of asking questions. You can't have it both ways."

David snorted. "That's strange advice coming from a professor." After a moment, he added, "But I have to admit that some days a lobotomy looks like a pretty good option."

MacFarlane considered briefly whether that comment signaled something in David that he should be concerned about, then changed the subject.

"What turns you on, Mr. Williams?"

David glanced at him and winked lasciviously.

"No, not that. You can tell that part of your story to someone else."

"OK, let's see. One thing I can tell you it's not, is being somebody's worker bee, sent to pollinate clover one day and dandelions the next."

"That's a rather strong indictment of international development assistance, don't you think?" MacFarlane asked in a cautionary tone.

"There are good people working hard in development, of course, and they make a difference in millions of lives. But at times the whole process felt like a laudable distraction. We worry about sharing the leftovers, but we aren't allowed to challenge who's gets the main meal."

"And once again, you ask the big question. I'm beginning to wonder what the world is going to do with you."

David was thrown a little off balance by the idea that he might be the object of an action rather than the actor. After a moment, MacFarlane picked up again on the subject of David's interest.

"From the way your eyes lit up when you were telling me about the India project, I can guess that helping people is at least part of what drives you, people who've been dealt a poor hand."

"Yes, I guess that's right."

"The World Bank should have been a good fit for you, then, but maybe it just has too many stakeholders with different interests."

"Some I agreed with, others I didn't," David said, acknowledging the point.

"I understand that young people these days are into meditation. Do you meditate, Mr. Williams?"

David wondered at the apparent change of subject, but answered, "No, it's too close to praying to have much appeal for me."

"Well, whether that's true or not, I'm not going to let you ruin my analogy. I think what you need to do is change your mantra."

David glanced quizzically at MacFarlane.

"That's right. You need to get away from the notion of a right answer and begin to ask instead, 'What's the best answer under the circumstances?' If that question gets you to look at the circumstances as carefully as you do at the options, it will be worth it."

The two men looked at each other and smiled, David recognizing the value of what he had just heard and MacFarlane wondering if the idea would take hold.

"Come on, enough is enough," he said. "I'm lecturing. I'm sorry. It's a professional hazard. Have a Danish."

As they each worked on a pastry, MacFarlane said, "You mentioned earlier that your wife moved back to Charlottesville. Does that mean the honeymoon's over?"

"The honeymoon and the marriage," David replied.

"I'm sorry. Another victim of the Bank?"

"No. I can't blame the Bank for that. She wasn't impressed with the whole thing, but we were having difficulties before we went to Washington. That's part of what I meant when I said earlier that the story started here."

"Oh?" MacFarlane had an idea what was coming.

"Yes, it sounds lame to say we drifted apart. I guess it's more accurate to say that when I came to UVA I went chasing after new ideas and didn't notice that she wasn't coming along for the ride."

"I'm sorry, but it's something we see a lot when young couples come back to school."

"It's interesting, you know. When the dean had all the wives over for coffee and dessert one evening that first semester, he called the MBA the Divorce Degree. Turns out he was right."

MacFarlane grimaced. "Our dean has many strengths, but marketing isn't one of them."

David chuckled at MacFarlane's comment but continued with his own story. "Then, as the situation deteriorated on the domestic front, I finished things off by breaking the rules."

"That will usually do it, all right," MacFarlane commented. He hesitated for a moment, then said, "Since I've already crossed the line and asked about your personal life, I'm going to go ahead and make a recommendation."

"By all means, please. I admit to being lost these days."

"Now that you have a little space, take some time to get to know yourself. Make some decisions just for yourself."

Pursed lips hinted at the effort David needed to remain composed. "Thank you," he said simply. "I appreciate that."

"Never mind. I'll put the bill in the mail."

They both laughed quietly and looked out onto the Lawn to give the exchange a moment to settle where it would.

"So, tell me. What are you planning to do now?"

"I really have no idea," David answered. "It feels like I'm starting over."

"Cheer up. Starting over is nothing new. If Robert McNamara can go from prosecuting a war in South-East Asia as Secretary of Defense to leading the World Bank's assault on poverty, you can certainly find a new challenge."

David took some encouragement from the analogy but didn't say anything.

"I remember Peter, ah, Dr. Dreyfus," MacFarlane continued, "telling me one time that you did very well as a teaching assistant and that you seemed to enjoy it."

"You know, I was thinking about that this morning. There is something very real about the interaction between a teacher and a student."

"Well, make sure to peel a few more layers off that particular onion before you make any decisions," MacFarlane cautioned. "Anyhow, an acquaintance of mine tells me that Shenandoah College is looking for a lecturer in economics."

As David made his way back to Northern Virginia that afternoon, he reflected on his time as a teaching assistant. MacFarlane was right. He had enjoyed the experience. There was a sense of accomplishment in seeing the lights come on in a student's face. Perhaps he saw himself in that face, in that struggle, as his own view of the world had begun to take shape.

Only a few sparse furnishings remained in the Alexandria apartment, the tangible remnants of his failed attempt at marriage. He sat at an old oak desk that had survived the negotiations, took out pen and paper, and composed a letter of interest for the position at Shenandoah College.

CHAPTER 3

Memories of his time in the Blue Ridge Mountains had helped Jerry survive Leavenworth. He longed to be back among them now, and it didn't help that they called to him each morning as he crossed the yard from the house to the shop.

By Thursday of that first week, the mountains and the constant interaction with people in the shop had begun to take their toll and he arranged to take Friday off.

Up shortly after dawn, he had expected to slip quietly out of the house, but his mother was already in the kitchen. There was no way her boy was going off without a decent breakfast.

"No, Mother. No more pancakes, really," he said, after the second helping.

"Just this last one," she insisted, putting another on his plate and adding a sausage link. "You haven't been up there for a while. You'll need your strength."

"Huh. Home a week and you're ragging on me already," he grumbled, then, with a wink, added, "If you're going to be like that, how about another splash of coffee?"

In the alchemy of motherhood, his comment felt like a hug.

*****

The mountains did not welcome Jerry back with open arms. Every bit the neglected lover, they pouted and played hard to get, as if to punish him for having been gone so long. They hid behind the intervening years of growth and decay. They flaunted their new Park facilities, distracted him with new signs and confused him with new trails. But gradually they did take him back and by early afternoon he had begun to accept their new reality.

He wasn't happy about the freshly groomed trail that ushered hikers through Fletcher Hollow, but the chimney and hearth of the old home place were intact. Grandpa Jake's abandoned garden patch labored under an enormous crop of sumac and pokeweed, but the bees were happy. Flash floods and spring runoff had cut through the bank and drained the pool where, as a boy, his father used to draw the family's water, but the spring was still there, singing its random lullaby.

"It's good to be back," he said aloud, watching cloud shadows climb the slope of Old Rag Mountain and disappear to the far side.

A decade of changes in tree growth and ground cover gave him trouble locating the cave where he used to camp, but eventually he recognized nearby features and made his way up the slope to its overgrown entrance. Selectively, he cut the brush and saplings so he could access the cave without exposing it. *It could be worse,* he thought. *There could be a marked trail right to the entrance.*

Inside, any trace of human scent had long since ceased to discourage wildlife and there were signs of a variety of occupants that had lived in the cave since he was last here. If he planned to use it this winter, he might have to do some serious negotiating with the black bear that had apparently nested by the back wall last year. But that was for another time.

With the remnants of his old wood supply, he started a fire and used a branch to sweep out the scat and nesting material of the interim tenants. Brush clippings from the terrace freshened the smell of the place. By the time daylight had faded from the entrance there was a new supply of firewood in a stack against the wall and a solid bed of hot coals glowed in the fire pit. The cave was beginning to feel the way he remembered it.

Dinner was a can of Dinty Moore stew and some soda crackers, but no meal was ever prepared or consumed with more pleasure.

His mother had been right about the demands of the trail. As Jerry lay back on his bedroll fatigue settled over him accompanied by a collage of memories of his time in the cave. They were joined by strangely comfortable memories of the other space that had been the center of his existence for so long. In those nights at Leavenworth his cell had been his cave. Instead of a doe's whistle or the bark of a fox, the silence was broken by a snore or the sounds of a nightmare, but either way the disturbances were beyond a secure perimeter. As he drifted into the last stages of awareness, the two spaces merged. His bedroll and his bunk became one, and he fell into a deep sleep.

The cave floor proved to be a lot harder than Jerry remembered, leaving him stiff and sore the next morning as he relit the fire, made his coffee, and ate a few handfuls of granola.

He had no plans for the day, other than to wander along some of the old trails, maybe check out the deer population in his former hunting spots. But after walking for a couple of hours, he found himself looking down into Page County on the Shenandoah side of the ridge. The Guersten farm was down there somewhere, in the patchwork of fields and hedgerows. A little to the southwest, he remembered, not far from that switchback in the South Fork of the Shenandoah River. Karen would probably be in the egg room now, supervising the packing.

Karen Guersten had been his best friend. They had fallen in love and become part of each other's lives in those last months before he shipped out to Vietnam. She hated the war and, in her letters, she described the anti-war demonstrations that she participated in. He had mixed feelings about that—not about the war, but the demonstrations. To him they had seemed noisy, futile displays, scarcely more than a nuisance to the machinery of power that he imagined alternately amused and annoyed by such distractions.

But, after friendly fire killed his sergeant and two of his buddies, Jerry had said in one of his letters, "You can protest for both of us now."

Every time he remembered writing those words, his mind skipped ahead to the day another letter was delivered to his cell at Leavenworth. This one was from Joan, Karen's sister-in-law. Karen had gone with college friends to protest in Ohio—Kent, wherever the hell that was. When the Ohio National Guard opened fire on the demonstrators, she had been gravely wounded. He should never have encouraged her to protest. Without that letter maybe she wouldn't have gone to Kent State, wouldn't have become cannon fodder for weekend warriors and dipshit patriots. Jerry had anger enough to go around, with plenty left for himself, and for that note he had scribbled in a moment of self-pity.

Some months after her release from the hospital, a letter had arrived in Karen's own hand. *She must be getting better,* he'd thought. But the feeling of distance was even greater than when her sister-in-law had been her scribe. It was pleasant enough, as were the ones that followed, but all she ever said about herself was "I'm doing OK," or "Things are fine at this end." And she didn't ask about him beyond "How have you been?" or "I hope you're well." There was something mechanical, something alien, about it all, despite the conventional words.

Jerry had begun to suspect that her feelings toward him had changed. Did she disapprove of his actions in Vietnam? Had she found someone else? With each exchange her reply was longer in coming, its content even less personal. Then, after a couple of years, and without any formal acknowledgment, the correspondence had ceased.

Thinking about her, however, had not. Other than the bond to his family, she was the one connection in his world that had felt like part of himself.

Looking into the Valley this morning, he realized that he couldn't be this close to Karen and not at least try to see her. But just picking up the phone or walking up to her door was out of the question. He couldn't take the chance of learning face-to-face that his worst fears were true, so he settled on a different approach.

He worked his way back to the trailhead where he had left his vehicle and by early afternoon was headed toward the Valley. Karen lived on the poultry farm with her older brother, Ed, and his wife, Joan. Jerry knew that if he hung around town he'd see Ed sooner or later at the co-op or one of the other agricultural suppliers. If he could set up a chance encounter and get some feel for the way things were, he could either arrange to visit Karen, or just say goodbye and keep going.

His search consisted of sitting in the co-op parking lot and cruising slowly through Luray, then driving seven miles to Stanley to check out Reid's Exxon, where Ed had all his tire and equipment work done. When he had no luck, he'd swing back to Luray and start the cycle again.

On one of these rounds, he turned up a side street on the edge of Luray and pulled into the yard of a small frame house. He had another errand to take care of. After accompanying the occupant to a nearby shed, chatting amiably, he returned to the van carrying a brown paper bag. Back in the co-op parking lot, he took one of two mason jars from the bag, spun the top off and poured a splash of homemade whiskey into the coffee cup that he had kept handy in anticipation of the moment. The hundred-proof shine burned more than he remembered but, in a few moments, its familiar warmth began to radiate through him.

He gave up watching for Ed when the co-op closed for the day and headed back to the Park. Instead of hiking all the way back to the cave, he decided to spend the night at the Big Meadows campground. The summer camping season was winding down so the area wasn't crowded, and he found a site with no immediate neighbors. With its side doors open next to the firepit, the van his father had suggested he use this weekend began to feel like a decent camper. He decided to ask when he got back if he could continue to use it.

First thing the next morning, back in Luray, Jerry saw Ed get out of a pickup and head into the co-op. Nerves and what-ifs pinned him to the seat for a few moments, but he had worried too long about Karen not to seize this chance. He opened the van door, walked purposefully toward the store, and went in. Ed was at a counter at the rear of the store, probably ordering feed. Jerry moved to an aisle where they could seem to bump into each other when Ed headed back toward the front of the store.

"Ed?" he asked, as they passed in the aisle a couple of minutes later.

Ed looked up and a smile broke out as he reached for Jerry's hand.

"Well, I'll be damned. How are you, Jerry?"

"Oh, doing all right, thanks. A few changes since I last saw you, but here I am."

"It sure is good to see you again. You've been through more than one flavor of hell since the last time, haven't you?"

"I guess you could say so, yeah."

Ed decided not to comment on how much older Jerry looked.

"Are you back in the area now or just visiting?"

"Actually, I guess I'm still trying to figure that out. I'm working for my old man for the time being."

"I bet he's glad to have another good mechanic in the shop."

"Well, one he can boss around, anyhow!"

There were a few moments of awkwardness as they ran short of subjects they could raise instinctively. This close to Karen's world, Jerry's need to know about her grew by the moment, but all he dared say was, "How's the family?"

"They're all doing well. The kids have grown like weeds."

"I bet they have."

"Karly heads to UVA next fall. Can you believe it?"

"Hard to imagine."

"Joan's done a great job with them." Then, Ed changed gears and, in a quieter voice, continued, "As you probably know, Karen's had it rough."

"So I heard," Jerry answered, relieved that the subject was finally front and center.

"Why don't we head on out to the truck?" Ed had glanced around when he mentioned his sister, and Jerry recognized that the celebrity of her case was not something he wanted to feed if he could avoid it.

"Sure."

"Do you have stuff you need to pick up?"

"No, no. It's not important," Jerry said awkwardly. "I can come back later."

As they walked, Ed gave him an update on the poultry operation, finishing his answer to Jerry's question about feed prices as they reached the truck. Resting his forearms on the tailgate and propping one foot up on the trailer hitch, he was silent for a moment. Then he looked at Jerry.

"I'm not sure how much Joan has told you, or Karen herself," he began, "but physically she's pretty much recovered. If that slug had been a half inch more to the right, it would have killed her. Nasty scar on the side of her skull but the way she wears her hair now it doesn't even show. The stiffness and the limp I guess are permanent, and she has migraines fairly often, but otherwise she does OK."

Jerry heard himself say, "That's good news," but with the description of Karen's continued suffering, his anger flared like dead pine boughs, and he had to force himself to be silent for a moment for fear of blurting something out that would distract Ed from his account.

"She's been keeping the books for us the last several years, and managing the egg sales. I don't know what we'd do without her. In fact, she's up in Pennsylvania this week talking to our chick suppliers. Joan's with her, of course. She wouldn't have gone otherwise, but we hope the change of scenery… you never know."

Ed paused and Jerry could see that he was trying to pull a thought together.

"The real problem," he continued, "is that she's not the same person since she was shot. I mean, us Pennsylvania Germans have never been known as the life of the party, but Karen was always livelier than the rest of us. That's all gone. She does what's needed—her work, helping with the kids and so forth—but nothing seems to interest her. Sometimes when I talk to her it feels like she's somewhere else, not even listening to me, and other times she'll overreact to something I say and go off half-cocked."

"She's been through a lot," Jerry said, forcing himself to control the anger that burned as Ed spoke. "She's lucky to have you guys."

"We've done what we can but, after all this time, it seems like she's settled into a kind of withdrawal. That's hard to accept in someone who used to be so full of life."

Jerry spoke now, giving Ed time with his reflection. "When her letters got more—distant I guess is the word—part of me actually hoped that she was getting on with her life, maybe with somebody else. But I guess not."

"No, there's nobody else." Then, as if the pieces came together out of the blue, Ed said, "Hey, when are you coming by?"

"I don't know. Do you think I should?"

"Of course. Everyone would love to see you and, who knows? It can't hurt. They'll be back the middle of next week, so why don't you plan to come by for lunch next Saturday?"

They agreed to keep everything casual, not even to ask anyone's opinion. Ed would just announce that he had bumped into Jerry at the co-op and invited him for lunch.

As Ed drove out of the parking lot, Jerry was left with two problems: He had a week to kill before the agreed time of the visit, and he was right back where he didn't want to be with his fears about Karen. Well, almost. At least he knew there wasn't someone else in the picture. Picking up where they left off wasn't an option, but he wanted her back in his life.

CHAPTER 4

The want ad in the *Warren Sentinel* read "For rent: two-bedroom farmhouse and outbuildings on ten acres. Fenced. Small pond. Eight miles from Front Royal."

It turned out to be eight miles in the wrong direction as far as the commute to Winchester was concerned for Shenandoah College's new professor of economics, but David loved the little farm from the moment he saw it.

The white clapboard house was nestled into a hillside, arrayed with its barn and clutch of weathered sheds against the backdrop of the Blue Ridge. The mountains cradled the rolling farmland and woodlots of the Browntown Valley, as though awaiting the return of the lord of the manor, as they had two hundred years before. Browntown, originally the commercial center of the manor, was a quarter mile down the hill from the little farmhouse. Its grist mill and tannery were long gone but there was a cluster of houses, a general store, the requisite Baptist church, and a paved road leading back to Front Royal.

"If you were planning to have livestock," the agent said, "there could be a problem because the owner has given the haying rights to the Stones on the farm next door. You'd have no year-round pasture."

"That's not an issue for me. No plans for livestock," David replied, as he surveyed the large field in the direction the agent was pointing. In fact, it suited him just fine that someone else would be caring for the bulk of the property. "It looks like Mr. Stone will have a good second cut next month."

"Yes, it's been a good year for hay."

In a smaller field that sloped gently toward the house there were half a dozen fruit trees, several rows of berry canes, and a garden patch overgrown with weeds. If he got the place, he'd reclaim at least a corner of the plot for a fall garden of beans and greens.

Passing through a small iron gate, they made their way along a flagstone walk toward the front porch. As the agent proceeded to unlock the door, David surveyed the front yard, recognizing several stalwarts of the Virginia garden scene from walks with his former mother-in-law around the family home back in Rappahannock County. Azaleas, barberry, and holly bushes anchored the gardens that bounded a slightly overgrown lawn. Daisies, coneflowers, and an array of annuals provided the finishing touch. Someone had loved this space and it returned the sentiment now with a medley of color and fragrance that fostered a sense of well-being.

"OK, got it," said the agent, as though it was always a relief when the new-fangled lockbox system worked. "Welcome," he said, pushing the door open and standing to one side.

The house was a story-and-a-half, center-hall model, bedrooms upstairs, kitchen in the rear.

"It's one of the old Sears Catalogue designs," the agent said. "The materials would have been hauled up here by wagon from the rail depot in Front Royal sometime in the 1920s."

Woodstoves by the chimneys on both ends of the house, as well as in the kitchen, were clearly not just for decoration. But the house did have a full bathroom, hot water, and modern kitchen appliances. Floral paper covered most of the walls, between high base boards and heavy crown molding. David would have preferred plain painted walls but, with a little glue on the curled edges, the old paper would be fine. He couldn't imagine needing a formal dining room, but that room faced west, with a view of the front gardens—a good place to set up his study.

The agent could see that his client liked the property. In fact, David was already visualizing where he'd put his desk, and a big old easy chair for what he fantasized would be long hours of reading as he settled into the routine of a college professor.

"You know, the owners mentioned to me that they thought they might put this place on the market sometime in the future. Maybe they'd consider an option to purchase as part of the rental agreement."

Buying real estate was well down David's list of priorities, but the idea sat well with the comfort he felt as he walked around the grounds and the house.

"OK. That would be good, but I wouldn't make it a deal buster."

*****

David arranged his office hours around the morning class so he could have blocks of time in the afternoon to work on the garden patch and fix-up projects that were starting to make the little farm feel like home. There were always stops to be made at Ramsey's Hardware or Southern States in Front Royal, but he could generally count on getting into work clothes and being in the garden or up a ladder with several hours of daylight still ahead of him.

His commute from campus to Browntown took the same forty-five minutes as the bus ride of his past life, between the World Bank offices in DC. and his Alexandria apartment, but there the similarity ended. Sitting, or standing, on a crowded bus with his face in a book while someone else did the driving through bumper-to-bumper traffic was a far cry from his new drive through farmland and wooded foothills, with the choice of country music or religion on the radio.

By the second week, he had begun to get comfortable maneuvering the last eight miles along the winding Browntown Road, with its narrow shoulders and deep ditches. But he still reached for the brake pedal every time a vehicle suddenly appeared over a hill in the oncoming lane, always seeming to take more than its share of the road.

One afternoon, topping a rise near Browntown, he had to slow quickly. A pickup truck was stopped on the opposite side of the road, partly blocking the oncoming lane. The hood was up, and the driver was bent over the engine. David rolled down the window and came to a stop.

"Anything I can do to help?"

"Not unless you got a new water pump you can spare," the middle-aged man said, wiping his hands with a rag. "Tell you what, though. Maybe you could make a telephone call for me."

"Certainly. Let me pull over."

He nosed into a driveway a few yards up the road and walked back to the disabled pickup. There were half a dozen crates of freshly picked tomatoes in the back. Ripe, too, he noted, as the fruit exhaled in the afternoon sun.

The driver had taken paper and a pencil from the truck's visor and was writing a phone number to give to David.

"'Preciate your stoppin'," he said. "There's nobody at home just now, but this here's my neighbor's number, name o' Hildebrand. If you'd give him a call and tell him where I'm at, that'd be a big help."

"And do you think he'll be there?" David asked.

"If he ain't, I'm up shit's creek."

"Yes, this isn't a good load to be leaving out in the sun, is it?" David said, with as much sympathy as he could put in a simple statement to a stranger.

"No. There's never a good time for a truck to quit, but this is bad. The buyer at Casey's pays an extra five cents a pound for ripe 'maters, but if he sees any juice leakin' out o' the bottom of a box, he'll reject the whole load. In this sun I don't figure I got more'n two hours to get 'em into his cooler."

"That's tight even if Mr. Hildebrand is home," David said, but his mind was clearing the way for a different solution. "I'll tell you what. I'm just heading home to do a couple of chores this afternoon and none of them are urgent. Do you think those crates would fit in the back seat and the trunk of my Chevy?"

"Well, I believe they might, mister, but I couldn't ask you to do what you're suggestin'."

"You aren't. I'm offering!" David answered, with an extra touch of enthusiasm to convince the man that he was sincere. "I'm David Williams," he added, reaching out his hand.

"Bruckman. Dan Bruckman," the other man replied, taking David's hand in his calloused grip. "That's mighty generous of you and I guess I'll just be acceptin' your offer."

Ten minutes later, the pickup had a handkerchief tied to the door handle and David's Chevy was heading back to Front Royal, with Bruckman in the passenger seat and a length of baler twine holding the trunk lid down over boxes of tomatoes that wouldn't fit on the back seat.

"I seen your car in the village a couple times. Guess maybe you moved into the old place next to the Stones, then, did you?"

"That's right," David replied. "I started renting there last month. Where's your place?"

"I'm about a mile south of the village, on the Loop. We run a few cows and do the vegetables mostly. And I work at the rayon plant in town."

"That's quite a load. Do you ever get a day off?"

"Well. I'll put it to you this way. A day off is worth about the same as a water pump for that truck. Can't have both, and there always seems to be somethin' like that pump."

David shook his head sympathetically and changed subjects. "From what I see, a lot of people have vegetables and cows, like you. That's the basic pattern for farms in this area, is it?"

"Yeah, that and the orchards—apples mostly, and peaches. Everybody's got some and nobody's got much. Makes for problems when it comes to gettin' a decent price."

"And how's that?" In fact, it was the same pattern he'd seen among small farmers during his Peace Corps and World Bank days.

"Well, we pay top dollar for our piddlin' amounts of fertilizer or whatever in the spring and then the buyers complain about the nuisance of dealing with small lots like this here," he said, pointing toward the tomatoes on the back seat. "Then they offer us twenty five percent less than the price on the radio that morning."

"Do you think buying or selling together with other producers might make a difference?"

"Now you're soundin' like the county agent."

"How do you mean?"

"That 'work with other producers' thing. It rolls off his tongue as easy as a church hymn, but the only thing he's ever organized is a field day. It's not like everybody has a phone in their ear so as you can agree on stuff when you need to. They don't plant the same thing on the same schedule. They don't take care of things the same way..."

"I see what you mean."

"It'd be like herdin' cats to try to put a combined load of anything together around here."

But David couldn't help but think of the small farmer cooperatives he'd seen in India, and others that he knew of elsewhere that found ways to deal with exactly the same issues. Now, they were giving their members better prices and helping them invest some of the proceeds in their farms and in their communities.

Figuring he'd laid the previous subject to rest, Bruckman asked, "What line o' work you in?"

"Oh, I just started teaching at Shenandoah College up in Winchester."

"Interesting. If you don't mind my sayin', though, you got a bit of wear on your tires for somebody just startin' out."

"That's a fair comment," David laughed. "Actually, I worked overseas for a while, on economic development projects before I decided to teach."

"What's that, economic development?"

"Oh, it's a high fallutin' term for helping people make a better living."

"Huh. Could use some o' that around here."

CHAPTER 5

Jerry knew that Karen was more than ten years older than when he had last seen her. He knew she had been critically wounded at Kent State.

It was still a shock to watch the woman with pale complexion and drawn features move tentatively up the back steps into the kitchen, one shoulder a little lower than the other, one step a little shorter.

The wisps of hair that escaped her headband had once been the finishing touch to the portrait of a carefree spirit. Now, prematurely salted, they spoke of disinterest in a world she moved through but wasn't part of. He had to make a conscious effort to see past this stranger, to look for the woman he knew. When Karen turned toward him, he caught a brief glimpse of her, in eyes that no longer sparkled but were hers.

Ed and Joan watched, awkwardly, hopefully, from their places at the kitchen table.

"Well, well," Karen said with the makings of a smile. "There's someone I used to know. How are you, Jerry?"

He didn't say anything but moved toward her and, ignoring her hesitation, took her in his arms. He felt her arms close tentatively around him, her palms rest on his back. They were together again, and for a moment the pleasure of that fact eclipsed everything else.

Then, her arms settled to her sides. She raised her head from his shoulder and shifted her weight so that it would have been awkward to continue to hold her. When he released her, she stepped back.

"So, how have you been, Jerry?" she asked over her shoulder, as she made her way toward a cupboard. He might just as well have been the regular mailman back from vacation.

"Good. Well, as good as can be expected, I guess. How about you?"

"As good as can be expected, I guess." She took a glass from the cupboard, turned on the tap and poured herself a drink of water.

"It's been a long time, Karen. A lot has happened."

"Yes, a lot has happened."

She looked about the room, seemingly preoccupied. At a loss, Jerry glanced from Ed to Joan and back. This wasn't a conversation; it was a game of Pong. How had Ed put it? It was as if she wasn't there.

"Krug's truck was supposed to be here more than an hour ago," she said to no one in particular. "I've got twenty cases of eggs waiting for him and they're blocking the rest of the cooler."

"Would you like me to move them for you?" Jerry asked.

"No, thanks," she said. "He should be here any minute. They've got to be where he can get at them."

Joan had busied herself with lunch and now made a suggestion.

"Why don't we sit down and have a sandwich. We can watch for the truck while we eat."

"Thank you," Jerry said, as brightly as he could. "These fixin's look good."

After five minutes of conversation that amounted to, "have some of this," or, "try this," and "please pass the mustard…" they all had a sandwich and a scoop of potato salad on their plates. Joan began to tell Jerry about the kids and Ed chimed in with a chuckle about Karly's first driving lesson. Jerry was enjoying the company and the updates, but he couldn't shake the fact that Karen was sitting in silence beside him. She glanced back and forth between her watch and the window or looked about the room, but she left her sandwich and the conversation untouched. Then she put her napkin on the table and pushed back.

"You all carry on," she said pleasantly as she stood. "I'm going to take my sandwich to the packing shed. I don't want to miss that truck."

Jerry glanced at Ed who shook his head discreetly and then he watched as Karen disappeared down the steps.

They sat in silence until Joan said, "I'm sorry, Jerry. I know you wanted this to be different. We all wanted it to be different."

When he looked at her there were tears in his eyes and he made no attempt to hide them.

"They've destroyed her," he said, his voice cracking.

Joan reached across the table and rested her hand on his.

"I feel so helpless," he continued. "There must be something I can do. Tell me what I can do."

"We've felt that way for a long time," Ed replied. "But the doctors tell us that all we can do is keep her from any further stress—they call it 'trauma'—and encourage her to be active."

"Like a goddamned trained bear," Jerry snarled under his breath.

Joan stood up and signaled to him to follow her.

"I want to show you something," she said. He followed, hesitating momentarily when he realized that she was taking him into Karen's room. "It's alright. We won't touch anything, and she won't be back now until that truck has come and gone."

The room looked like something out of Good Housekeeping, in an article that could have been titled 'And Everything in its Place.' He stared for a long moment at the bed where they had made love before he left for jump school, then remembered he was with Joan and looked awkwardly away. She nodded toward a large bulletin board on the wall next to Karen's dresser. It was filled with newspaper and magazine clippings, articles, and photographs about the events of that day at Kent State and investigations in the years since.

"She never talks about Ohio," Joan said, "But look at this. She collected these clippings over the years and, even after all this time, I still notice new items… an anniversary, a memorial, a retrospective. Part of her still thinks about that day, about those people. It's like she's stuck there. No damned wonder, but if there was just some way for her to let it go, maybe—some kind of closure."

Jerry moved to the board and began reading some of the headlines.

"Thank You, National Guard… Mayor Praises Action of National Guard… More Should Have Been Killed…"

"Are these for real?" he asked.

"Yes, unfortunately. I guess you didn't get the coverage in Leavenworth, but you'd think the Guard had done the world a favor by opening fire on those kids. Look at that one about the Guard mail down in the right-hand corner."

Jerry read a highlighted sentence aloud: "The greatest volume of mail ever received by the Ohio National Guard showed support for the Guard's action by a fifteen-to-one margin."

"Can you believe that?" Joan asked. "And look at the one next to it. The President himself blamed the protestors."

Jerry read aloud the bold type at the top of Nixon's speech: "When dissent runs to violence, it invites tragedy. "

"The bastard," she hissed. "If they'd just been good little robots, none of this would have happened. I sometimes wonder if it's not only the shock of her injuries that has taken her away from us, but the shock of realizing how things actually work. If your view of the world gets shattered by that piece of metal just as much as your body did, how do you put it together again?"

As Joan spoke, Jerry continued to stare at the bulletin board and his eyes settled on a clipping with a picture of the Adjutant General of the Ohio National Guard: The caption read:

GUARD COMMANDER'S CLAIM OF SNIPER NOT SUBSTANTIATED

"What's this business about a sniper?" he asked.

"The Guard's top general called into a talk show that night and told people that his men had fired only after a sniper had shot at them. Makes a good story but there was never any evidence to support it. In fact, it contradicted what the guardsmen themselves had said. Even the FBI report said there was no sniper."

After his eyes wandered back over the board for a few moments, Jerry shook his head.

"I can't believe how fucked up—sorry—people were over this. They decide that some lieutenant and his dumb-ass platoon fighting in Vietnam are devils for shooting civilians at My Lai, but then they turn around and praise a bunch of weekend warriors for doing the same thing over here."

He turned to move toward the door and noticed the small record player on Karen's desk. Absent-mindedly, he reached to rotate the 45 sitting on the turntable and read its title: Subterranean Homesick Blues by Bob Dylan.

"I used to hear this a lot around base camp when I was with the 173rd outside Saigon," he said. "Not the brass's favorite song."

"Some evenings she plays that over and over," Joan said, reciting the lyrics. "'You don't need a weatherman to know which way the wind blows.' I don't know whether it comforts her or feeds some deep anger."

Rejoining Ed in the kitchen, they finished their lunch together, in tacit agreement to stick to small talk, to distance themselves, if only briefly, from a reality they could not resolve.

As he left the farm, Jerry stopped into the packing room to say goodbye to Karen. Her pleasantries were even more painful to him now, given what he'd seen of her life on that wall.

Casting about for some way to get beneath the protective surface, he had an idea. "Hey, Karen. How about we go for a hike sometime? Maybe a picnic at Lewis Spring Falls. You liked it there, remember?"

"Oh, I don't think so. I have a lot to do around here these days."

"I'm sure Ed and Joan would be happy to cover for you for a few hours."

"I know, but they have a lot to do, too." She began to rearrange some papers on the top of the small desk where she sat, and Jerry leaned over the desk and put his hand on hers.

"Karen, I've missed you and I'd really like to spend some time with you again. Come on a picnic with me."

She pulled her hand from under his and looked about the room, a hint of panic in her movement.

"That's a nice idea," she said absently, "But I shouldn't, really. I shouldn't leave my work."

"Promise me you'll think about it," he said, stepping back from the desk. She nodded but still did not look at him. The conversation wasn't going any further, so he turned slowly toward the door.

"OK, take care," he said lamely.

"Thank you. It was nice to see you, Jerry."

It was all he could do not to drive his fist into the side of the van as he approached it. Not only had Karen been reduced to an anxious shadow of her former self, but the people who did this to her had reveled in their self-righteousness. His mind wandered back over the bulletin board, to the picture of the Guard's commanding general and, for the first time in many years, he saw something else: the crosshairs of his rifle telescope began to appear over the image. Gradually an idea took shape. If the general wanted a sniper, maybe there should be a sniper.

CHAPTER 6

The cheapest gas in the area was at an independent service station in Front Royal so David generally planned his refills around a stop there. As he leaned against the fender one afternoon while the tank filled, his gaze settled on a Chevy van at the next island. They were a common sight on the road these days, but the driver of this one looked familiar. A dozen years had made some changes, but after a few moments he recognized his old high school classmate, Jerry Fletcher. His story, gleaned from talk around town on visits home, came rushing back. After living through so much, would Jerry even remember him?

When David's fill-up was complete, he paid the attendant and approached the van. "Jerry? Is that you?"

Fletcher looked at him, disoriented for a moment, and then said, "Hey, Preacher. Long time."

"Ah, you remember me. Yes, it has been a long time. And it's certainly been a while since anyone called me Preacher!" David strode over to him with his hand out. "How are you, Jerry?"

"I'm doing OK," Jerry said, wondering if he was beginning to sound like Karen, or if he'd always been this noncommittal toward people.

"How's the ankle?" he added, recalling the time he'd come across David after a hiking accident and helped him off the mountain.

"It's good, thanks. I've put a few miles on it since then. But none of those miles were as tough as yours."

Jerry smiled and said nothing.

"I must say," David continued, "if the papers and the talk around town were anything like accurate, you wrote a pretty tough script for yourself."

"They probably got the details twisted up, but if they said I shot someone and then had a ten-year holiday courtesy of the government, they got the main points right."

David shook his head slowly. "I don't think anyone would ever be able to appreciate what you went through," he said, "but it doesn't take a genius to get the importance of what you did. My hat's off to you."

Something in the way he said it Jerry appreciated. None of the empty kinship that often went with salutes to valor.

"Well, some situations just need fixing," he said.

"I'll tell you a story sometime about a man on a bicycle." David was thinking of the schoolteacher in rural India who had bicycled over a hundred miles in the blazing South Asian heat to try to save his village. "The rest of us are lucky that some people have that courage."

"Most of the time it's a pain in the ass," Jerry said with a shrug. "What have you been up to yourself?"

"The quick-and-dirty version? I went to Tech, lived in the Philippines for a couple of years, got married, went to UVA, worked in India for a couple more, got divorced and lost my job."

"Hell, that's a trip, too. What are you doing now?"

"I'm kind of starting over, teaching at Shenandoah College and living in Browntown."

"That's nice country over on that side."

"Yeah, and close to our old stomping grounds. My place is less than half a mile from the Park."

Jerry was always on the lookout for another place to leave a vehicle when he went into the mountains, especially if a particular visit might include moonshine or venison. Avoiding any pattern to his movements was an important part of staying under the radar. So, he was pleased when David said, "Listen. I'm headed home now. Why don't you follow me and see where your gimpy hiking partner ended up?"

"All right, maybe I'll just do that."

David gave him directions in case they should get separated and they set off for Browntown.

*****

Stepping out of his van in front of the house twenty minutes later, Jerry looked around. "This is very nice," he said admiringly and followed David toward the barn. "And is that your garden?"

The plot behind the house didn't have a lot of produce in it, but it was weed free now, and the few remaining rows of greenery were neatly tended.

"Yeah. I got the place too late to do any summer gardening this year, but I've got greens finishing up and winter cress coming along—not bad for my first year, huh?"

"Not bad. How come the interest in the garden?"

"Well, I studied agriculture at Tech, but it started to become real for me when I worked with small farmers in the Philippines. Farming isn't just what those people did. It was part of who they were. They belonged, and they knew it."

Jerry pictured Grandpa Jake and his single-bottom plough back in Fletcher Hollow. It was the family's eviction, the government taking his land, that ultimately killed him. He thought of Y

Nur Kpa and his people in the central highlands of Vietnam, their dignity, and the rich spirit in their simple lives.

"I saw it in India, too," David continued. "Then when I moved here, I realized that the same reality exists right in our own neighborhood. You can do lots of other stuff, too, but it's the connection to the land that grounds you."

"I guess I can see that. So long as you don't have cows to milk at five o'clock every morning."

"I'm with you on that," David assured him. "No cows."

A quick tour of the house ended in the kitchen, where David took two bottles of Coke from the fridge, passed one to Jerry and led the way to a couple of lawn chairs outside the back door.

"Best seats in the house," he quipped as he passed the bottle opener to Jerry.

They sat in silence for a few moments, enjoying what the late afternoon light was doing to a tapestry of pines, bronzed oaks, and patches of bare poplar along the western slopes of the Ridge.

Then Jerry asked, "Did you and your old man ever make peace?"

"No, not really. I guess he resigned himself to my decision to go to college instead of becoming a preacher, but just to the point of being civilized when I went home for holidays. Then when things came unstuck with my marriage and my job last year, that basically did us in. I don't go over to that side much these days." He jutted his chin toward the Ridge. In fact, he'd only been home twice since moving back from DC, and they had been awkward visits.

"Too bad," Jerry said. "His loss."

"I think about that sometimes but, you know, my family was never really close growing up. The blood-and-water thing was true—still is—but most of the time there were too many rules and expectations for us to have the kind of closeness some families have.

After a few moments he added, "I call over there once in a while when I figure he won't be home, just to see how my mother is doing."

"I guess I'm lucky," Jerry said. "My old man rags on me sometimes but it's usually for something silly like cheering for the Cowboys, or something I deserve to be blasted for, like forgetting to lock the shop. And it's worth keeping the peace because my mother still makes the best pancakes in the county."

Jerry took a drink of his Coke. David looked out at the mountains and remembered his mother's raisin spice cake.

"So, are you living at home these days?" he asked.

"Yeah, 'til I figure out what I want to do," Jerry answered, in his head adding, *or 'til I shut down the goddamned Ohio National Guard.*"

"Maybe it's time you found some cute young thing and settled down," David suggested.

Jerry dismissed the subject with, "Yeah, sure," And in the brief silence that followed, the tumblers fell in David's memory. He suddenly recalled the big gossip on one of the trips home from Tech during his senior year. Jerry Fletcher's girlfriend had been shot at Kent State.

"Oh, man, I just remembered. What a total ass I am. I'm sorry, Jerry."

"No big deal," Jerry replied, trying to avoid being drawn into a conversation he had no taste for.

"Do you mind me asking how she is?"

"She's OK, I guess. Kind of keeps to herself these days."

It was clearly a subject he didn't want to pursue, so David didn't inquire further.

"And what about you?" Jerry asked. "Did you marry that Atkins girl?"

"Yes, I did. It didn't last, though."

"So, you're divorced now, you said. Do you have a new flame?"

"Yes, I am. And, hell, no!" David answered.

"OK. There's a story there, for sure. You haven't switched teams, have you?"

It took David a moment. "Oh, no," he said with conviction. "Nothing like that. I just made such a mess of my relationships with women that I don't want to risk it again. Letting someone rip out my intestines with a bale hook has lost its appeal, at least for now."

"Jesus. Put like that, I can understand," Jerry said with a grimace.

The fact that he might have been the cause of similar pain for the woman he had married was an inconvenience that David could ignore, as long as someone kept the conversation moving along, and Jerry rose to the occasion. Looking toward the base of the mountains he said, "You know, I think the fire road that leads up to the old Browntown trail across the Ridge is just off the end of your road."

"That's right," David answered. Nodding toward his bad ankle, he continued, "I don't do any serious hiking anymore but if you're in shape, it's only four or five hours to Flint Hill."

Jerry had his own memories of the area David was talking about; the switchback trail to the gap at Skyline Drive, the remote meadow on the eastern slope where he'd poached deer on more than one occasion, the branch of Jordan Hollow where Sam Kaiser had his still....

"Maybe I'll just take that walk one of these days," he said.

"Speaking of hiking, have you been back to the cave since you got home?" David asked.

David was the only person Jerry had ever revealed the cave to. Stuck on the mountain in bad weather back in high school, with David unable to walk, he'd taken him to the only nearby shelter he knew. But there was something of a sacred trust in that revelation, and he wasn't happy to have the cave tossed casually into the conversation.

"Yes, I have," he replied flatly.

David picked up on the insular silence surrounding the words. "I haven't forgotten your request," he said. "No one knows you helped me off the mountain and no one knows about the cave."

Jerry seemed more at ease as he answered, "I appreciate that."

"You know, you saved my ass up there," David said. "So just remember what I told you the day you left for Basic Training. If there's ever anything I can do…"

"Well, maybe I'll help myself to a few raspberries when I leave the van in your yard to go for that hike."

"Anytime. On both counts."

CHAPTER 7

The following Friday evening, Jerry was headed west again, back toward the Park, with a single mattress in the back of the van, a kerosene camp stove, and a wooden box for supplies. The cave would always be his home in the mountains but now it wasn't his only alternative to sleeping in the open.

He put the new set-up through its paces that night at the Big Meadows campground. After a shower and a hot breakfast the next morning, he was in the van again and, from the cassette player, Bob Dylan's energy and dissident lyrics set the tone as he left the Park.

Karen's bulletin board had set him to thinking about a gun more and more during the week —not any gun, but the sniper rifle he'd used in Vietnam. He'd seen the notice of a gun show at the Winchester armory and today he was going shopping. Were Garand M1Ds even available outside the military?

Browsing casually along a row of vendor displays an hour later, he heard a familiar voice coming from a couple of tables further down the aisle. The man was sitting with his back to him, talking with a couple of customers, and when that conversation ended, Jerry said, "Can't figure what a New York Italian is doin' in this neck of the woods."

John Ceruti, the team leader of his long-range reconnaissance patrol in Vietnam, stood and turned to face him, a broad smile on his face.

"Well, I'll be damned. If it isn't the marksman. How are you, recon?"

"Pretty good. How about yourself?"

"Hangin' in there, you know."

Their handshake was strong, and they held each other's grip as if to substitute for words that neither of them would have been comfortable expressing.

Jerry broke eye contact with a glance at the display table.

"This all your hardware?"

"Yeah, man. Nothing but the best. Ceruti Firearms at your service."

"You still sleep with your M-16 or did you get a better offer when you got home?"

"Well, things were different for us all when we got back, but let's just say my bed was warmer than yours."

"That wouldn't be hard," Jerry answered, acknowledging the sympathy in Ceruti's comment.

"There were a lot of guys really pissed at what happened to you, man. You got the shaft for doing what needed to be done."

"Well, I appreciate that," Jerry said, "but I'm sort of trying to put it all behind me these days. You know, a little hunting, a little fishing." Then he added with a wink, "A little warm bedding." It all sounded very normal and that was what he wanted.

"I hear ya, man."

"But really, you in the gun business full time?" Jerry asked.

"No. I couldn't escape my old man's machine shop completely, but this is a pretty demanding sideline. I do a dozen shows a year and work on some refits and restorations when I'm home."

"You're a busy man."

"Yeah, but you know how it is. I've got a good woman and two brats to put through college someday."

"Ceruti, the family man. Hard to believe, but that's great. I'm happy for you."

"How about you? Was it tough inside?"

"Once I got over being claustrophobic and powerless, you mean? It was numb, that's what it was."

Ceruti shook his head in silence as a surge of disgust and respect gradually receded.

"Anyhow, here I am," Jerry said. He locked his thumbs and waived his hands to indicate a pair of wings. "Free as a bird."

Recognizing the code for a change of subject, Ceruti asked, "What are you working at?"

"I'm back in the auto shop with my father, at least for now. It puts cash in my pocket, and living at home works fine—my mother's a great cook."

"Solid."

Casting about briefly for the next topic, Jerry asked, "Do you ever come across any of our buddies from Second Squad?"

"It's funny you should ask. We've never done any of the reunion stuff but a couple of months back I took some pistols to a show in Houston, and guess who showed up, just like you did today?"

"No idea."

"Butch Carter, the Alpha Team scout. You remember him?"

"Oh, yeah. Big quiet dude."

"That's the one."

"But wasn't he from Ohio?"

"That's right, but he was also from the steel industry and while you were killing time in Kansas and I was turning gun barrels in Brooklyn, the steel industry died, at least the big old mills like in Ohio and Pennsylvania."

"Sorry I missed it."

"Well, I guess his old man was some kind of big shot at one of the mills that closed in Cleveland, and he bought into a new smaller kind of mill in Texas. That's how Butch ended up working steel somewhere outside of Houston."

"And he just came to the gun show out of curiosity?"

"I guess so. Didn't buy anything, but we had a good visit and talked about mods to the M-16."

"I'm glad he's doing alright," Jerry commented. "He was an OK kind of guy."

"Oh, one other thing," Ceruti said. "He travels the Southwest for his work. He told me he did a little reconning on company time and found where Sergeant Douglas is buried. Outside some small town near Socorro, New Mexico. And he actually called on the widow one time in Albuquerque. Imagine that."

Jerry didn't respond immediately and Ceruti backed off. He knew Douglas and Fletcher had become close in the few months they were together in Vietnam, and when Douglas was killed, Jerry took it hard. Dropping the sergeant into the conversation no doubt brought back tough memories.

After a few moments, Jerry said, "Maybe I'll get that address from you sometime if you have it."

"Sure. And here's my card so you can write me and remind me."

Jerry slipped the business card into his wallet and took a deep breath to clear his head. Looking around the room, he asked, "Do guys at these shows ever carry military stuff?"

"What, you going to start an army?"

"No, nothing like that. I was just thinking back on those days and trying to remember what my old M1D felt like. It was a heavy son-of-a-bitch, but I remember thinking it would make a good long-range hunting rifle. If it was legal, of course."

"Man, you live in the land of the free, as in free to buy and sell anything. Garand M1s show up in these shows all the time. Just be careful that you're getting the real thing and not some retrofit with homemade parts."

"For now, I'd just like to see one again, maybe heft it a bit."

He needed Ceruti to think his interest was purely sentimental.

"Not sure if there are any here but you can leave word with some of the dealers and arrange to meet them at another show. Hell, I'll get you one for that matter. Ammo, too."

"No. No. That's not necessary. It's sort of idle curiosity."

"Your choice, Jerry, but I'd be happy to find you one. For you, no commission and guaranteed quality. For old time's sake."

"Maybe if I get serious I'll take you up on that."

"And ammo's no problem, either. Armor piercing or incendiary rounds, you name it."

"You're kidding, right? Jerry used shock to conceal his pleasure at what he was hearing. "Armor piercing? Incendiary? What the hell do people need that stuff for?"

"Usually just for messin' around but, hey, some of these survival types are planning for the worst."

"Is that what we fought for?"

"That's freedom for you," Ceruti shrugged. "Like a gun. It's not the thing that's right or wrong, it's the use."

"I hear you."

A customer had begun to show an interest in a pistol on Ceruti's table and Jerry took advantage of that to wind up their conversation. "I'd better let you take care of business."

"It's been good, man" Ceruti said, and a firm handshake and smile ended their visit.

Jerry's risk in asking about the M1D had paid off. He now knew he could get the weapon he wanted, even the ammo he had scarcely dared to hope for, and without any formalities. As a bonus, he'd also learned about Douglas's grave and his widow. It would be best to avoid any further contact with Ceruti.

Backing out of his parking space at the rear of the armory, he had to turn sharply to avoid the fenced area around a large propane tank. *Dangerous place to put that thing,* he thought.

As he pulled onto Route 540 and headed back down the valley, he began to accompany Bob Dylan on the cassette player and he heard himself singing, "Light yourself a candle…"

Operation Weatherman had begun to take shape.

CHAPTER 8

David spotted Dan Bruckman standing by the barbeque in his back yard with several other men. He started toward them, exchanging smiles with other guests as he went. At the general store the previous week, Bruckman had described this as a casual get-together for a beer and some barbeque, so he was surprised to see so many people.

Men stood around the yard in threes and fours, beer bottles in hand. Women chatted happily as they shuttled an array of covered dishes from the kitchen to tables in the yard. Several older ladies sat in folding chairs, carefully arranged for their own conversations while they oversaw the younger women's work with stern or approving glances and the occasional direct order. Youngsters ran about the yard, amusing themselves with makeshift games.

"Welcome, David," Bruckman called out. "Come on over and meet some of your neighbors." David approached the men looking in his direction, some pleasantly, some with indifference.

"Gents, this here's the guy who kept my 'maters from rottin' on the side of the road a couple weeks back."

The men's sun-leathered faces broke into smiles as David reached in turn for their extended hands. The calloused grip and tentative shake were the hallmarks of a country greeting.

"You shoulda left him there," one man said with a wink. "Maybe he'd learn and get a truck that runs."

"Never," another chipped in, introducing himself as Roger Atkins. "He's married to that old Ford."

David laughed with them. "Maybe I should just keep on going next time then!"

It was clear from the long-handled basting brush in Atkins' hand that he was in charge of the barbeque.

"Roger..." David wondered out loud. "Of course, "Jolly Roger." You have the barbeque set-up by the bridge in town on the weekends."

"Yeah, the wife and I try to put a few extra bucks in the coffee can that way."

"I guess that was her I met when I stopped by to pick up lunch a couple of weeks ago," David said. "Good ribs, I must say."

"You mean hers or the barbeque?" someone asked to general chuckles.

"Never mind them," Bruckman said. "They're all nuts, but they're harmless. Listen, there's Millers and Schaefers over in that wash tub." He pointed toward an old galvanized tub on the ground near the kitchen steps. "Help yourself. And Roger also brought some of that new Stroh's beer from Detroit, if you're of a mind to try it."

A television sat on a card table next to the beer tub, its snowy image catching just enough signal to keep die-hard fans up to the moment on the first game of the Redskins' regular season.

When he returned with a Coke there were some curious glances, but David just said, "I'm thirsty, so I thought I'd start out slow."

The chatting moved easily back and forth—a mix of local news, compliment, and complaint. A baler wasn't packing the hay tight enough. Somebody's son had been hired by VDOT after finishing up at the community college. The vet had preg-checked Dan's cows and two of them were still open, so they were headed for a change of career.

"Change of career?" David asked.

"In the cow business," Dan explained, "You're either a momma or you're meat."

The families gathered that afternoon were all small farm producers, and their talk frequently circled back to production and marketing issues. As David moved about the yard visiting with other guests, it occurred to him that Bruckman might not have dismissed his earlier comment about cooperation as lightly as it first seemed.

"Dan says you got some ideas to get better prices for our vegetables," one man said.

"So, you're the fella suggested we work together," said another. "Don't see how that'd work, really."

An older man, wearing a straw hat that had seen better days said, "Hear tell you're a cooperatives man."

Some of the comments had a cynical note, but for the most part there was just the normal mix of curiosity and skepticism toward anything new. He knew from his work in economic development that the greatest enemy of the poor was risk. These people might not see themselves as poor, but they surely had the risk aversion of those who couldn't afford to take chances.

"Well, there's nothing mysterious about it, really," David said at one point. "As you know, buyers like to deal with larger quantities, and they like to keep the costs down to assemble what they buy. As suppliers, if you work together to give them larger shipments of more uniform product, you can usually bargain to get some that advantage in the form of a higher price."

"Sounds too easy," someone said to a chorus of concurring grunts.

"You're right, but a lot depends on how far you go in the coordination," David said, matter-of-factly. "You could just make a few calls to friends during the week and put all your stuff in one truck. Or, at the other extreme, you could plant the same variety at the same time and manage the crop the same way."

"Huh!" a woman grumbled, just beyond the group. "I've got a life-sized picture of that happening with this bunch."

One of the men nudged the guy next to him. "That's what you get for marrying the smartest girl in the class."

"Well, as Dan pointed out to me," David continued, "It's not easy to coordinate production or harvesting. Putting together a combined shipment of anything is tricky."

Again, a wave of agreement.

"But the real payoff comes when you can standardize your production. You know, the same quality at the same time. Or when you can even agree with the buyer ahead of time and give him exactly what he wants."

The silence and spaced-out expressions told him he'd gone too far, so he backtracked to conclude.

"Of course, the idea would be to try something easier first, maybe like two or three of you putting together whatever's ready on the day you'd like to ship, sorting through it and dressing it up a bit. Or maybe some of you get together and set up a few tables somewhere in Front Royal on the weekend. You could take turns setting it up and manning it. There's lots of space where Roger has the barbeque, for example, and I imagine something like that would be good for both."

With those last comments people began talking among themselves, agreeing or disagreeing, coming up with their own interpretations, their own examples.

As David finished the last of his Coke, Dan Bruckman began to move through the group, carrying a mason jar and a tray of small glasses.

"Y'all are getting too serious. Time for a break. This here's the good stuff," he said and, looking at David, added, "It's imported."

"Really?" David asked, unable to reconcile the mason jar with a foreign origin.

"For sure," Roger said. "Dan had to go all the way to the next county for that whiskey." David laughed, happy to be included in this long-standing witticism.

"You've got kin over in Greene County, don't you, Dan?" Roger asked.

"Yeah. On my wife's side."

"Just as well, too," one of others chimed in. "Strangers still aren't welcome in some of them hollows back of Williams Fork."

Opinions on the moonshine's kick and discriminating discussion of its oak flavors displaced any further talk of farmers' cooperation. David put the glass to his nose several times and smiled in agreement with the comments but left the drink untouched. Excusing himself with a nod, he moved in the direction of another group, discreetly setting his glass down among some empties on a table as he passed. At last, the call came that everyone had been waiting for: "Food's ready!"

David assumed his suggestions would be lost in the wake of the afternoon's events, but two weeks later there was an array of tables in the vacant lot by the bridge in Front Royal, offering a variety of produce and homemade preserves. By the road, a freshly painted sign read "The Best of the Shenandoah."

CHAPTER 9

Jerry recognized the feel of the gun the moment he picked it up, not only its weight and balance but the subtle warmth of its walnut stock. As he raised it to the firing position the wood rested, gentle and familiar, against his cheek and the trigger guard nestled in his fingers. He could almost smell the vegetation of the central highlands.

"Brings back memories, does it?" the dealer asked.

"Yeah. Sort of like an old friend."

Jerry had done some homework since talking to Ceruti, so he knew what to look for when he came to the Hagerstown show. This gun was the real thing, complete with the original firing mechanism, the Springfield Armory stamp, and the same telescope he'd used in Vietnam.

"Well, if that's the case," the dealer suggested, "you ought to take her home."

"Oh, I don't know about that," Jerry shrugged, as if the idea had never crossed his mind. Holding the gun at arm's length to admire it, he asked, "Just out of curiosity, what kind of money would it take?"

"I'll tell you straight up, I've got three hundred dollars in this piece, what with cleaning and bluing and all, but there are several 'D's in the show this week and there seem to be a bunch around these days. They're not as nice as this piece, but I'll tell you what. Give me two seventy-five and it's yours."

"That sounds pretty good, but let me give it some thought," Jerry said, handing the weapon back to the dealer. "I'll go ahead and finish looking around and then come back and see you." With that, he started to move away but the dealer apparently needed to make the sale.

"Listen. Make it two fifty and she's yours, here and now."

It was a decent price, and he didn't want to make the transaction memorable in the dealer's mind, so he turned back with a smile and said, "OK, guess you sold a rifle."

There were gun shows most weekends within easy driving distance, so Jerry had no difficulty finding the special 30-06 ammunition he was looking for. Buying a few cartridges here and there, he avoided catching anyone's attention. To the dealers, he was just like a thousand other guys who picked up gung-ho stuff at the shows to play with in the back forty.

Within a month, he had three dozen armor piercing rounds and a couple dozen incendiary rounds—all the most accurate Denver Ordinance M2s—stashed in a wooden box in the back of the cave.

It wasn't hunting season yet, but hunters had begun to do some weekend shooting in preparation for opening day. So, when Jerry wanted to use the rifle, he would take back roads to an area where he knew hunters were welcome and leave the van in plain sight. The .30 caliber cartridges were common among hunters, so anyone hearing his weapon would just assume he was part of the seasonal incursion that came with living in the rural piedmont. They couldn't know that when he trained the rifle on his target, what he imagined wasn't game but a man's head, a particular man's head. And they couldn't know that he saw it as clearly as if the target were a photograph.

*****

The general in command on the Kent State campus the day of the shootings had since been promoted to Adjutant General of the Ohio National Guard. In the Governor's appointment speech, as reported in a clipping on Karen's wall, he had referred to the general's "heroic leadership on that difficult day."

Heroic leadership, my ass, Jerry thought. *A back-bench general playing Stonewall Jackson issues live ammunition to a bunch of weekend warriors. Then, when they decide to vent their anger at what they saw as punk demonstrators, he hides behind a story about a sniper.*

It galled him that a charade like that should be even remotely connected to the uniform that Sergeant Douglas and his buddies in Second Squad wore. Operation Weatherman was still just a vague idea, but he was going to sort this bastard out one way or another. *Let's see how he manages when the real thing comes calling.*

After work one day he picked up a five-gallon propane tank and filled it at the farm supply store in Marshall, where he was unlikely to be recognized. The larger tanks outside the armories were no doubt made of heavier steel, but this would do as a first experiment. He waited for a rainy day, drove to an abandoned quarry, and set the tank against a gravel bank.

With the first shot he learned two things: The armor piercing round went through the tank like butter; and there was no explosion. The sour smell of the escaping gas began to fill the quarry as he collected the cartridge shell and headed back down the dirt road. He wasn't concerned about the risk of a delayed fire at the site because everything was wet, and the continuing light rain was absorbing the gas quickly.

But why hadn't the tank exploded? He felt like an idiot when he realized his mistake. Of course! Propane, like gasoline, doesn't burn in liquid form. It only burns when it's a gas. So, another piece of his plan fell into place. It would take one round to rupture a tank and a separate incendiary round, a few seconds later, to ignite the escaping propane vapor.

Using a state map and the list of Guard armories, he located ten units within a six-hour drive of Flint Hill. In the next month he made two weekend trips to Eastern Ohio to get the lay of the land around them, noting vantage points for an attack and alternate routes to depart each area. He confirmed that above-ground propane tanks like the one he'd seen in the parking lot of the Winchester armory were virtually stock issue for all locations.

He got good at disconnecting the odometer on the van and carefully reconnecting it on his return so only a hundred miles or so would show after each trip—about what he'd put on over a typical weekend in the Park and the surrounding counties. He paid cash for everything and disposed of any receipts that weren't from stores around his usual haunts.

During the week he made extra efforts to appear to be settling into a normal life. He took most of his meals at the kitchen table with his parents. He stayed current on Redskins football and the fading chances of the O's to get past the American League Division Series. In the lunchroom at the shop, he argued vehemently over the choice of quarterback between Billy Kilmer and Sonny Jurgensen for the previous week's game or the proposal to introduce the Designated Hitter in the American League. But in most cases when someone proposed a weekend activity, he found a way to beg off. Operation Weatherman and keeping up a presence in the Park needed as many of those weekends as he could find.

"He's a bit of a loner, isn't he?" the shop gofer said one day.

The senior mechanic replied matter-of-factly, "Got the mountains in him."

CHAPTER 10

Teaching at the college and working with the farmers around Browntown had begun to restore a sense of purpose in David's life. Talking with Jerry, however, had reminded him of a loose end, and a few days later he called home.

"Well, hello there," his mother said in the quiet, tentative voice he knew so well. "How are you doing?"

"I'm fine. Busy, but doing fine. And how about you?" He always meant it as a sincere question, but he had learned a long time ago to expect his mother's ambivalent response.

"Oh, pretty good."

To some she may have come across as just choosing to stay under the radar, preferring not to trigger curiosity or judgment. In the congregation this might have been seen as modest reserve, but it was more than that. It was, in fact, an accurate reflection of the range of feelings Ruth allowed herself to experience. Joy and sorrow were two sides of a coin whose toss she was no longer willing to risk.

"So, the rest of the clan isn't driving you crazy, then?"

Ruth chuckled. "Oh, well, their big brother cleared a wide path for them." Her first-born held a special place in her heart, and mischievous comments like this were about as close as she would come to revealing it.

"Why, thank you. I'll take that as a compliment," David said cheerfully.

He went on to share a couple of anecdotes from his class and to ask in turn about each member of the family.

"And Dad?" he asked finally.

Ruth hesitated, "Well," she began, "he's having a difficult time these days."

David was immediately alert because it was unusual for her to signal a problem so clearly.

"What's going on?"

"I guess I don't really know. There's been some unhappiness in the church lately. Your father says it's the Devil's doing, trying to undermine the work of the Holy Spirit, but apparently Deacon Miller said something to him that was hard for him to accept."

"Like what?"

"Well, maybe that his business was beginning to interfere with his ministry."

"Ouch. What do you suppose he meant?"

"Word seems to have gotten out that he's having trouble making payments to a couple of subcontractors."

"That's not new, but he's always made good."

"It may be worse these days. I hear him pacing around the house in the middle of the night, and there have been some angry phone calls."

"The silly ass," David blurted out. "I told him years ago he needed to manage his cash flow better."

"David! Don't talk like that. He's your father." David held his tongue, and after a moment she continued. "Anyhow, Deacon Miller went on to say that some of the congregation thought that wasn't setting a very good example."

"That pompous bastard," David growled.

"Your language, child!"

"Miller's never known what it's like to have to make ends meet. Ask him which of his in-laws paid for that new tractor."

"Oh, David, please. That's a terrible thing to say. I knew I shouldn't have said anything to you."

"Of course you should have. Don't worry. I'm just letting off steam. So where do things stand with the church now?"

"A couple of the new families have left and there's a meeting of the Board this Thursday evening." She was silent for a few moments and then, trying to hold back tears, she said, "I'm afraid they're going to begin the search for a new pastor."

* * * * *

David knew the location of the little house in Front Royal that his father was currently renovating and decided to drop by the next afternoon. Maybe a bit of idle chat, a few smiles—he couldn't think of much he could actually do to help, but at least he could offer a show of support.

On his way back from Winchester the following day, he began to imagine how the conversation might go. His father would probably say he'd been rereading the Book of Job lately, that the Lord was testing him. If he could only get subcontractors to do what they say they will. If the city inspectors weren't completely unreasonable. As far as the church was concerned, Deacon Miller couldn't even see how he was being used as an instrument of the Devil. Then he'd conclude with something like, "Never mind, the Lord never gives us more than we can handle."

By the time David had turned off Main Street and headed toward the house, he was fuming over this imagined litany of excuses and rationalizations. He pulled to the curb and stopped short of where his father's Suburban was parked.

What the hell am I doing here? This is a no-win situation, he thought. *Either he's still his old self and we'll just be rehashing the old conversations, or he's really hurting and he'll think I'm there to gloat. There's nothing I can do. He won't listen anyway.*

David struck the steering wheel with the palm of his hand and, without looking at the house, turned back toward Main Street.

He didn't get far. The worry that had brought him here resurfaced and he couldn't just drive away. Muttering to himself, he pulled into the café next to his usual gas station, bought two coffees and a couple of glazed donuts and headed back toward the house.

James was there on his own when David walked in, framing a new interior wall. He greeted his son awkwardly, strangely unsure of himself.

"Welcome," he said. "This is a first, at least in a while." He pushed some two-by-fours to one side with his foot in a self-conscious gesture of tidying up. "What brings you up this way?"

"Just thought maybe I'd come by and say hi."

"Of course. Good." His father brushed sawdust from his shirt and pants and led the way toward the kitchen.

"I like how you're opening things up in here," David said, looking around, and then added, "There'll be more light as well as more space."

"That's the idea. The electricians were here earlier but I let them go to another job this afternoon."

Code, David thought, *for "they only work here now when they don't have a cash job."* He set the coffee and donuts on the unfinished counter and opened the bag.

"Cream and sugar, right?"

"Yes, thanks. That's great. You know, your brother came by yesterday."

"Two visits in two days: You'll never get any work done!" They laughed.

"And he had that new baby of his with him. Jacob's the cutest little fella."

"Maybe when he gets a little older, I'll become his 'Uncle Marvin' and tell him all sorts of stories his parents would rather he didn't hear."

James' brother was the black sheep of the family and his influence during David's teen years had been a source of concern. But that was all in the past and James didn't pick up on the comment. Instead, he smiled briefly and changed the subject.

"How's the teaching going?"

"OK, I guess. There are always some in the class who seem dead between the ears, but I'm trying to learn that that's not always my fault."

"How is it ever your fault? Teach truth and the rest is up to the Lord."

"Yeah, I know. 'And the truth shall set you free.'" He tried to keep the sarcasm out of his voice. "But try this: If you know the answer, you ain't heard the question.'"

"That doesn't make sense."

"For me it all has to do with peeling layers off the onion, Dad. The questions change with the layers, and I think teaching is about getting people to peel off more layers."

"That's interesting. I guess for secular subjects it makes sense."

David knew where it would lead, so he didn't challenge the line his father had drawn between the secular and the spiritual. Instead, trying to get back to how things were with his father without cornering him, he asked, "Are you happy with the way things are going on this job?"

"A few more headaches than usual," his father said, "but the same kind of thing with subcontractors and permits."

"The banes of your existence."

"For sure, and there's a new manager at my bank these days who doesn't understand the facts of life in this business. He's not as flexible as the last manager was on my line of credit."

David saw different facts of life in his father's comment and for a moment he was tempted to point them out. Instead, he took a sip of coffee and looked admiringly at the new skylights over the island.

"You've got a good eye for these old places," he said. "Too bad the business end of things is such a pain."

"You can say that again."

"And, with the church, I always thought you were taking on too much but, actually, maybe the church work helps you offset the stress of the construction work."

"That could be the selfish take on it, I guess, but the fact is that that's the work of the Lord. That's the most important thing I do."

"Yeah, I remember: "Where your treasure is, there will your heart be also."

"Ironic, isn't it?" James said. "It was the apostle Matthew who said that, and he was a tax collector before he followed Jesus. Just shows you no one is beyond redemption."

They both chuckled, but David was concerned that James might be reading his willingness to let religion into the conversation as a sign that he could be ready to return to the fold.

"You know, I pray for you every day," his father said.

"And believe it or not, Dad, I've done a bit of growing up and, in my own way, I pray for you every day, too."

"But the Bible says there's only one way to pray, Son, and that's in the name of Jesus."

"I don't mean to be insulting but that's very self-serving of the authors, don't you think?"

"God is the author. You know that."

"OK, it's self-serving of His representatives who wrote it down."

The conversation was going off the rails very quickly. David had to find a way to salvage the visit.

"Look, Dad, I know Christianity works. I know people can find fulfillment in the teachings of scripture. I've seen it. Hell, I've seen it in you." The profanity triggered a brief glance between them, but David continued, "It's just that I've seen that same fulfillment in the lives of people who took different paths."

"That's utter heresy and it saddens my heart to hear you say it."

There was an awkward silence as the two men realized that their conversation was over.

David drank the last of his coffee and said, "Listen, one reason I came by, actually, was to ask if you might be able to take on a small job for us, I mean for me and some growers around Browntown."

"I don't think so," his father said. "I'm very busy here."

"OK, but I'll just mention it. There's a shed that we'd like to use for grading and packing but it needs some work. We'd get the materials for you." Casually, almost as an afterthought, he added, "And the budget's already set aside."

James didn't need to know that David would be paying for the work. Scribbling the address of the Bruckman place on the bag the coffee and donuts had come in, he wished his father well and left.

Disappointment settled over him as he drove away. He hadn't managed the conversation well at all. Not only had he not been helpful, but he had added to the anxiety that dogged James' path between body and spirit. The last thing he wanted to do was upset the poor bastard. He'd only tried to let his father know that his changing view of the faith wasn't simply the result of apathy. Yet his father could not have reacted any other way. It was a bedrock tenet of his faith that Christ had said, "No man cometh unto the Father but by me."

Looking to salvage something from their visit, David reminded himself that at least he hadn't rubbed his views in his father's face. And he had made a practical offer that could help James financially, although there was no way he'd take the work on now. By the time he reached the main road out of town he had accepted that this was just the first difficult round of many if they were ever to find common ground.

*****

After class the next day, David knocked at the open door of the office next to his.

"Hey, David," the occupant said when he looked up and saw the newest member of the Shenandoah College faculty.

Jack Stockton was a criminology professor, and the twenty years he'd spent as a Special Agent with the FBI were good credentials for the job. But he'd gone that one better, completing a law degree at UVA after his FBI retirement. What's more, he continued to consult with the FBI on a part-time basis, making him a poster boy for the careers theme of the college's recruitment campaign.

As it turned out, none of that prevented him from being an agreeable, approachable colleague. The coffee pot on the window ledge behind his desk had been the excuse for several very pleasant exchanges since the semester began.

"Hi, Jack. I hope I'm not disturbing you."

"Not at all. Come on in. I was just grading mid-terms and wondering where some of these students were when we covered the material."

"You, too, huh? That's reassuring," David said as he took a chair opposite Stockton's desk. "I've wondered the same thing, and just assumed it was my poor teaching."

"Teaching is a humbling experience, isn't it? You think you're passing on information in a clear, orderly fashion and then you see the gobble-di-gook that comes back. Man, it's disturbing!"

They had a good laugh and then Stockton changed subjects. "So, how's life in the country suiting you after your high-octane existence in international development?"

"You know, I think it's going to be just fine. Actually, I grew up not too far from here, over in Rappahannock County. So my ten-mile drive to the grocery store these days is a piece of cake."

"That's right. You don't live in Winchester, do you? You're in some village in the Valley."

"Browntown, below Front Royal."

"What's the big draw there?"

"The scenery. And the farming."

"That's beyond me. My Philadelphia roots were stretched about as far as they would go when I went to law school in Charlottesville, and that's a college town! Hell, even here I have nightmares about Conestoga wagons!"

"Of course!" David recalled with a laugh. "That's right. They used to rumble down what's now Route 11 on their way west, didn't they? The Great Wagon Road. In fact, some of the people I'm working with in the Valley are Pennsylvania stock. Their people came to Virginia in those Conestogas."

"Working with?" Stockton asked.

"Yeah, it's turning out to be a sort of community thing. The farms around Browntown are all small mixed operations and I've been helping them organize their marketing."

"That's not too far off what you were doing in India, right?"

"I suppose. Anyhow, they're excited with the early results, and they're talking about formally organizing their efforts."

As the two men drank their coffee, Stockton offered some useful tips on organizing the growers under Virginia law and when their visit ended David said.

"Thanks very much, Jack. I think the Shenandoah Valley Small Farmers Cooperative is a step closer to becoming a reality."

*****

Two days later David stopped into the Bruckman place to take another look at the shed the group planned to renovate. His father's old Suburban was parked in the yard and James was standing on the loading dock, a tape measure in one hand, talking with Dan Bruckman. Apparently, the visit with his father had not ended as badly as he thought.

CHAPTER 11

Jerry's juggling act to keep up a normal work routine at the family garage during the week and reconnoiter Ohio Guard locations on weekends kept him busy, not to mention making sure that he was seen from time to time around the Park. But Karen was never far from his mind.

He tried to convince himself that she had been clear in her disinterest- that he had to let her go. But time and again he came back to the idea that maybe it was just the effects of the attack. If he could get through her defenses, he'd find the person she had been and the feelings she had for him. He was sure of one thing: it wouldn't happen without trying again. So, one day, when he was sure Karen would be in the packing shed, he called Joan.

"I've kind of been going crazy thinking about Karen," he began, not knowing any better way to fill the silence while he got his thoughts together.

"We love her, too, Jerry, so I know what you're talking about."

He'd have to think about that word later. For the moment, he pressed on with the makings of an idea.

"I was thinking that maybe if I got her to go for a hike with me... I asked her the day I went to lunch at your place, and she said she couldn't get away, but I thought I'd try again. Just a walk in the woods, you know? No serious talk or anything, but just some time on the trails. Maybe she'd see some things that she could remember feeling good about, things she could talk about without feeling..." he searched for the unfamiliar word. "...vulnerable. You know?"

"I see somebody's been doing his homework."

"It's a fuzzy subject," he continued, ignoring her comment, "but some of the ideas I've come across seem reasonable. Anyhow, I just wondered if it was worth a shot. What do you think?"

"I think it's a great idea. I don't know if she'll go and I wouldn't want to force her, but it's worth a try."

"Good. That's good," he said, relieved.

"Maybe there's something Ed and I can do to encourage her," she said. "We'll look at the schedule for the day you want to go and when she objects, we'll just list off the deliveries and the chores and who'll be covering for her."

"That's great. Thanks."

The following Saturday morning, Joan went down to the packing shed with a message for Karen.

"Jerry called a little while ago" she said. "He's going to come by."

"Oh? Any idea why?"

"I suspect it's because he wants to see you, silly."

Karen didn't answer but busied herself crating the last of the eggs from the washer.

"You know, he's called a couple of times to see how you are," Joan continued.

"Just tell him I'm fine. It's better that way. You know I'm not much for conversation."

"My guess is that he'd be happy just to spend a little time with you. You wouldn't have to make conversation."

"It makes me nervous to have anyone close to me. It's not necessary. And then, if people get upset, who knows? Maybe someone gets hurt. It's better just to stay in your own space."

It was unusual for Karen to talk this openly, and Joan was saddened by what she was hearing.

"What about Ed and me?" she objected. "We basically share the same space, and it works for us. In fact, I can't imagine not having him near me. He makes it for me."

"Yeah, but you guys are different. You're not normal."

"Everybody makes their own normal."

"Well, I like my normal the way it is."

Lines were being drawn, so Joan took a different approach.

"Do you remember when it was different, when he used to come calling before he went to Vietnam? You'd flit around the house getting ready, nervous as a wren. I don't think I've ever seen a bigger smile than yours when he came to the door."

The hint of a smile on Karen's face vanished as quickly as it appeared.

"I've done a lot of growing up since then." she said dismissively.

"What's happened since then is that you and your world were viciously attacked. You've done a lot of changing. Where you got the strength to recover, I'll never know." Joan knew she was treading on thin ice, but it had been so long since Karen had opened up that she felt she had to take a chance. "But I can't help but think that you lost something of yourself in the process."

"You think maybe I've lost something?" Karen asked incredulously. "You mean like the part of my skull I left in that parking lot? The part of my life I left in that ICU? You're goddamned right I lost something!"

"I'm sorry. Of course. I shouldn't have put it that way."

"But you know what I really lost? I lost the desire to give a shit. It died with the words and the faces on that wall in my room."

Joan was brought up short by the intensity, the bluntness of Karen's response. How clearly she had captured in those few words what life had become for her.

"We love you, Karen, and we'll do anything we can to make you safe and happy."

"I know that. I know that you guys made it possible for me to recover and start over. I just don't want you to think that we'll all wake up some day and things will be back to where they were. It's not going to happen."

"I see that now," Joan admitted. "It was absurd of us to think that it could after what you've been through." She paused. "But now I want you to do something for me. I happen to know that Jerry is going to ask you to go for a hike with him in the Park. I want you to go with him. You don't have to confide in him. You don't even have to talk for that matter. He'll understand."

Karen turned away and fidgeted absent-mindedly with some packing materials, but she didn't say anything.

"And who knows?" Joan continued. "With him nearby maybe you'll find that there are other things out there to enjoy. Maybe a different view of the Valley than you get from this window every day, maybe a breeze in the hollow. Maybe you'll find a puffball for us to fry for dinner."

"You make it sound harmless," Karen said, hesitantly. "Kind of nice, actually. Puffball's not my favorite but I know Ed likes it." Then, as if running through a mental checklist, she shook her head and said, "But I can't go. There are a couple of shipments going out this afternoon and I was going to start disinfecting the feed and water troughs before the new pullets are moved into House 4."

Joan was quick with an answer. "Never mind all that. We'll cover everything here. The place never ran this well before you came, but we got by, and we can certainly manage for an afternoon!"

Karen smiled a little reluctantly, and she didn't pull away when Joan gave her a quick hug before heading back toward the house.

That evening, as Jerry's van made its way back down the lane after dropping Karen off, she came into the kitchen carrying a bunch of wildflowers.

"No puffballs," she said, "but I thought these might be nice on the kitchen table."

*****

Since coming home from Leavenworth, Jerry had found it easy to fit back into the quiet evening routine of the Fletcher household. It suited him to sit down with his parents at the appointed hour, dig into his mother's hearty fare, and be part of the easy conversation that drifted through points of interest in their day. After the meal, he would take a copy of Field and Stream to his room or join his father in the den to watch TV.

Faith worried that her son didn't seem to have any social life or any interests outside the house. Nothing, that was, but those infernal mountains where he went every weekend. They were in his blood. Might just as well try to change the color of his eyes as break that connection. But why couldn't he meet some nice girl from a good family, maybe settle down somewhere in town, have a couple of kids? It was a standard-issue picture of happiness, she knew, and her son wasn't standard issue. But it was hard to imagine what might take its place and still make him happy.

Following the hike with Karen, Jerry was late getting back to Flint Hill. He rinsed his hands quickly in the sink by the back door, tossed the towel in the direction of its hook, and moved jauntily to the table where his mother and father had already begun the evening meal.

"Good evening, Mother," he said, leaning to kiss her cheek. "Dinner smells great."

"Good evening yourself," she replied, looking inquiringly at him.

"And what am I? Swiss cheese?" Gerald grumbled with makeshift indignation.

"You, too, Pops."

"You must have had a good day," Gerald said.

"What, can't a guy just be happy?"

"Happy, yeah, but the Cheshire Cat thing? That's a bit unusual."

"Ah, you old folks have just forgotten how beautiful an Indian Summer day can be around here."

"Maybe," Faith said, looking at Jerry coyly. "Or maybe there's something else in the mix."

Jerry ignored her comment and reached for the platter in the center of the table. "Pot roast, huh. Great! Pass the bread, please."

When supper was finished they moved off in their usual directions, but a few minutes later Jerry came back into the kitchen. Without saying anything, he picked up a dish towel and began to dry one of the plates that rested on the drain board.

"To what do I owe the assistance this evening?" Faith asked with a lilt.

"Oh, nothing. Just a bit restless, I guess. It really was a nice day on the mountain today."

"I'm sure it was. And who did you share it with?"

"What do you mean?"

She smiled as she sponged off the counter.

"I've never smelled that particular fragrance in your bathroom, and I don't think it's one you'd find in the men's section at the drug store."

"You always were one step ahead of me, weren't you?"

"Oh, no, it's just that I like to watch for signs that you're happy."

Jerry smiled and, after a moment, said, "I haven't given you a lot to work with in that department, have I?"

"No, that's true. But I'm not sure happiness will be an easy fix for you." She cut herself short, then added, "And stop trying to change the subject. This interrogation is not over."

"Oh, it's like that is it? OK. Her name is Karen, Karen Guersten."

"From over in the Valley then, is she?"

"Yeah. But how'd you know that? Do you know the family?"

"No, but being German, it was a safe guess."

"Her people have been on land south of Luray for generations. Her brother and his wife have a poultry operation. You'd like it."

The downside of her vision for his happiness was that it included another woman. In part to vent the twinge of jealousy and in part to tease him, she said, "Chicken litter isn't my favorite aroma."

"Yeah, but it sure can grow nice tomatoes," he parried.

"I assume, since you're speaking to your mother, that you are referring to the garden variety," she said with an air of propriety.

He winked at her. "Yes, ma'am. Of course."

"You're rotten," she exclaimed, and tossed the sponge at him.

There was a pleasant silence for a few moments as he put the plate in the cupboard and reached for another.

"That name has a familiar ring to it somehow. Have I met her?"

"She's a cousin of one of the guys in the shop. Maybe that's it."

"No, I don't think so."

"Well, I guess your memory's pretty good then. Her name was probably in the paper around these parts about eight years ago. She was shot at Kent State."

"Of course!" Faith said, "That's it. And where did you meet her?"

Somewhat hesitantly, Jerry answered, "We were seeing each other before I went to Nam."

"You mean you knew her when the shooting happened?"

He nodded and she suddenly felt the awful weight her son had been carrying for so long.

"She was your... Oh, Jerry. Dear Lord! Why didn't you tell us? I'm so sorry."

"Hey, Mum. Easy. I wasn't the one who was shot."

"Yes, I know, but that must have been horrible. What did you do? How on earth did you cope?"

He thought back to the morning in Leavenworth when he had received Joan's letter, back to the flood of anger and helplessness that had overtaken him, the rage as he stormed about his cell; the pain and confusion that filled him, body and mind, for days as he lay in solitary.

"It wasn't easy," was all he said.

"How is she now? Has she fully recovered?"

"She moves with a limp and has nasty migraines, but other than that she's physically OK."

"And emotionally?"

"Well, that's the problem. The whole thing really messed her up. She's not the same person. She doesn't trust anyone. She doesn't want to be around people unless it's like a customer or a delivery man or something."

"And what about you? Are you close to her again?"

"That's why I was so happy when I came home tonight. Today was the first time she treated me different than the mailman. We picked some wildflowers below Tanners Ridge. And when I took her home, she put her hand on my arm, and she said she'd had a good time. It was amazing, Mother. I got a glimpse of the old Karen."

Faith had tears in her eyes as she came over to him and put her arms through his. "My dear, dear boy," she said. "Where do you get your strength?"

He smiled at her, and his voice was gentle. "That's a silly question. I'm hugging the source of half of it. And the other half is sitting in the den!" Then he added, "Don't tell him, though. We don't want it going to his head."

She giggled despite herself and pushed her hand dismissively against his shoulder, but he drew her to him. This was a rare moment, to be sharing something important in his life with her. Yet he knew he could never tell her the whole story, his plans for the bastards who had hurt Karen.

"You're my main squeeze," he said reassuringly.

"No," Faith said, looking up at him. "I don't think I am anymore. But, you know, that's OK. It's good." She touched his cheek.

From the other room, Gerald called out, "Hey, you two. Archie Bunker's on."

CHAPTER 12

David didn't know whether to chuckle at Dan Bruckman's discomfort or feel sorry for him as they approached the Warren Bank building on Main Street. When they stopped near the entrance of the imposing Greek revival structure to wait for Roger Atkins, Bruckman continued to fidget, glancing about, and pulling at his shirt collar.

Mrs. Bruckman must have gone heavy on the starch, David thought. *After all, the newly elected chairman of the Shenandoah Valley Small Farmers Cooperative needed to look proper for his meeting with the manager of the bank. And from the hint of mothballs, it's been a while since he wore that jacket.*

But clothes weren't the main reason for Bruckman's discomfort. Until this morning, banking for him had consisted of standing in line at a teller's window. Being asked into the manager's office evoked the same instinctive fear as being called to the principal's office back in high school.

David tried to lighten the moment by nodding in the direction of the two Grecian nudes that reclined on the pediment above the doorway. "They were probably fully dressed when they got here," he speculated, "but they couldn't make their payments."

It didn't help.

When Roger Atkins arrived, the Executive Committee of the cooperative's Board of Directors was complete, and the men entered the bank. David led the way across the marble-floored chamber in the direction of a large corner office and they presented themselves to a woman at the nearest desk. More accurately, they came to a halt at an oak knee wall that separated her desk from people the bank insisted she refer to as clients. She wore her smile as though it was part of a mandatory dress code, and she used it sparingly.

"Good morning," David said. "We're from the Shenandoah Valley Small Farmers Cooperative. I believe we have an appointment with the manager, Mr. Jenkins."

The woman looked at them skeptically, then glanced at the appointment calendar on her desk.

"Ah, yes." Again, the conforming smile. "Are you Mr. Williams?"

"I am, with Mr. Bruckman and Mr. Atkins." She acknowledged the others with a quick appraisal and then said to David, "Mr. Jenkins is engaged at the moment. Please take a seat and I'll let him know you're here."

It sounded a bit like 'take a number' but the men smiled and moved to the nearby arrangement of chairs. *Apparently, the waiting routine is alive and well in Virginia, too,* David thought, recalling its practice as a fine art in his India days.

After a couple of minutes, Jenkins came out of his office and greeted his visitors with a generous smile. Holding a gate in the knee wall open with one hand for them to pass, he shook their hands with the other and directed them into his office. He wasn't from the Valley—Loudon County, David guessed from the accent—but he knew the routine. After enough small talk to conform to local etiquette they got down to the business at hand.

On David's recommendation, the cooperative had applied for a line of credit to bridge the gap between buying farm supplies at planting time and receiving payment for members' produce after harvest. Today's visit was to clarify some of the information the bank had been given, and to give the branch manager a chance to size up the men who would guide the enterprise.

As a new organization, the cooperative had little by way of assets or performance history, so the bank had also asked for financial background on the officers who now sat in Jenkins' office. The Bruckman and Atkins wives had no doubt been involved in providing that information, and David had shuddered at the thought of the conversations in the respective kitchens and bedrooms before that matter was settled. The mention of wives having any say in financial matters outside the home would have set tongues wagging in pews and corner stores for miles around, but woe betide any man who failed to pick up on the signals his wife had mastered to convey her view on decisions beyond her jurisdiction.

David determined before the meeting that he would encourage Bruckman and Atkins to handle as many of the questions as possible. Jenkins would see quickly that he was the force behind the financial control of the cooperative, but to get a feel for the business itself—the farming, the markets, the commitment to working together—he'd have to hear from the others.

Fortunately, Jenkins was good at his job. He didn't need to appear aloof to control the meeting or cynical to get the information he wanted, so a pleasant atmosphere developed during the interview and Bruckman and Atkins relaxed enough to give credible performances.

After half an hour or so, Jenkins expressed his satisfaction and, with a smile and a hint of ceremony, closed the file and said, "I think we should be able to get this to the loan committee for their meeting next week."

Outside the bank, David took his leave from the others and headed to Winchester for a session of his economics class. The feeling of accomplishment with the meeting's outcome was much like he had experienced with the achievements of the project team back in Rajasthan. It was a simple thing really, not glamorous or sophisticated at all. He had just helped to create an opportunity for good people to achieve more of their potential.

*****

David's routine had begun to include long evenings in the front room where he graded student term papers and attended to co-op documents at his desk or reclined with a reference book in an old leather chair. On one such evening in late November, the wood stove was throwing a pleasant heat and he had dozed off in the easy chair. The phone startled him when it rang, and he grappled for the receiver, managing to place it to his ear after the third ring.

"Hello," he said, with as much clarity as he could muster.

"Is that you, young fella?"

"Ray? How the hell are you?"

It was Ray Baker, his closest friend from the World Bank days. He had coached David in project design and taught him about living and working across different cultures. But more than that, Ray and his wife Teresa had seen him through the early days of his recovery from a serious bout of depression and alcohol. Ray had stayed nearby in the weeks and months that followed as David gradually got his feet under him again.

"I'm not bad," Baker replied. "Other than the pain of trying to find you. I was beginning to think they didn't have phones in your neck of the woods."

"Of course, we do. And some of them don't even need to be cranked."

"Cute. And how are you? How's the teaching going?"

"Very well, actually."

"Does it beat preaching?" There was muffled coughing before Ray continued with, "Sorry. A bit of a cold these days."

"Well, preaching and teaching both seem futile sometimes, but I prefer the message with this gig."

"And what about women? Are there any women out there in the boondocks?"

"Fuck," David said, dismissively.

"Well, that's a bit Pavlovian, but it is part of the concept, all right," Ray replied.

"You mean they didn't teach you the difference between a verb and an expletive where you went to school?"

There was laughter at both ends of the line.

"It's really great to hear from you, Ray. How's Teresa?"

"She's good. In fact, it's partly her fault that I'm calling you. There's a rib roast in the fridge here that she wants you to come and help us take care of for dinner this Sunday."

"It would be hard to say no to a request like that!"

They chatted a little longer about some projects Ray was working on, and when they hung up it was with, "See you Sunday, around four o'clock."

CHAPTER 13

"You'd better bring an extra sweater," Jerry said as Karen finished putting the makings of a picnic into the knap sack that sat on a kitchen chair. "There's a cold front coming through this afternoon and that jacket might not be enough,"

"I suppose," she replied. "It is almost December, after all."

What a perfectly mundane conversation, Jerry thought happily. *How perfectly normal.* Karen had gone to the Park with him twice more since their first outing together, each time wandering farther, each time talking more and guarding her space less. She no longer did a mid-course correction if they accidentally touched. On occasion she would even reach for his hand to navigate a tricky part of the trail. Last week, as they sat on a log finishing their lunch, she had put her hand on his arm to reinforce some point she was making. He didn't remember the point, but he remembered that touch.

On the way back to the car that afternoon she had asked, "Can I tell you something?"

"Of course." He stopped and turned toward her.

"I like being here with you," she said, smiling gently. "I'm glad you asked me to come with you."

It was all he could do not to reach and take her in his arms, but he had the presence of mind to limit his response to something she had already accepted. He put his hands on her arms and said, "In my mind you have always been here with me."

This morning, as she moved around the kitchen preparing for another outing, she showed no apprehension whatever. It looked as though she was beginning to reconnect with her world before the shooting and, thank God, it seemed he was still part of that world. He hadn't thought of Operation Weatherman for weeks, savoring instead the fact that Karen was back in his life.

"What do you say to a tougher trail this time?" he asked.

"You mean 'Am I up to it'?"

He glanced quickly at her and was relieved to catch the wink. "Maybe woman no good for hard trail," he said, ducking as the bag of chips flew in his direction. "I guess that's a yes," he chuckled. He'd chosen the trail not only because South River Falls would be an attractive destination but also, if she started to tire along the way, there were options to shorten the distance back to the van.

Three hours later they were sitting on a large rock near the base of the falls. As he suspected, recent rainfall had been enough to swell the creek upstream. From their vantage point, the view was magical as the water tumbled over ledges toward them and plunged through its own mist into the pool below. The pool and its surrounding rocks calmed the water before sending it on downstream.

"Tonight, the Rapidan," Jerry said. "Tomorrow the Rappahannock. Chesapeake Bay by the weekend."

"Sounds like a nice trip," Karen said wistfully.

"Yeah. Except for a dam and a few sewage outflows!"

She glanced reprovingly at him but said nothing, and they continued to watch the water for a time in happy silence.

When Karen did speak again, she said something Jerry wasn't sure he had heard correctly. *Had she said, "Would you take me to Kent?" That couldn't have been it.*

"What's that?" he asked.

This time she looked at him as she repeated, "Would you take me to Kent?"

He couldn't have been sure whether it was the fragility of her progress that frightened him with such a request or the threat to his own happiness. As it was, he sensed only the risk. It put a twist in his gut that he needed to get under control before he could answer her.

"Are you sure you want to do that?"

"I guess they call it facing your demons," she said. "But I need to go back and see where it happened. There's been so much shit in between that when I try to think back, I can't remember what it was like. I know what they did. I know how it messed me up. But the images from the press and from my nightmares have destroyed my memory of what it was actually like. I don't remember the people, the place, the grass, the parking lot. I don't remember how I felt, why I moved in one direction and not another when the shooting started. Was there something I missed that would have told me what was happening?"

"Is this something you should talk with Ed and Joan about maybe?"

"You mean as my employers or as my medical advisors?" she snapped.

Then, in an important sign of the progress she was making, she caught herself and said, "I'm sorry. That was nasty. I know you mean well, but I need to start making some decisions for myself. I think this is something I have to do."

Jerry thought back to the evenings spent walking by the river in Ban Me Thuot, looking across to where the mortar shell had killed his buddies and Sergeant Douglas, and he understood.

He smiled at her. "When you're ready to go to Kent, I'm your man."

On the way home they agreed that they'd head north the following Saturday. That gave him only six days to worry about the outcome, and if his state of mind on Sunday and Monday were any indication, it was going to be a tough week. By Tuesday, sleeplessness and a short fuse had built to the point that he needed to talk to someone, so mid-morning, when Karen would be in the packing shed, he called Joan.

"What do you think about this trip to Ohio?" he asked, keeping his voice as calm as he could.

"It's a big step, that's for sure," Joan answered, "but she seems determined to do it."

"I gather it's important," he said, "and I can see that, but I wonder if she's ready for it."

"She's very different now than she was a month ago, Jerry. You and the mountains have been a big part of that. But even at the worst of times she's been a very determined person."

"You mean pig-headed. Yeah, I've noticed."

"It runs in the family," Joan replied with a chuckle. "Try living with it."

Living with Karen. As the idea registered, there was a moment of wildflowers and dappled sunlight before his mind caught up to the conversation and he heard himself say, "I'd be willing to give that a try."

CHAPTER 14

It was such a pleasure to David to hear Ray's voice again, and to dabble in the repartee that had kept their cylinders lubed in the World Bank days. Why had they let so much time go by since they last spoke? It was easy enough to do when both people led normal lives, but when one of them was out of the country for weeks at a time and the other was drying out and starting a new career, weeks could become months, and they had. That didn't make it right.

Ray had always been big brother in the relationship, but in the months following David's breakdown he had also become caregiver and therapist. It wouldn't be beyond him to have recognized that David needed space and time to get his feet back under him if they were ever to shed those relationships and return to the friendship of earlier days.

As to his own role in the hiatus, David was inclined to see it as neglect, plain and simple. But if that was the case, he would have felt guilt or regret when Ray called. He felt neither. On the contrary, he had experienced the kind of relief and anticipation one might associate with bandages coming off. Somewhere beyond the reaches of consciousness, something had told them the time had come to rekindle their friendship. That they should both have thought so at the same time was a mystery for another day.

Arlington was only seventy miles away, but he'd had no reason to go back to Northern Virginia since moving out of his apartment. As he drove toward Ray and Teresa's that Sunday afternoon, memories returned. Like the tufts and twigs of an old nest, they were part of something he had once known, but he no longer felt at home here. This was now just familiar territory.

He might have felt the same way about the Baker's little brick colonial as he came up the walk, were it not for the affection with which Ray and Teresa greeted him. He had spent the first phase of his recovery in this house, as the bourbon worked its way grudgingly and painfully out of his system, as his mind struggled with the tangled strands of a broken marriage, a lost love affair, and disillusioning career. But with their caring, their unobtrusive attention, Ray and Teresa had seen him to the point where he could face the work to reclaim his life.

Their smiles and hugs now touched that same cord. Chatting easily, collaborating on the final meal preparation, he felt once more the warmth of their friendship and support.

After they settled at the table, Ray turned to David. "Tell me, is your passport still valid?"

"Yes, I think so, and I might even be able to find it, but why?"

"There's a job in the Philippines that has your name on it."

In the moments it took him to organize his thoughts, David couldn't decide whether to be flattered that Ray saw him back in the international development business or offended that he didn't take his new life in Virginia seriously.

"You're kidding, right? I have a job, Ray, and it suits me."

"I know that. It's all over your face. But if I remember correctly, teaching isn't a year-round thing." He winked at David, who immediately regretted his churlish response. "What I'm talking about is a short-term consulting job. It's normal for faculty to take leave for a couple of weeks between semesters to work in their field. Some schools even encourage it because it adds to the experience you can use in class."

"Come to think of it, the guy in the office next to me consults regularly with the FBI."

Ray grinned and raised his hands, palm up. "There you go, and I bet they don't dock his pay, either."

For the rest of the evening, the wide-ranging chat of good friends kept circling back to the work to be done in the Philippines.

"To be fair," Ray said, "Land reform is a massive undertaking, even under the best of circumstances. But in the Philippines the political motives and a completely inadequate administration have made the whole thing a quagmire of expropriations and unmet promises. Owners have no interest in land they're going to lose. Former tenants have no place to turn for the inputs and technical help they need. Rice production has plummeted."

David listened, increasingly convinced of the futility of adding another consultant to the mix.

"But, finally," Ray continued, "we're starting to see significant areas of land being transferred. There's a growing demand for farm inputs and services to help the new smallholders."

"Here's the challenge," he said, in an attempt to summarize, "There are two million rural families that are used to being told what to grow and given the tools and the inputs to grow it. How do they now get the services and the know-how to become productive family businesses in their own right? How do they become capable of feeding themselves and generating the surplus production that a country needs to survive?"

"Oh, well," David replied, "When you put it like that I can see where an expert for a week or two might come in handy."

"Smartass!" Ray said. "Look. We've got the best know-how available on the mechanics of land reform. The Government's on board with good people now, too. But these small farmers have been burned so often that they don't trust government officials or outsiders. With your hands-on experience with village life in Luzon, maybe you could navigate the social barriers they've set up to protect themselves. You could gain the confidence of some village leaders.

As Ray spoke, David was remembering times in his village when just such barriers defined the outcome of a conversation or a barrio council meeting. It was only when he had gained the confidence of the community that even his commonsense inputs were taken seriously.

"A little bird told me recently that you had a good way with the farmers in those districts in India, too." Ray added. "You've got a good sense of how small farmers think, and somehow you managed to keep those MBA skills from going to your head. A post-grad who remembers how to screw in a light bulb? That's a scarce commodity.

"I think if you could just sit and listen to these people for a couple of weeks, get a fix on their concerns and give us an idea who some of the real local leaders are, you could help us put together an approach that the government and the donors could consider.

As if to concede his interest, David asked, "When would this need to be done?"

"Yesterday, of course, like everything in this business!"

By the end of the evening, David had agreed to approach the college about the assignment, with a view to getting approval to head for the Philippines during the Christmas break. He had a suspicion that the holidays might be difficult for him this year, and there was a certain comfort in the prospect of not being around to find out. The extra money wouldn't hurt, either.

He went to sleep thinking about a walk-in cooler for the co-op's packing shed and a power tiller for his garden.

CHAPTER 15

For most of the drive through West Virginia and Pennsylvania, Jerry and Karen chatted with the ease that was finding its way back into their relationship. Crossing into Ohio, however, and nearing their destination, Karen became increasingly quiet. She would alternate between spells of stillness, staring at the dashboard, and restless shifting and fidgeting, not knowing what to do with her hands or feet.

"Would you like to stop for a nature break?" Jerry asked.

"No. Yeah. That would be a good idea."

He pulled off at the next exit and they went into a local café.

"What'll it be, folks?"

"Hot chocolate," Karen said, without looking at the waitress.

"Sounds good," Jerry chimed in. "Make it two."

Their booth was next to the windows. After Karen had gone to the ladies', Jerry surveyed the landscape beyond.

Under normal circumstances, he would say his mind was wandering. In fact, he was searching for something useful to break the silence when she returned, something to take her mind off the pending encounter with her demons. Just outside the building, a stream emptied into a small lake.

When she returned to the table he said, "See that water out there?"

She looked out and gave a disinterested, "Uh huh."

"I saw a sign a few miles back that said we're in Portage County. That creek is strong enough that I'm guessing it was part of one of the old portage routes from the Saint Lawrence to the Ohio for the fur trade three hundred years ago."

"Poor beavers," she said.

"I was thinking more about the trip those guys were on," he continued. "If they made it this far, they'd travelled the best part of a thousand miles, and the rest of the trip was downstream."

Karen smiled at him, then reached across the table and rest her hand on his.

When they arrived on the Kent State campus, they parked in a lot on the north side of an open, grassy area Jerry recognized from the photos on Karen's wall. They were at The Commons, the site of the protest rallies.

Before getting out of the car he made a suggestion. "I'll play this any way you want. But maybe, if you'd tell me what you remember as we walk, it would give me a better picture of what I'm looking at." Perhaps making her his guide would help her talk about her memories, maybe burn off some of their energy.

She didn't answer him, but as they walked across The Commons toward the hill on the south side, she began to speak.

"We were gathering over there," she said, pointing ahead toward the base of the hill. "People were coming from different directions. Some of them were just passing through between classes. Some, with signs, obviously came for the rally. Around noon, someone began to ring the bell." She gestured toward the Victory Bell that was mounted on a low brick wall just ahead of them.

"Then the speeches started. But while we were listening to the first speaker, the troops began to move toward us from back there." She pointed back toward where they had parked. "Somebody got on a bullhorn and told us the gathering was illegal, said we had to disperse."

Now there was a longer pause as Karen looked around, distracted.

"That pissed everybody off," she said eventually. "The idea that they weren't allowed to protest. Says who? And what the hell were soldiers doing on a university campus, anyhow? They started shouting back and refused to leave." She paused again, and then, "Things got really loud, and the teargas came."

Karen was standing next to Jerry, but her stare was fixed on things only she could see.

"I had never experienced that thing people talk about," she continued, "where everything moves in slow motion. But that's what happened. Teargas canisters tumbled across the ground, leaving white trails of smoke. People screamed stuff at the soldiers and threw the canisters back at them, but everything was happening in slow motion. I guess they threw rocks, too. Then one of the incoming canisters hit a girl standing over there."

Karen moved toward a spot on the lawn that only her memory could distinguish. Standing over it, she said, "She fell, here, screaming. Her friend was really pissed, and he picked the thing up and threw it back at the soldiers. I put some tissues on the nasty gash on her head and wrapped my scarf over it. That's all I could think to do."

"Man, you were right in the thick of it, weren't you?" Jerry said.

She didn't answer, but the comment seemed to encourage her to continue.

"My friend and I had parked in front of Prentice Hall, over that way," she said, pointing to the space between two buildings that dominated the horizon at the top of the hill. "So we headed in that direction, but the Guard had moved around and blocked that path. It's crazy, you know. They said they wanted us to disburse, but then they were funneling everyone out the other way." She pointed to the right side of Taylor Hall. "It's like they were herding us. I still don't get it. Why the hell, if you're trying to disperse a crowd, would you concentrate them into one exit route?"

Jerry's mind flashed back to his days on the long-range reconnaissance patrols. He remembered his platoon moving in an arc toward a village and the men (or were they just boys) sneaking out the only remaining escape route, directly into his field of fire.

"They wanted you gone," he explained, "but they weren't willing to give up control."

For the first time since they had begun their walk, Karen looked at him. There was something strangely discomforting in her expression. But again, no response. Instead, she turned to lead the way up the hill to the left. They passed between the buildings and came to the parking lot in front of Prentice Hall.

To Jerry's eyes, this area looked less ominous than The Commons. A parking lot, an athletic field beyond, and to the right, a hill with a few mature trees—all presided over by Taylor Hall, set into the brow of the hill. But as he glanced at Karen and saw her withdrawing into herself, he realized that this was where the massacre had taken place.

When she did speak, her voice had a derisive edge.

"If you wanted a Pulitzer Prize that day, all you had to do was take a picture of a student lying dead over there." She pointed to a spot near the parking lot fifty feet from where they stood. "Someone kneeling next to him would be a nice touch. Someone who actually cared."

Then, as she scanned the parking lot, she suddenly tensed, and growled, "Un-fucking-believable."

Jerry followed her glare to see a service vehicle from a local plumbing and heating company in a parking space to their left.

"That's too much!" she said. "It's bad enough that there's no memorial to those people, but to park on Allison Krause's memory while you go somewhere to fix a toilet...?"

He didn't know what to do. Her look moments earlier had warned him off trying to comfort her, so he waited.

"We were standing here when the soldiers came down the hill and lined up on the athletics field. Over there," she said, sweeping her hand from the right to indicate a spot beyond the parking lot in front of them. "It was bizarre seeing all those guns pointed at us, like we were extras in some movie."

"M1s," Jerry said, without realizing that he had spoken aloud.

"Of course," she said. "You'd know about such things, wouldn't you?" And again, the strange look.

"There weren't many protesters still around, maybe a couple hundred. But some of them were really mad. They shouted at the soldiers and threw stuff at them as they finally took their guns—excuse me, *their M1s*—and started back up the hill. They were leaving.

"It's weird. On TV or in the movies, soldiers are always silent, professional. Anything but personal. But some of those guys were shouting back at us, even throwing rocks back at us and threatening individuals. It was really personal, like they were psyching themselves up for a street fight.

"But as they neared the top of the hill, there was more distance between them and us, and it seemed like things had started to settle down."

Karen stared intently at the top of the hill. When she spoke again, her voice broke.

"My friend said, 'I guess that's it for today. I wonder what the organizers have planned for tomorrow', and we turned to head back to the car. Then it happened." She was crying openly now, her fists clenched in front of her.

"Why?" she sobbed. "It was over. Why shoot then? They'd won. But suddenly there was that incredible noise, and people starting to fall, everywhere. I saw Allison go down, right there." She gestured toward the van in the nearby parking space. "And blood ran onto the pavement, like she'd broken a bottle of it when she fell.

"Then we were running for the car, and something hit the side of my head. Everything seemed to be flying apart and collapsing in at the same time. It was all piercing the inside of my head like broken glass. The last thing I saw was the ground rushing up at me. I was awake, but I was tumbling and suffocating in some dark space. I heard my friend scream, but I couldn't reach her. And then everything stopped."

Karen was shaking and looking around desperately, but when Jerry put his arms around her, she pulled away.

"I've got to get out of here," she said. "I can't do this."

Then she buckled over, retching loudly, and again he grabbed her to keep her from falling. She spun away from him and, with her hands over her ears, started to run back toward The Commons. When she fell, she fought both him and gravity to stagger to her feet and move forward, crying, stumbling in the direction they had come.

Afraid she'd fall again, he struggled to support her.

"Leave me alone," she shouted, pushing his arm away. "Don't touch me."

Softly, insistently, he said, "Karen, listen, it's OK. Just stop a minute and take a breath." She fell again and tumbled the last few feet down the hill before regaining her footing and heading across The Commons. He caught up to her, and this time he used whatever strength he needed to contain her.

Her eyes wide with panic, she screamed, "Let me go! Leave me alone!"

"Karen, please," he said. He had forgotten how strong she was. As she flailed and kicked at him and he worked to restrain her, it looked more like a fight than a rescue.

He didn't see the campus security truck racing across the grass toward them, its lights flashing. It wasn't until two security guards stood on either side of them that he realized they had been the subject of an emergency call.

"Sir. Please release the woman."

"I need your help," Jerry said, still holding her as securely as he could. "She's going to hurt herself."

"Let go of me, you bastard. You knew what they were going to do," Karen shouted as she continued to twist and kick at him. "You're one of them!"

The accusation stunned him, but he held onto her.

"Sir," the officer repeated, "you need to release the woman, now."

"Look, you've got to understand," Jerry insisted. "She's having a panic attack. I brought her here to visit where she was shot, and she panicked."

The two officers glanced uncertainly at each other for a moment, then quickly concluded that this was a case of domestic violence. They moved in, one with a night stick at the ready to subdue Jerry if necessary. Jerry realized what was happening and decided that the only way to get help for Karen was to cooperate. As he relaxed his grip on her, she collapsed to the ground.

"Sir, back away," the older officer said. "Back away. Now."

Reluctantly, Jerry did. The officer moved between him and Karen with his hand on his weapon as his partner knelt and put his jacket under Karen's head. Then he called for an ambulance.

"I need to go to her," Jerry said.

"No, sir. I can't allow that just now. Please keep your hands where I can see them and walk over to the truck."

"What? What is this?" he asked in disbelief.

"Sir, move, now." The officer tightened his grip on the still-holstered weapon and pointed toward the campus security vehicle with his other hand. In his mind, Jerry rehearsed the quick jab and the fist that would take care of this guy, and the kick to the midriff that would disable the other one before he could get to his feet.

But then what? He heard the question as clearly as if his friend, Y Nur Kpa, had been standing beside him as he asked it.

The officer spoke again, "The lady will be taken care of, sir, but until I understand what's going on here, you need to stay with me. Please move to the truck, now."

Jerry complied and when they reached the side of the vehicle he submitted to a weapons search and let the officer pull his driver's license for ID.

The ambulance came quickly. Karen was conscious, but she was sufficiently disoriented that the paramedics were able to keep her subdued while they secured her on the gurney, loaded her into the ambulance, and headed away from The Commons.

"Where are they taking her?" Jerry asked.

"Robinson Memorial, sir."

"Where is that? I need to get there quickly."

"Sir, you need to stay with us for now."

"What the hell are you talking about? My girlfriend and I drove here from Virginia. Now she's going to a hospital and I need to go with her. Then I need to take her home."

While this exchange was going on the other officer had been on the radio checking Jerry's ID. He signed off now and came around the truck as a police squad car pulled up alongside. The police officer had apparently been part of the radio exchange on Jerry's ID. He introduced himself and asked, "Sir, have you recently been in prison?"

"Yeah. What's that go to do with anything?"

As far as the officers were concerned, Jerry's prison term was evidence of a violent crime by a man now being interrogated about a situation that looked like an assault. More than enough to hold him and investigate. So, Jerry found himself handcuffed and seated in the back of the squad car. He was seething, but he had the presence of mind not to resist.

"You've got it all wrong," he told them, before going silent for the trip to the police station.

It took about six hours and a long phone call to Ed and Joan, but eventually the Kent Police Department was satisfied with Jerry's version of events. He was released with a perfunctory apology and driven back in the darkness of late evening to his van. In the meantime, Karen had been examined at the hospital, sedated, and admitted for observation.

Jerry asked for the nurse on duty and gave her Joan's phone number but, on her advice, he did not wake Karen. Instead, he drove around town until he found a strip mall with an all-night convenience store, parked the van in a far corner of the lot and fell asleep.

*****

It was a long drive back to Virginia after Karen's release the next day. Snow that had started to fall during the night in Kent continued to make things difficult as they crossed Pennsylvania. More than once the rear tires lost their grip and sent the van askew toward the shoulder of the road—a no-nonsense refresher for Jerry's rusty winter driving skills.

The snow transitioned quickly to rain as they dropped out of the mountains east of Hancock. The demands of keeping the van on the road were no longer a diversion from the silence and tension inside the vehicle. When Karen wasn't staring out the window, she appeared to be sleeping. Occasionally she flinched or made involuntary sounds as events replayed themselves in her mind. Jerry preferred to think it was the sedative that kept her so distant from him, but when she did respond—when he asked if she would like to stop at a restroom—she looked at him with that same troubling stare.

When he decided to pull into a service plaza, she stepped out of the van and moved unsteadily toward the building. He reached to support her, and she jerked her arm away so forcefully that she almost lost her balance. Heartbroken, he watched as she continued up the path. The progress she had made—they had made—was gone.

Ed and Joan were waiting for them when they reached the farm. With as little fuss as possible, Joan opened the passenger door for Karen. She smiled at Jerry and mimed the words 'thank you' as she and Karen turned toward the house. Jerry handed Karen's small travel bag to Ed and shifted indecisively for a moment. "I'm sorry," he said. "We shouldn't have gone."

Ed looked at Jerry sympathetically. "I know it was rough," he answered, "and you may be right, but it was worth a try. Who knows, maybe she'll bounce back after she's had a rest."

"Don't hold your breath. She's really pissed at the world, and at me, too."

Something in Jerry's voice troubled Ed. "Don't take this the wrong way," he said, "but don't do anything stupid, OK?"

Jerry smiled lamely and wondered what Ed would think if he knew about his plans for the Ohio National Guard.

"No," he said absently. "Maybe I'll just go hunting for a few days."

As he drove away, Jerry glimpsed Karen in the rear-view mirror, standing at the bottom of the steps, clinging to Joan, and crying uncontrollably.

His time with Karen in recent weeks, and her improvement, had pushed Operation Weatherman to the back of his mind. Now, as he crossed the mountain toward Flint Hill, it was all he could do not to head for the cave and his stockpile of munitions. The bastards had to pay, once and for all.

As he drove, he could feel the Garand in his hands. The sensation of looking through its sights, of squeezing the trigger came close to overwhelming him. At Thornton Gap, he turned into the Park, but pulled immediately into the Panorama parking lot. He had to talk himself down. Going back to Ohio now would be just plain dumb.

He was too embroiled in anger and loss to think, but in the turmoil, a process was at work that gradually brought order to the impulses ricocheting through his mind. Going off halfcocked in winter conditions would be stupid. Tire prints and footprints, limited mobility, reduced cover, reduced traffic to mix in with, reduced target access—it all amounted to one thing: lower impact and greater risk of mission failure.

But how the hell could he survive 'til spring without taking some kind of action? The idea of attending to a brake job back in the shop or trying to focus on a carburetor tune up—of being one of the guys—made him suddenly so claustrophobic that he had to get out of the van and walk it off.

As he took in the mountain air and his breathing returned to normal, the solution came into view as if it had been there waiting for him all along. It was time to visit Sergeant Douglas's grave. Operation Weatherman could wait 'til spring when conditions would be more in his favor. To seal his decision, he reached for the mason jar in the box of camping supplies, spun the top off and raised it toward the southwest.

"New Mexico, here we come," he said, and took a long slow draught.

CHAPTER 16

Shenandoah College agreed to David's request to take on the Philippines assignment. As the end of the semester approached, he spent any time he could find digging into issues he might encounter in the field. Time and again he found himself wondering what Dr. McFarlane would think on a particular aspect of the work. His experience with smallholders and his understanding of rural economies will be a gold mine in preparation for the assignment.

Thoughts of McFarlane meant thoughts of Charlottesville, and that kept returning him to another preoccupation in his life these days. The final order of divorce had been sitting on his desk for several weeks. He hadn't had the stomach to read and relive the details of the failure it represented, but the deadline for his signature was fast approaching.

Sherry, his soon-to-be ex, had been adamant when they first separated that she was going to divorce him on the grounds of adultery. When it came down to it, though, the shorter waiting period for a no-fault divorce, and not having to go through court appearances had convinced her to go the no-fault route.

No fault. What a stupid expression, David thought. *If there was no fault there would be no divorce.* But the law only recognized certain faults, like dipping his wick where it didn't belong, and not others, like impulsiveness, fear of being alone, securing the future, trying to stop time, or better-the-devil-you-know. Why did so many things start out feeling like love, being called love? Some huckster in the Darwinian past must have been so anxious to perpetuate the species that he had devised this oral sleight of hand to lure couples of breeding age into the wedding tent.

Virginia's waiting time for the divorce had come and gone, and Sherry was keen to get on with her life. Her interest in the insurance business had taken on a personal dimension, and that suited David. If she and her boss had discovered something more than insurance policies in their time together, good. Her happiness would be one less thing he'd have to worry about.

Dealing with the order also meant getting it back to Sherry. If he put it in the mail now, there was a chance she'd receive it a few days late. *That wouldn't matter*, he told himself. But it would. It would be one more thing she could hold against him, one more thing he had failed at. On the flipside, delivering it in person might earn him a few points, even in a lost cause. And a meeting with Dr. McFarlane would give him the excuse for going to Charlottesville.

When David called the next morning, McFarlane was in his office and took the call personally. "Of course, I'd be happy to talk with you," he said. "It sounds like a very interesting assignment." There was a brief silence before he continued. "But since you're coming this way, could you come Thursday morning and join the class? We'll be looking at the effect risk has on decisions by smallholders. Your experience in India and the Philippines would fit in nicely."

*****

Sherry stood in the doorway of her apartment and smiled as David handed her the envelope. Acknowledging the personal delivery, she said, "Still the good guy, huh?" There was more observation in her voice than acrimony.

"Well," he shrugged, "I dragged my feet a bit on signing it, and then I was coming this way anyhow, for a meeting on campus."

Beyond her, he caught a glimpse of a modest, comfortable apartment. Something of Sherry's that he wasn't part of. She had a life of her own now and, in that moment, he felt a distance from her that he hadn't experienced even in those bewildering first hours of their separation.

"I wonder what you'd be like if you weren't always trying to please other people," she said.

"You don't think that's just who I am?" he asked.

"Oh, you've got a good heart. But it must be tiring to be constantly thinking of others as a way to protect yourself."

David sensed they were rapidly using up any reserve of goodwill that the time apart might have restored to their relationship.

"This isn't the kind of conversation that normally occurs in a hallway," he said, uneasily. "And maybe a little late in the day, too." Glancing at his watch, he leveraged the comment into a change of subject. "Listen, I'm sorry, but I have to run."

"Of course. Thanks for dropping this off. Good luck, David."

"And to you. Let me know if there's anything else you need."

He had always valued time alone, sought it out like a sanctuary. Loneliness was not a feeling he had ever recognized. Until a few moments ago he had always assumed that there was someone waiting for him when he went off to be by himself. He could rejoin the tribe anytime he wanted and that knowledge had taken the risk out of being alone. It was an emotional safety net that made a joke out of his sense of what it meant to be alone.

As he descended the stairs from Sherry's apartment, the net was gone. Thoughts didn't form to that effect, but the message in the pit of his stomach was clear. Life on his own had become real for the first time. Both frightened and exhilarated, David felt like he was in freefall. Did he have what it took to enjoy the ride?

CHAPTER 17

Jerry awoke with a shiver sometime after dawn in a church parking lot in Greensboro North Carolina. The fog covered windows robbed the sun's first rays of any warmth and he shifted to pull the lightweight travel blanket more snuggly around his shoulders. If he could regenerate the frail envelope of body heat in his makeshift cocoon, he wouldn't have to reach through the cold air to restart the van.

Struggling at the juncture of fatigue and cold, he became aware of the sound of another vehicle nearby, then the sound of its door opening and closing… He was fully awake by the time the form of a man moved along the walkway in front of the van. Even through the fogged up windshield there was something familiar about his gait. It was a long time since Jerry had last seen it, moving purposefully down a dirt path in the village of Plei Gong Krek, but it was unmistakable. He rolled down the window and called out, "Paul?"

The man stopped and looked toward the van. It wasn't unusual for travelers to approach church representatives for material assistance, and that's what he assumed was about to happen again. He was startled, however, to have been addressed by name.

"Yes. May I help you?"

Jerry got out of the van, made a brief gesture of straightening his clothes and then smiled as he approached the tall lean figure.

"It's been a long time. You probably don't remember me. Jerry Fletcher."

But recognition had already flashed across Paul Anderson's face. He quickly closed the distance between them, grabbing Jerry's hand enthusiastically.

"Remember you!? You've been in my thoughts and my prayers ever since Vietnam. What a pleasure to see you, Jerry!"

"I didn't expect to see anyone here this early," Jerry said.

"Getting up early is an old habit from the highlands," Anderson replied, and Jerry smiled.

"Dawn was a special time in the highlands, for sure."

"That seems like such a long time ago," Anderson continued. "These days I like to come over here to the church when I get up, make a cup of coffee, and just sit back for a little while before people start filling up my schedule. Come on in and let's get the pot on."

"Sounds good."

And with that simple exchange, they bridged the more than ten years since they had last talked.

"What brings you to Greensboro?" Anderson asked, holding the side door of the church open for Jerry.

"Oh, I decided to take some time off and go find my sergeant's grave in New Mexico, maybe look up his widow. This time of year, that means a southern route."

"Oh, yes. I remember Sergeant Douglas," Anderson said, adding with a wink, "We met over dinner."

"Yeah, back in Buan Ken Hmek. We sure sent the dishes flying that night, didn't we?" They both laughed heartily, remembering the chaos that had ensued when Anderson suddenly appeared in the dimly lit longhouse where the village elders were hosting Douglas's squad. The shock of a stranger's voice so near to them had sent the recon soldiers scrambling for their weapons, scattering food and dishes in all directions.

"How did you find me?" Anderson continued.

"My parents kept the letter you sent—that meant a lot to them, by the way—so I had the address of the church's regional office in Durham. Some lady in that office told me you were here now. I hope you don't mind me just stopping in like this. I was in the area, so I figured..."

Anderson held up his hand. There was sadness back of the smile.

"Listen. A lot has happened since we last met, some big changes for both of us," he said. "But when I saw you just now it was like a glimpse back to a better time. OK, it wasn't easy then, either, but we were part of something very precious in those days."

There was a suggestion in Anderson's voice of news that Jerry feared. For the moment he didn't ask.

"Memories of village life with the Montagnards are touchstones for me now," Anderson said. "Gifts from the Lord that have kept me grounded ever since. And those memories include sitting by the fire with a young reconnaissance soldier, and seeing the way Kpa's eyes used to light up when that recon was with his people. Thank you for bringing those memories back."

Jerry had been looking reflectively out the window of the church kitchen as Anderson spoke.

"I'm afraid to ask," he began, turning back to him. "But I have to know. How's Kpa? Do you ever hear from him?"

"Yes, in fact we correspond regularly these days. He's much older now, and frail. He spent the first two years after the takeover in prison, where he was beaten and tortured. But he was released last summer, and I think he's OK. The trouble is that conditions aren't much better on the outside. Since the Americans left, several thousand of the Montagnard men have kept up the fight as guerilla, and that hasn't helped the cause of the non-combatants. Everyone's being forced into what the SRV calls restricted areas."

"SRV?" Jerry interrupted.

"Socialist Republic of Vietnam. The people have lost their lands. They can't get medical care or supplies. They're forced to speak Vietnamese, and everything written in their languages is being burned. The slightest resistance gets them beaten or shot."

The anger that grew as he listened to Anderson's account and the helplessness he felt in the face of such atrocities met in the pit of Jerry's stomach. He leaned over to rest his arms on the edge of the sink as faces of the men, women, and children he had known passed through his mind. With the thought of Kpa being beaten, revulsion overtook him, and he retched.

"I'm sorry," he said, wiping his face with the paper towels Anderson handed him.

There was nothing to add and Anderson sat quietly, respecting what he had just witnessed.

When Jerry appeared to have regained his composure, Anderson continued. "The SRV calls it cultural levelling, but it's genocide as far as I can tell. When we left, there were about a million Montagnards in Vietnam but they're being killed off and driven out at such a rate that there's no telling what token skeleton of their culture will be left."

"What's the State Department doing about it?"

"Nothing."

"What do you mean, 'nothing'? The 'Yards were promised protection when they began to work with us."

"I guess they didn't read the fine print, about only getting help if it was convenient to us," Anderson said scornfully. "As far as the policy types are concerned, Montagnards are just an aberrant two percent of Vietnam's population. It's more important to juggle face-saving and business interests. You can't do that and worry about the plight of some disenfranchised minority just because they once helped your cause."

The bitterness, the hardness in Anderson's words was something new to the man Jerry had known. Apparently even soldiers in Christ's army weren't immune to disillusionment. Jerry wanted to ask him where his God was while all this was going on, but he guessed Anderson had already asked that question. To have one's faith challenged at such a fundamental level must be a terrible thing. There was no way an outsider could be part of that process. Loyalty would require that he defend the faith no matter what, and that energy would be better spent on the issues at hand.

"I guess it was some of the guerillas who helped Kpa escape," Anderson said. "I don't know how they did it, but they crossed Cambodia on foot, through the hell of that war. Can you imagine? The Kmer Rouge has driven millions of people from the cities and towns into the rural areas. What kind of murderous chaos must that be causing? Just think what it's doing to the people in the north of the country who are trying to survive on rainfed crops. Are there any paddy fields left, any livestock? How are the people surviving?"

Anderson shook his head and returned to Jerry's question.

"Anyhow, Kpa and his guides made it to Thailand. Now he lives in a refugee camp somewhere southeast of Surin. He works day and night, writing letters, talking to donors and the UN, visiting embassies—anything he can do to try to get help for his people. I got a letter from him the other day postmarked in Bangkok. That's a long bus ride for an old man. I think working for his people, grieving for them, will kill him one day. But in the meantime, that's what he lives for."

Jerry leaned against the counter, listening intently.

"Some of the guys around Fort Bragg get together regularly," Anderson continued, "and send money and supplies to the people in the refugee camps."

"Good. At least somebody's doing something."

"Come to think of it," Anderson continued, "your partner in Plei Gong Krek, Sergeant Walton, is part of that group. He came back to this area several years ago. What they do is a big help but there's so much more that needs to be done."

"Say hello to Sergeant Walton for me, would you, the next time you see him?"

"Certainly."

"Come to think of it, if you happened to have his address, maybe I'll drop him a line."

Anderson led the way to his office, where he took an address book from his desk drawer. As he began to write down Walton's address, Jerry said, "I heard that a few the 'Yard scouts managed to leave with the troops."

"That's right. A handful, maybe a couple dozen, who happened to be with American units when they were evacuated. There was no organized help for them when they got here and they ended up scattered around the country, near the bases the troops returned to. Some settled east of here to be close to their Special Forces friends at Bragg, but they're starting to move to this side because the country is more like the highlands."

"How are they doing?"

"Very well, under the circumstances. It was a big upheaval for them, as you can imagine, but they are hardworking and very stoic. The local people admire them."

Jerry shook his head. "That's a hell of a change for anyone to have to go through."

"It's a sad thing to have to admit," Anderson said, "but the idea of the people returning to their homes and their lives in the highlands is no longer realistic. I guess maybe it never was. It's looking now like the best option is to help them leave, get more of them to America or elsewhere. It's the only way they can be assured of any safety."

"Is that what Kpa's working on?" Jerry asked.

"Mainly, yes, although trying to get other governments to put pressure on the SRV to ease up on those remaining in-country is also a big job. There are some hopeful signs among smaller European countries, but the US and France are more worried about positioning themselves for the future. To them the Montagnards are just an awkward footnote to the main agenda." After a moment he added, "Makes you wonder where they'll end up in the history books."

Jerry thought for a minute. Somewhere in the Great Beyond, Kpa and Grandpa Jake would have a lot to talk about.

There wasn't much more Anderson could add to the story of Kpa and his people, and after what Jerry had heard, small talk would have been decidedly out of place. So, after a second cup of coffee and some catching up on personal fronts, Jerry took his leave with the promise to stay in touch.

He headed south on I-85, but fatigue finally overtook him and he pulled over at the first rest area. After the Ohio trip, last night's drive from Virginia, and the anger and sadness at the plight of his friends the last of his reserves were gone. Sleep was no longer just a good idea; it was a necessity. He reclined the driver's seat a couple of notches and lay back. Thoughts of Karen and Kpa began to trade places in his troubled mind, clearly at first, then with less distinction, less separation, and he fell into a deep sleep.

A spate of images from Kent State and the Vietnamese central highlands began the visit to his unconscious, as a dream reworked the recent pain of watching Karen confront her past, folding it seamlessly into memories of the confrontation in Y Bam's longhouse. Karen became the woman being assaulted on the floor of the longhouse; the commander of the Ohio National Guard troops stood over her, hissing about a sniper as he pulled her head back by the hair. From the distant past, another figure appeared. The old man lying beaten and bloody in the doorway of the longhouse was no longer Y Bam. It was Grandpa Jake.

The dream ran its course without waking Jerry. When he did open his eyes, he felt rested and strangely calm. He sat for a few moments in silence, exploring the sense of purpose that filled him. Without even framing a conscious thought, he knew what he was going to do.

Reaching under the dash, he disconnected the odometer and got back on the highway. At the next exit, he turned around and headed north.

*****

Two days later, the frontpage headline in the Daily Record in Wooster Ohio shouted:

EXPLOSION AT GUARD ARMORY

Complete with pictures of the smoldering ruins, the article went on to say that the explosion occurred as a Guard unit drilled nearby. The ensuing fire had destroyed an adjacent mechanical service facility. Losses included jeeps and armored personnel carriers being serviced at the time. Newspapers across the state treated the explosion as second page news, speculating that the reduced military budget and poor maintenance probably contributed to the event.

The next day, a letter arrived at the Ohio National Guard headquarters in Columbus, addressed to the Adjutant General. The nondescript envelope was postmarked in Wooster the day of the explosion. The address was typed, as were the five words on the back, where the return address would normally have been: "Which Way the Wind Blows." The envelope contained a single sheet of notepad paper with two words, also typed: "For Allison."

That afternoon there was a second explosion, this one at the Mount Vernon armory about forty-five miles from Wooster. The

THE PURPOSE BREAKS

FBI's Cincinnati office that had taken charge of the investigation knew it would prove to be more than a coincidence, even before the second letter arrived. This one read: "For Jeffrey" and was otherwise identical to the first. The letters that followed successive explosions over the next two days a hundred miles apart read "For Sandra" and "For William."

The night after the last letter was received, one of the investigators was working late in the archives of the *Cincinnati Enquirer* when he found the link among the four names. The students killed at Kent State almost eight years earlier were Allison Krause, Jeffrey Miller, Sandra Scheuer, and William Schroeder.

As they discussed the case among themselves the next morning, one of the investigators who had worked in Chicago in the late sixties recognized the words on the back of the envelopes.

"Son of a bitch," he said. "'Which Way the Wind Blows.' That's from the Bob Dylan song where the Weather Underground got its name."

"But that outfit's long dead," another investigator said from his desk nearby.

"The outfit maybe, but not the people or the ideas."

As the conversation wandered over the finding, another fact occurred to the former Chicago agent.

"Hey, I just remembered. It was the Weathermen who bombed the Haymarket statue a couple of years back."

"What the hell's the Haymarket statue?" someone asked.

"Short story? It honored the cops that put down a riot in Chicago in the late eighteen hundreds. Bunch of people shot and killed."

"Come on, that's a bit of a stretch, isn't it?"

"No, I don't think so. Just look at it. Both there and at Kent, the government used lethal force to put down a demonstration. In both cases people were killed. It was that bombing that really put the Weathermen on the map, and there's still a lot of bad blood because of Kent State. If somebody wanted to rekindle the Weather Underground, there's fuel there for a damned good fire."

"And here, look at this," another agent said, with his finger on a page in a file he was leafing through. "That bombing in '68 was on May 4th, the same date as the shootings at Kent State."

*****

The commanders of the four targeted Guard units sent notices to all guardsmen that operations at those units were suspended until alternate arrangements could be made for the resumption of regular drills. The next day, every newspaper in the state reported the Adjutant General's decision to instruct all Guard units to cease outdoor drills and reduce exercises until further notice. One headline read: "ONG Grinds to a Halt." Another said: "Domestic Terror Hits Our State." In Kent, the *Record-Courier* asked: "A Ghost from the Past?"

As the headlines began to hit newsstands and front porches around the state, the salt covered 1974 Chevy van that had travelled unnoticed through Ohio's winter slush on second-hand snow tires was cruising into Georgia, sporting a wash job and its own regular tires. The radio had found some blue grass music and the odometer was once again happily counting off the miles.

CHAPTER 18

The vagaries of a mid-Atlantic winter began to yield to the longer days of late February. The approach of spring meant growing demands on David's time, both at the college and in the cooperative, and he was feeling the pressure. Curriculum changes and textbook selection for the next semester, agreements with produce buyers for the new season, a final round of edits to the Philippines report.... It was all interesting work, sure, but it would be so much better if he could take the time to enjoy it. Instead, he struggled to complete each task before the calendar swept it into the past with the mindless resolve of a combine.

Driving home one evening after a co-op board meeting to face yet another late night at his desk, he recognized the threat of overload in his life. He was quick to conjure up explanations as to how his situation was different from his father's, but he eventually had to admit that the apple hadn't fallen far from the tree. Add a wife and kids to the mix and somebody would be bound to get shortchanged. *Note to self on adding family to the mix: Hell, no!*

There was also something new in the works. Several county agents were impressed with what they'd seen on the farms of co-op members —the fresh approach to problems confronting most small producers in the Valley. They invited David to do short radio broadcasts following the noon market report on area stations. The idea was to feature a mix of timely tips on production and marketing as well as reports on current events of interest to growers.

The Communications Department at Shenandoah College gave him access to a small recording studio linked to several radio stations in the Valley. He'd be able to broadcast live or produce taped programs for times when his other activities made live transmission impractical. The Faculty Committee agreed to fund a research assistant for him, a student with prior radio production experience. For quality control, David had a simple test: would Dan Bruckman find the program interesting enough to take the time to sit and listen?

He began the first broadcast with a Virginia Tech report on starting seedlings in cold frames and tunnels. With a very small investment and some changes in planting technique, growers could cut the time from seeding to transplanting by up to ten days. That meant bigger transplants and earlier production. Or, if things got off to a late start—because of bad weather, for example—they could still salvage a regular growing season. He kept the style casual as though he was talking with friends at the kitchen table.

Other topics each week were timed to current farming activities, but he kept the programming flexible enough to include a current event if it could be useful to his listeners. He ended the Thursday program that week with the following announcement:

"Finally, folks, a note for those of you in Page County. VDOT has closed the low-water bridge on Route 613 outside of Bentonville until they can clear a dangerous buildup of flood debris upstream of the bridge. So, if you had planned to travel that way in the next couple of days, you'll have to find a different route."

Word of mouth at auction yards and farm supply stores quickly began to build an audience for the 12:10 pm radio program that became known as The Farm Notebook.

*****

April marked the start of the second operating quarter of the co-op and, as its treasurer and controller, David was invited to drop into the bank manager's office to discuss the first quarterly report. Mr. Jenkins was his usual pleasant self—a performance made easier by the fact that the coop's financials were at the upper end of the expected range. Even the dutiful Mrs. LeHew at her post outside Jenkins's office seemed to have picked up on the fact that David and the cooperative were now being counted among the bank's favorite customers.

"Well, congratulations, David," Jenkins said after they had gone over the summary report. "It looks like things are in good shape to start the season."

"Thank you," David answered. "I think the members are excited about what they've been able to accomplish so far. You should come out some day and see our new packing shed."

"I'll do that," Jenkins said as he set the co-op's file to one side. "Incidentally, we have another visitor to the bank this morning who would like to meet you."

"Oh?" David was at a loss, and his first reaction was to worry about who or what might be about to descend on him.

"As you know," Jenkins explained, "the Virginia Inland Port is scheduled to open next year, north of town, and we are expecting some large new industrial and commercial clients." He paused as if to savor the prospect. "To be better able to serve those clients, we've affiliated the Warren Bank with Riggs National Bank out of Washington. We bring local knowledge to the relationship and Riggs brings a broader range of financial services."

The way he put it, one would think it was a partnership of equals, although the balance sheet of the Warren Bank would scarcely warrant a footnote on the financial statements of its new

Washington partner. Nevertheless, David was careful to make sure his smile was of a congratulatory nature.

"Anyhow," Jenkins continued, "their Regional Manager of Corporate Accounts is here today and when she saw your name associated with the cooperative, she asked for the chance to say hello." Without waiting for David to inquire further, he picked up the phone and asked Ms. LeHew to invite the Riggs Bank visitor to join them in his office.

David hadn't seen Linda since they were teaching assistants together at UVA. When she appeared in the doorway of Mr. Jenkins's office a few moments later, he was stunned.

How do you laugh, cry, and stay composed all at the same time? You don't. You just hope that the kaleidoscope of feelings that suddenly tumbles across your face conveys what you'd like each person to see. As Jenkins watched and Linda wondered, David's mind flashed back to their months of collaboration in graduate school, their growing friendship, the night of innocence at River House, and then through the years of his own failure in affairs of the heart since they had gone their separate ways.

By the time they reached each other in the middle of Jenkins's office, joyful smiles had gained the upper hand. They embraced with such affection that Jenkins wondered if perhaps he should excuse himself.

"Well, well," Linda said, stepping back from David's arms to look at him. "So, this is the rural innovator of the Shenandoah Valley."

"No. That's crazy. Somebody's been exaggerating big time. You look wonderful, Linda. Banking agrees with you."

"Well, on balance it's OK. Working with people like Mr. Jenkins makes up for some of the other aspects." Linda smiled and glanced toward Jenkins.

"I can certainly appreciate that," David concurred, also turning to include the bank manager in the conversation.

"Linda's been a big help in familiarizing our staff with the way Riggs works with its clients," Jenkins said. Then, looking at his watch, he added, "If you two will excuse me, there's a matter I need to see to," and discreetly left the room.

They sat in the two chairs in front of Jenkins's desk and looked at each other, suddenly shy. Uncertainty shadowed their smiles. Linda was wearing an impeccably tailored woolen suit, a silk blouse, and dark shoes with practical heels. Her blonde hair was done in a French twist, and she wore just enough makeup to highlight her natural good looks.

David gestured toward his own plaid shirt, jeans, and windbreaker and said, "If I'd known I was going to meet the Regional Manager of Corporate Accounts I'd have dressed for the occasion."

"Nonsense. Tell me what you've been up to since grad school."

"Not much, really," he shrugged. "I joined the World Bank and traveled a lot, threw the cat into the pigeons a few times, had a few drinks, got divorced, went back to teaching and rented a small farm south of town."

"Sounds like quite a story. Am I going to get a chance to hear it sometime?"

"If you'd like. I'll leave out the gory details."

Linda cocked her head and looked at him out of the corner of her eye. "Oh, no. That's the good stuff!"

David changed the subject. "Listen, I have an idea. Do you have time for lunch today?"

"Not much. I need to be back in the city later this afternoon, but I can certainly take a quick break."

"Good. I make a mean tuna fish sandwich, and the view from my kitchen window is perfect."

He promised to have her back by two o'clock and went off to run errands until lunch time.

A couple of hours later they pulled into his driveway and Linda stepped out of the car. "Oh, David!" she exclaimed, as she took in the house and the outbuildings, and then stood looking up at the Blue Ridge. "This is wonderful. Was it all like this when you found it? Or have you fixed it up?"

"Well, the mountains are basically the way I found them," he said modestly.

"Cute," she said, but there was a warmth in her smile that spoiled the attempt at sarcasm.

"Actually, everything was in good shape when I came. I've kept up the yard and gardens. And that's my vegetable project," he said, pointing at the newly tilled area on the side of the hill.

Linda wandered around the yard in silence for several minutes, clearly enjoying the views, the fresh air, and the spring smells of earth and plants returning to life.

"If you had the time and the footwear, I'd suggest we take a walk up the Browntown trail." He pointed toward the base of the mountains. "The maples and the redbuds are finished blooming, but the dogwood and the paulownias are in flower. There are fiddleheads, trilliums, all sorts of ground plants."

He hesitated when he noticed that she was looking at him and smiling. "What?"

"You've always loved this country, haven't you?"

"Well, you have to admit, what's not to love?" he answered, but he felt self-conscious and gestured for her to follow him. "Come on. Let's get that sandwich."

He gave her a quick tour of the house, finishing in the kitchen where they teamed up to chop the gherkins, mix the mayo and tuna, and put generous helpings on multigrain bread he'd picked up fresh at the bakery that morning. Sandwich plates in hand, they moved to the kitchen table, where iced tea, and a plate of cookies waited to complete the lunch.

"Do you invite all your women home for tuna sandwiches?" Linda asked.

The question caught David off balance, and he hesitated for a moment, not sure how to respond. Then he heard himself say, "You're the first woman in this house since I moved in."

"You're kidding. So, you go on a lot of sleepovers, then, do you?"

David shrugged. "No, that just hasn't been part of my life for a while."

She looked at him, eyebrows raised.

"Lots of other stuff going on, I guess," he said, then rose and walked toward the fridge. "More iced tea?"

"No thanks, I'm fine. I didn't mean to make you feel uncomfortable. It's just that women were always a big part of your life. It's kind of strange to see you on your own."

"I guess I got tired of hurting people. Or being hurt," he said, returning to the table without looking at her. "I obviously didn't understand what was going on in that department. Now that I'm used to it, it's just easier being alone and focusing on other things."

"But don't you get the feeling that something's missing, David?"

"Sometimes I guess I do, but so far I've decided it's not worth the risk." After a moment he asked, "What about you? Anybody significant?"

"No," she replied. "I'm not keen on the risk either."

He nodded his understanding, and they ate in silence for a few moments before Linda added, "There could have been somebody once, but he was otherwise engaged."

A forgotten longing subdued his smile, but no words formed, and the moment passed.

They reclaimed the safe ground of friendship with small talk about the intervening years in their lives. When they'd finished the sandwiches and cookies, they took the last of their iced tea out onto the back porch. The April sun lit the spring countryside with every hue imaginable. Its warmth touched their faces, and the two drifted aimlessly, just beyond reach of the feelings their time together had stirred.

"When I look at the mountains this time of year, I realize the Irish were right," David said. "There really are forty shades of green."

"I can believe it," Linda said and then added, "I think I'd better be getting back. My VP's a stickler for prompt attendance at his meetings and I have a long drive to get to the office."

David was uneasy as he pulled into the parking lot next to her car about twenty minutes later. She had made him aware of a missing piece in his life and now she was about to say goodbye. He didn't want to let her go. He needed to give her some kind of signal about how he felt, but how could he do that when he didn't know himself?

"Next time, I want to take you up one of the trails into the Park," he said, as matter-of-factly as he could.

"I'd like that," she replied, "and maybe I'll bring a pair of gloves so I can help with the garden."

*****

That evening, as David sat in the study trying to concentrate on a batch of term papers, the telephone rang. He reached for it quickly, hoping it might be Linda.

"David?" the voice asked, weakly. "It's Teresa. Ray's sick."

CHAPTER 19

Jerry's van struggled, as it always did, on the ten-mile climb out of the village of Magdalena into the juniper and pine-studded mountains of southwestern New Mexico. It seemed to breathe a sigh of relief when he finally pulled off the dirt road two thousand feet above the valley floor. Leaving the vehicle by a dry creek bed, he picked his way carefully across its stones and boulders and climbed the last hundred yards through open woodland to reach a small patch of ground surrounded by a weathered fieldstone wall.

The Douglas' family cemetery was set on a shallow slope, with a majestic view of the mountains and the distant valley. Passing through the simple entrance, Jerry stood among a couple dozen stone markers in varying states of uprightness and legibility. The newest was a slab of granite with a single polished surface:

SFC Thomas J. Douglas
June 15, 1932 – October 12, 1968.
Proud to serve.

Jerry stood by Sergeant Douglas's grave for a few moments. Then, he sat on a nearby boulder with its overhanging juniper bush and let his eyes wander over the setting. The other graves dated as far back as the mid-eighteen hundreds, when forty thousand acres of this land had been deeded to Tom's great grandfather and become the Douglas ranch. Over the years there had been some attempt to align the burial plots, but the imperative of digging a hole deep enough in the rocky ground to protect the remains had prevailed, resulting in an agreeable randomness to the layout. Wind, sun, and soil had made the placement decisions for the shrubs and bunch grasses that completed the sanctuary.

The air was still brisk at this altitude, but anywhere there was shelter from the wind the spring sun had begun to work its magic. An array of green shoots and tiny wildflowers was putting in an appearance. Meandering trails in the surrounding hillsides were evidence that cattle still grazed the area, but they were no longer Douglas cattle. This land was now part of the Cibola National Forest and the US Park Service had issued grazing permits to other ranchers to run livestock on the now-public lands.

Looking back toward the road, Jerry remembered his first visit to the cemetery. Even with Mrs. Douglas's directions, it had taken him the best part of a day to find it. By early evening, when he started back down the mountain, the light had begun to fade, and he hadn't realized how deep the ruts were. At one point the muffler had dragged on the crown of the road, separating it from the exhaust pipe. Rolling down the main street of Magdalena sometime later, the van made such a racket he knew he'd have to do something about the muffler if he wanted to avoid a run-in with some eager deputy.

Fortunately, the lights were still on at the one garage in town, so he had pulled onto the lot and turned the motor off. The proprietor of Crossroads Automotive turned out to be Sergeant Douglas's cousin and a friendship had developed quickly. Some wire was all Jerry would have needed for a quick fix but, in less than an hour, he had acquired new brackets, put the van on the hoist and done a proper repair. He had also accepted a part-time job as a mechanic and been given a lead on a furnished mobile home off Second Street that was available by the month. Just like that, Magdalena had become the base of operations for his stay in New Mexico.

Now, it was time to head back to Virginia. He had put the last of his things in the van this morning and said his farewells in town. This trip up the mountain was for the same purpose.

There were times after he'd been here with Douglas's remains that Jerry couldn't be sure whether the conversation had been entirely in his mind or if he'd actually spoken. It was that feeling of a reality beyond his senses that made today's visit difficult. What he may not have said, or heard, he had felt, and he would miss the communion with this place, the way he missed the eastern slope of the Blue Ridge's Pinnacle, or his village in Pleiku Province. But it wasn't just the land; it was the people who bound him to that land, the people who were part of who he had become.

Passing through Albuquerque that afternoon, he stopped to say goodbye to Tom's widow. It was a pleasant visit, as it had been when he first arrived in New Mexico. She was still somewhat distant, but maybe that was normal. She didn't know him, and after all it had been more than ten years since her husband's death. She had gone on with her life. But it was more than that. When she talked of Tom it wasn't of times they had spent together or things they had shared. It was of marriage to a soldier serving successive tours in combat, of life on the home front and how he hadn't been much of a letter writer.

Jerry was left with the impression that they hadn't been close. While he might have wished for something more for his friend, he had to admit that it certainly made the transition easier for his wife when Tom didn't come home. For the same reason, Karen's withdrawal from him was probably a good thing. What future could he give her, especially now, after his Ohio project? It was selfish to want to be close to her. It would just be setting her up to be hurt again. It was time to resume the pieces of his life in Flint Hill, but he would do his best to leave Karen out of it.

*****

"What a heavenly aroma," he said, walking into the kitchen in Flint Hill on his first morning home.

"Just the usual," his mother said, delighted at his reaction.

"Well, pancakes and sausage beat PopTarts and Spam all to hell, I'll tell you that."

"That's disgusting," his mother gagged. "You need to learn to take better care of yourself."

"Why, when I've got you to sort things out for me?" Jerry replied, as he poured himself a cup of coffee and sat at his usual place.

That he would always be nearby so she could sort things out for him pleased Faith too much for her to risk pointing it out. She set a plate in front of him with sausage links and a stack of buttermilk pancakes.

"So, other than living on junk food, how was New Mexico?" she asked as she poured batter into the skillet for another batch of pancakes.

"It was OK. Pretty good, actually. The landscape's very different but it's impressive in its own way."

"And you said in one of your letters—your two letters, by the way, two letters in more than two months—that you'd seen your sergeant's widow. How did that go?"

"Come on, now. I also sent you a postcard from Houston."

Faith waved her spatula in the air dismissively. "That doesn't count."

He ducked any further discussion of his communication practices by answering her question.

"Mrs. Douglas—Mrs. Rowland now—is doing OK. Hard to tell, really, how things affected her but frankly I got the impression that she and Tom weren't all that close."

"It's hard to know what a couple is really like together, even if you see them every day," Faith said. "But I wouldn't be surprised if you were right. Time and memory tend to bring out the best in something. If it didn't show after all those years, maybe it wasn't there." Noticing a small package on the table she added, "What's that?"

"I don't know. Open it and see."

"I can't." She was suddenly flustered. "The pancakes will burn."

"OK, then, I'll just work on my breakfast. Nice weather we're having."

"I swear, you are incorrigible."

She finished the batch of pancakes, flopped them onto Jerry's plate and turned the stove off. Then she sat opposite him, wiping her hands in her apron.

"Go on, open it."

"I hope you didn't go and do anything foolish."

"Of course not."

It was a silver pendant with inset turquoise stones arranged to complement their natural shapes. The workmanship in the leaf pattern of the silver was exceptional.

Faith looked up, tears in her eyes, cradling the piece in her hand.

"Oh, Jerry. This is beautiful. But you shouldn't have. It must have cost a fortune."

"No, but never mind that. So, you like it?"

"I love it. Tell me about it."

"It's Navajo, of course. There are some good craftsmen in the bands around Socorro County, but they don't always have cash for the stuff they need, so they trade jewelry for it. The guy I worked for had a display case by the cash register for the pieces he'd taken in exchange for repairs. I kind of liked this one so I traded him a few hours of work for it." He didn't mention that a few hours were actually two days. Seeing his mother's pleasure with the gift made it worth every minute.

They spent the next few minutes with casual pleasantries and updates on how the time had passed since he last sat in her kitchen. Then Jerry looked at his watch.

"I guess if I want my old job back, I'd better get over to the shop."

"I suppose. Your father did say something as he left about some front wheel bearings that needed to be replaced if you were up to it."

Jerry took his dishes to the sink and began to make the mental shift to his work at the shop.

As if it had just occurred to her, Faith said, "By the way, there was some guy here a couple of weeks ago asking about you. Had an FBI badge."

CHAPTER 20

David had not faced serious illness among close friends or family before, but now his closest friend had cancer. He hadn't pressed Teresa for details over the phone, but it didn't sound like something they were going to fix with a pair of tweezers. As he made his way through the crowded halls of George Washington University Hospital toward Ray's room, the mingled odors of sickness and cure did nothing to help his state of mind. Every doorway and every nursing station confronted him with a dose of reality that he would just as soon have done without.

When he finally reached the room, Ray was lying on the bed, propped up slightly, his eyes closed. His face was thinner than when David last saw him and the ruddy complexion from his years in the tropical sun had been drained to the color of old tallow. An oxygen tube wandered over the pillow and across his face. David sat on a chair near the bed and stared blankly at the presence that resembled his friend.

The gentle hiss of oxygen in the nasal cannula and the rhythmic sparkle of medication dripping into the IV tube had a mesmerizing effect and he must have closed his eyes because when Ray spoke, it startled him.

"Hey, young fella," Ray said hoarsely. "When did you come in?"

"Just a couple of minutes ago. You were resting or sleeping, I don't know which."

Ray smiled. "Good to see you," he said, "but you don't look so good, like you lost your best friend or something."

"Still the smart ass, huh? I guess that's good. What's going on, Ray? You look like you've been kicked pretty hard."

"Yeah. All that coughing wasn't a cold after all. Do you believe it? I guess I should have switched to filters a long time ago."

"So, what's happening? What are they doing to you?"

"You mean other than poking and jabbing at me? If they can get my vitals up to where they want, they're going to cut me open tomorrow and take a look. The x-ray shows a fairly good chunk of cancer so hopefully they'll be able to get it."

"Good. Then what?" David grabbed onto the hope as though it was a certainty.

"Well, then they'll use chemotherapy to get what's left."

"Sounds good."

"Yeah. Sick as a dog and lose all my hair. That sounds great." He made an effort to clear his throat and it triggered a cough that quickly became a deep rattle, even through the tissues he held over his mouth.

"Come on, now. It beats the alternative."

"I don't know," Ray said between gasps for air. "After you've been around the track a few times, maybe not."

The comment hit David like a cold draft, and he stared at Ray without speaking.

Once he had his breathing under control Ray smiled at him and said, "Relax, I'm just messing with you." But even in a good cause, deception wasn't Ray's strongest suite and David's expression didn't change.

"But never mind all that," Ray said, "What's new in the country?"

"Not much." David reluctantly set his concern aside. "Unless you consider becoming a radio personality significant."

"Is that right?"

"Yeah. For five minutes a day I'm now one of the voices people skip over when they're looking for news or music."

"That's great. What's the purpose, other than fame and fortune?"

"Local farm coverage, mainly. News, tips, events."

"Good for you. That'll keep you sharp. Have you got some help on research and production?"

"Yes. That's really what makes it possible."

Ray smiled for a few moments, enjoying David's accomplishment.

"You've settled into the scene out there pretty well, haven't you?"

"I guess I have. It feels right. In fact, I've decided to buy the place in Browntown."

"Why not? The whole set-up seems to suit you."

"When you get out of here you'll have to come out and spend some time with me. Now that the mud is drying up and things are starting to grow, it's really very pleasant. And I won't even make you cut the grass."

"In that case I'm ready to go right now," Ray said and pulled the blanket back with his free hand as if to get out of bed. The effort triggered another coughing fit that left him struggling for air. Finally, he lay, exhausted, looking up at the ceiling. "Well, maybe in a week or two."

*****

David was standing at the door to his college office, fumbling with his key ring, when Jack Stockton approached his office next door.

"Good morning, David."

"Good morning, Jack. How are you this morning?"

"Good. Great, actually, but if you don't mind me saying so, you look like you could use a cup of coffee."

"Ever the detective, huh?" David smiled.

"Maybe, but that was an easy call. Come on. Dump your stuff and I'll put the pot on." Stockton's tone was sympathetic and the idea of a cup of coffee in good company had its appeal.

"OK, thanks. I'll join you in a minute." David put his briefcase on his desk, glanced quickly through the sheaf of messages he had collected from his mail slot and went next door.

Gesturing toward David's overall appearance, Stockton said, "So, is this the product of a night of carousing or a night spent with term papers?"

"Neither," David replied, taking a seat. "My best friend is in surgery this morning. A pretty serious case of lung cancer."

"Oh, I'm sorry. And I'm sorry to be making light of it."

"Not at all," David said quickly. "He'd be the first one to get a kick out of your observation."

"He sounds like an interesting character."

David smiled, "Yeah. Ray's a cross between a professor and a farm boy."

"Wow. Everybody should have a friend like that."

"I'm very lucky," David said, reflecting for a moment. "He's taught me a lot. Saved my ass a few times, too."

The coffee pot sputtered and hissed to signal that its work was done, and the two men turned their attention to fixing their beverages.

"When will you know how the surgery went?" Stockton asked.

"His wife will give me a call after she's talked to the doctor," David replied. The brief conversation seemed to have pointed him toward Ray's recovery and he was more relaxed as he returned to his seat with the coffee.

"And what's got you feeling so good this morning?" he asked Stockton.

"Well, it looks like we may be making some progress on that case I've been working on for the Bureau."

"You mean the explosions in Ohio?"

"That's the one. I think we're getting somewhere on the profile of our boy."

"Narrowing down the search, huh? That sounds like progress, all right."

"Well, I think we're at least looking in a more promising area."

"Oh?" David wasn't sure how curious he was supposed to be on something like an FBI case, but Stockton seemed happy to chat about it, so it couldn't hurt to at least show interest.

"Yes, the early leads pointed to a connection with an anti-war group from a few years back, the Weather Underground. As the Regional Director said in his press briefing last Friday, we're still pursuing that possibility but, as you can imagine, the files are pretty dusty. There are a lot of dead ends. What he didn't say was that the Bureau had been forced to back off from its Weathermen investigation after some of its agents were caught using illegal wiretaps and other tactics frowned on by the constitution."

"As I recall," David said, "Mr. Hoover didn't seem to think the constitution applied to him."

"He did write his own rules sometimes," Stockton admitted. "Anyhow, the government decided not to prosecute some of the Weathermen the Bureau was building cases against so, as you can imagine, we're not getting a lot of support now from the guys whose work was put on the shelf."

"That could certainly limit your progress," David offered.

"You said it. But I would still have thought that kicking around in those coals would stir up at least a spark or two on the Ohio case if there was anything there."

"And nothing?"

"Not so far." Then Stockton continued, "Anyhow, one afternoon I decided to go back and take a look at the findings from the crime scenes again. As I probably told you at some point, the forensics people decided it was an incendiary round from a rifle that triggered the explosions. What's more, they found a couple of fragments of the propane tanks at the point of entry that were large enough to give them a fix on the size and speed of the bullet. It was a 30-06 cartridge. That wasn't a big help in itself because that are a lot of Springfields, Brownings and such out there with that cartridge, used as hunting rifles. But it's also the caliber of the Army's sniper rifle, and the AP fragments and the residue of the explosive indicate that it was military grade ammunition."

"AP?" David asked.

"Armor piercing."

"So your guy is military or ex-military?"

"Not necessarily," Stockton said. "All this stuff is available at gun shows and in mail-order catalogues."

"You're kidding! Why on earth would anyone need that kind of ammunition?"

"Some people just use it to get their rocks off," Stockton replied, "but there are groups out there that are planning for some sort of Armageddon, and they have stockpiles of stuff like this."

"What a scary thought. Who do they see as the bad guy?"

"The government, big business, the Hatfields, the McCoys—there's no limit to the choices if you're inclined to explain your own failures as the result of some conspiracy."

"So, other than making me paranoid about my neighbors and confirming your hunch about the incendiary device, what does any of this get you?"

"Well, even though it doesn't point conclusively to a military connection, I think there is one. If only some of the pieces of the puzzle were military grade, I'd figure it was some wannabe, but with everything up to that level of quality and accuracy, my hunch is that our boy does in fact have a military background. What's more, he's meticulous—the only evidence we were able to find was the fragments and the residue. And," he emphasized, "he's a damned good shot."

"Come on, Jack. Those propane tanks are the size of a water buffalo. Even I could probably hit one."

"Yeah, but could you hit it in exactly the same place each of the four times, to get the maximum rupturing of the tank? And could you do it from far enough away that even experienced observers couldn't tell where the shots came from? Two of the guardsmen who were drilling that day in Wooster were Vietnam vets and they couldn't tell us where the shots had come from."

"So, it's someone who has a grudge against the military?"

"Or the government, or maybe just the Ohio National Guard."

"That's right," David said, snapping his fingers. "The letters. The shootings at Kent State. I remember that you were annoyed when the information was leaked about the names in the shooter's notes."

"Yeah. I think it might have put him on guard. Anyhow, we interviewed families and friends of the four students who were killed, and now we're doing the same thing for the wounded students. From film and photos of the demonstrations we also identified half a dozen ringleaders and made the rounds of them as well. About a hundred profiles in all so far. It's taken most of the winter but we're nearing the end."

"Any interesting leads?"

"Not yet. There's the usual mix of good and not-so-good, but no one stands out."

"That's got to be frustrating," David commented.

"Then last week I decided to go back over them with my idea about the military connection, someone with military experience that included real time behind a long-range rifle. That narrowed the list down to eight."

"From one hundred to eight? Yeah, that's progress all right," David said, approvingly.

"I'd be a lot happier if we had something that would point to an individual instead of just a profile—a glove, a tire track, a motel receipt—but our boy was very careful, like he was trained not to leave any tracks. I wouldn't be surprised if he spends a lot of time in the wilderness."

*****

On his way home after class, David found himself thinking back over the conversation. Stockton was looking for someone with a military background, combat experience and excellent rifle skills, someone with a grudge against the government or the military, someone who probably spent a lot of time in the wilderness and someone close to one of the victims at Kent State. *Someone like Jerry Fletcher,* he thought, as easily as if he was reading the name on a passing billboard.

When the reality of the thought struck him, it took all the effort he could muster to sandbag his brain against it and stop the car safely on the shoulder of the road.

The twist in his gut, the frozen stare… it was that same deer-in-the-headlights feeling he had in the moments after Sherry had asked, "What were you and Diane doing at River House?"

To the adrenaline that surged through him, there was no difference between *what have you done* and *what will you do*.

"It can't be," he said aloud. But as the adrenaline subsided and David began to think, nothing but outright denial could block the obvious fit between his friend Jerry and the FBI profile. *Of course, it's all hypothetical,* he assured himself. *There's nothing that would drive Jerry to do such a thing.* Then he remembered how Jerry had dismissed his inquiry about Karen.

"Keeps to herself these days," he had said. That could certainly be the result of the shooting, and David was sure he detected a sense of loss in the long pause that had followed. *So, while he's in prison for something he might just as easily have been honored for, his girlfriend gets shot protesting the war and the effects of her injuries include ruining their relationship.*

He finished the drive home resigned to the fact that Jerry was probably the man the FBI was looking for, and at a loss about what he should do.

CHAPTER 21

"Hey, Jerry," the Fletcher's bookkeeper shouted from the doorway into the shop.

Jerry came out from under a hoist and looked in her direction. "There's someone here to see you."

He put his socket wrench on a tool tray and headed toward the office, wiping his hands on a rag as he walked. He hoped it might be a customer with a question about his car, but his mother's comment about an FBI investigator wouldn't concede the field. As he entered the small office, sure enough, a suit was standing there with a serious, clean-cut face.

"Mr. Fletcher?" he asked, "Gerald Fletcher?"

"That's me, unless you want my old man."

"I'm Special Agent Johnson, Mr. Fletcher. FBI," the man said, ignoring the question of Senior or Junior and holding up a badge that Jerry glanced at. "Is there somewhere we can talk?"

"Sure, right here." Turning to the bookkeeper, Jerry said, "Hey, Katie, how about taking a break for a few minutes?" With a brief glance of concern at Jerry and the agent, she took her purse and headed toward the lunchroom.

Jerry moved casually to his father's desk in the corner of the room and took what everyone in the shop called the boss's seat. Gesturing toward a chair in front of the desk for Agent Johnson, he made a quick judgment call: Since there was only one agent, the FBI was probably treating this so far as a background investigation. If he was a suspect, Johnson would have had a partner.

"What can I do for you, Agent Johnson?"

"Mr. Fletcher, do you know a Karen Guersten?"

"Yeah, sure. Why?"

"What's your relationship with her?"

"I don't know. Has something happened to Karen?"

"No, she's fine," he said. Then he corrected himself, "I mean nothing has happened to her recently."

"Then what's this about?"

"What do you mean you don't know what your relationship is to her?"

Johnson's refusal to answer his questions grated on Jerry but he knew he couldn't afford to lose his temper, so he stopped pressing the agent and took a different tack. A nice chatty answer might take the edge off the conversation.

"I'm sure you know that Karen was wounded at Kent State," he began. "Before that, and before I went to Vietnam, we were an item, but when I got out of Leavenworth, I went to see her, and she'd changed."

Johnson didn't blink at the reference to Leavenworth, confirming Jerry's assumption that he already knew about his background.

"Hell, I guess I'd changed, too," he continued. "Anyhow, we've had lunch a couple of times, gone for a couple of hikes in the Park... it's all pleasant enough, but that's about it." He was ticking off items he was sure were in Johnson's notebook and he decided to volunteer another biggy. "She did ask me to take her to Kent last fall, 'to confront her demons' as she put it, but that didn't go too well, and she had a setback. I haven't seen her since."

"How did that make you feel?"

Jerry glanced at the agent as if he couldn't believe he'd asked such a stupid question. Forcing as friendly a tone as he could manage, he said, "You've been watching too much Merv Griffin lately."

"It's a stock question," Johnson said, a little sheepishly.

"I wasn't very happy at the prospect of having to jerk off in the shower for the foreseeable future," Jerry said, as dismissively as he could. "But Karen seems happy enough with her set-up in Stanley and enough has happened in my life that the fantasy of the little woman and a white picket fence doesn't keep me up nights. I guess that's sort of how things will stay. Something else might be nice someday, but I don't know."

Johnson decided that Jerry was being cooperative enough that giving him more information would be more of a help than a hindrance.

"Mr. Fletcher, as you may have seen, there was a series of explosions at National Guard facilities in Ohio last winter."

"Oh, yeah. They made Cronkite a couple of evenings."

"We're investigating those attacks."

"Flint Hill is a long way from Ohio, Agent Johnson."

Johnson continued, "One theory we're looking into is that someone close to one of the victims at Kent State might see this as a way to get back at the Guard."

He watched for a tell-tale flinch, but Jerry didn't move, except to shrug and say, "Makes sense, I guess. I imagine a lot of people were really pissed off." *But not as many as should have been*, he thought, without changing his expression.

"Do you own a rifle, Mr. Fletcher?"

"Yeah, well, it's my old man's actually, but I'm the one that uses it. A 30:30. Got a shotgun, too. Why do you want to know?"

Ignoring the question, Johnson continued, "What kind of a 30:30 is it?"

"Winchester, lever action."

"Do you know where the weapon is?"

"Sure. In the gun cabinet in the house." He suddenly realized it had been a long time since he'd used it and he hoped that it hadn't been moved."

"How about showing it to me?"

Jerry led the way across the sales lot to the house and, as they went in the back door, he called out, "Hey, Mom. Got a visitor."

Faith looked up from the sink as they passed through the kitchen.

"This is Special Agent Johnson. FBI" Jerry said, as offhandedly as he could.

"Good morning, Mrs. Fletcher."

Innate hospitality vied with concern in Faith's expression as she acknowledged the stranger,

"Good morning, Agent."

"We're just going to take a look at the gun cabinet," Jerry said, without breaking stride. Fortunately, the Winchester was there, along with the 12-gage and his old 22.

When Jerry opened the cabinet, Johnson reached for the rifle, opened the chamber, and turned the weapon to look down the barrel. It was clean, but not recently oiled.

"Any other weapons, Mr. Fletcher?" he asked, handing the gun back to Jerry. "Either yours or anyone else's who might live here?"

"No, that's it. Don't need anything else for deer, turkey, or varmints."

The contents of the cabinet apparently weren't of further interest to Johnson because he began to look about the room.

"Would you mind if I had a look around while we're here?"

Jerry smiled as pleasantly as he could and said, "I'm sure it would be fine, normally, but this is my parent's home. My father's away this morning at an auction and my mother is not used to visitors being anywhere other than the parlor or the dining room. So, unless you've already gone through the formalities," he said as an oblique reference to the search warrant he knew Johnson didn't have, "I think it might be best to wait 'til my father's home."

Jerry knew the house was clean, but he couldn't resist tossing a little chum in the water. Maybe it was an unnecessary risk, but if the sharks came back and found nothing, they might be more inclined to look elsewhere and leave the Fletchers alone.

"That's fine," Johnson said, abandoning his attempt to short-circuit the search procedures.

As they made their way back to the shop office, he began a different line of questioning.

"Have you ever had an M1, Mr. Fletcher?"

"Yeah. Uncle Sam gave me one for a while in Vietnam, an M1D."

"What did you think of it?"

"It was heavy and awkward. If you stuck it between a couple of trees it could help you get up a riverbank, but that's about all it was good for."

"I don't know," Johnson said. "I hear it was pretty accurate."

"Yeah, sure. With that long barrel it was accurate, all right. I'm sure that was useful for the guys who didn't grow up with a rifle in their hands, but most people around here wouldn't need a clunker like that to bag their limit."

It was strange, but talking about the M1 like that, Jerry felt like he was badmouthing a friend. It was the closest thing to guilt that he'd felt for a long time, and he suddenly needed to change the subject.

"Is there anything else I can do for you, Agent Johnson?"

"Yes, you've been very helpful but there is one more thing I'd like to ask you about."

"Shoot," Jerry said and then winked when Johnson glanced at him. "Couldn't resist," he added.

Johnson couldn't decide whether he wanted to buy this guy a beer or put a watch on him twenty-four-seven, but his training kept him on track and with just enough of a smile to acknowledge the humor, he continued with his question.

"When I came to your house a few days ago, your mother said you were traveling. She was good enough to tell me when you were expected back, but do you mind me asking where you were?"

"In New Mexico. I went to visit my squad leader's grave and meet his widow."

"Where in New Mexico?"

"He's buried in the mountains near a little place called Magdalena and she's living in Albuquerque."

"Did you know him before Vietnam?"

"No."

"How long was he your squad leader?"

"A couple of months."

"Isn't that a long way to go to visit the remains of someone who was just your boss for a short time, a long time ago?"

Jerry was suddenly angry. Who the hell did this prick think he was to decide how he should feel about Tom Douglas? They reached the office in silence but when he closed the door it hit the jam with the same force as if Gerald had just returned from firing a belligerent employee. Johnson tensed in anticipation of an outburst, but Jerry stood still in the middle of the room, staring at a wall. When he spoke, it was in a hard, measured tone.

"I'm guessing you've never been in combat. You've never had somebody protect your green ass until you learned enough to up your odds of surviving. You've never watched the blood drain out of what was left of him as he lay in a hole in the mud, still worrying about his men."

He looked at Johnson and his expression changed from accusation to something like sympathy, as if what he had just described was a privilege that Johnson had never experienced.

"As for why I waited so long to go and see him, I was, as you well know, otherwise engaged."

Johnson struggled with gut-level sympathy for the situation Jerry had depicted while he searched for a way to salvage the interview.

"I'm sorry," he said. "That's part of the story I wasn't familiar with."

While Jerry processed the apology, Johnson assessed what he had just witnessed. This guy could be pushed to anger, all right, even if it was fairly well controlled, but it had happened on the subject of his squad leader in Vietnam, not his former girlfriend. On that subject he had shown a remarkable degree of equanimity, but it seemed genuine. Maybe they had never been that close.

"How long were you in New Mexico?"

"Not far off three months, I guess. I left here before the end of the year, after I brought Karen home from Kent." He intentionally made the connection that he was sure Johnson would already be wondering about. "She wanted to be alone and I had been thinking about Tom—Sergeant Douglas—ever since I got out, so I decided it was a good time to leave."

"Weather can be rough going across the country that time of year," Johnson observed.

"Yeah, that's what my mother thought, too. I went south first and then took I-10 across." He said nothing about his visit in North Carolina. It was unlikely that the Bureau would have come across his connection there, other than his days at Fort Bragg. Contrary to appearances, he had no intention of volunteering anything other than to get credit for candor by telling them things they already knew or would likely find out.

"Why'd you stay so long?"

"Well, when I left, I didn't know what I'd find, you know, like maybe the widow would need some help or something, so I didn't just take a couple weeks of leave. My old man was good about the work here, said he'd hold a place for me, so I didn't feel like I had to rush back. But that left the matter of making a living when I got there."

"So, what did you do?"

"Mechanic. I got a job at a garage there in Magdalena."

"Can you give me a contact so we can confirm that?"

"Sure," Jerry said, reaching for a pen and notepad. As he wrote, he continued to talk. "It's weird how things happen sometimes. This guy turned out to be Sergeant Douglas's cousin. A nice kind of a guy, too, so I was happy to help him out for a while and learn about the Douglas family. Nice country, as well. Do you know it?"

"No, never been."

"Different from around here, that's for sure, but nice."

"Did you spend a lot of time hiking and such?"

"A fair bit, I guess. The grave was up in the hills on the old Douglas ranch. That area's now part of the Cibola National Forest, like a national park."

"You're close to a national park here, too, aren't you?"

"Right out that window," Jerry replied. "Lots of good hiking there if you need a workout."

"Do you go to the Park often," Johnson asked.

"Whenever I can. The trails are a lot steeper now than they used to be!"

Johnson chuckled. The pleasant flow of the conversation and the ease with which Jerry volunteered information was having the desired effect on him. It didn't come across as a practiced presentation, more the awe shucks style of a confident small-town guy who had nothing to hide. SAT tests buried in the dusty files of Rappahannock County High School might have cautioned Johnson to reserve judgment on that score. As it was, his decision to recommend continued surveillance was more a matter of his careful approach to the work than to any particular suspicion that their interview had raised.

The following afternoon, as Jerry pulled off the lot on his way to the NAPA store in Front Royal for a couple cases of motor oil, he saw the dark blue sedan parked in the shade at the farm supply depot next door.

CHAPTER 22

"What do you mean they didn't do anything?" David asked, almost shouting into the phone at Teresa. He immediately regretted his abruptness, but he couldn't believe what he had just heard.

"They opened him up," she said, "but the cancer was everywhere, so they just sewed him up again." There was something methodical in her voice, remote, as if it was performing a service for her while she huddled somewhere nearby.

David was silent as he tried to come to terms with the idea that Ray was in trouble, that Ray was going to die. Then a whimper at the other end of the line reminded him that there was someone else to think about.

"I'm so sorry, Teresa. How are you managing?"

"Not very well," she said. "It doesn't seem real."

"No. Exactly. Would you like me to come in? I can be there in a couple of hours."

"No, it's all right. My friend Edith from the office is coming over tonight."

"OK, I'll cancel my class tomorrow and come in in the morning. Do you want me to come to the house or go to the hospital?"

"You'd better go to the hospital. The doctor is going to speak with him when he makes his morning rounds, so he will just have learned about the surgery when you get there. Spend some time with him. I'll come in later."

They agreed on times and said good night.

David left a phone message at the college office asking that someone put a note on his classroom door cancelling class the next morning. Then he went about his after-dinner clean-up routine. The noise as he put the dishes in the sink was strangely offensive and when he tried to wipe the counter the sponge sprang from under his hand. The second time it happened, he kicked it across the floor, left everything else as it was, and made his way toward the back porch.

His eyes adjusted quickly to the last of the nightly struggle between blue and grey. The fight was never the same, but the outcome was never in doubt. As darkness overtook the fading colors stars appeared, to be mimed by fireflies in the fields and woodland below the ridge. *I wish Ray could see this*, he thought, and he began to cry for the first time in a very long time.

*****

At the hospital the next morning David stopped at a nursing station to ask where Ray's post-op room was. A middle-aged man carrying a clipboard looked up when he heard Ray's name.

"Are you a member of Dr. Baker's family?" he asked.

"No, I am a close friend."

"I see. I'm Dr. Baker's doctor and I just checked on him a few minutes ago."

"How is he?" David asked, the concern plain on his face.

"Well, he seems to be recovering from the surgery about as we would expect. We have him on a sedative, not just for comfort but because we don't want him coughing. He's awake though, and I'll leave it to him to fill you in on our conversation."

The room was only two doors down from the nursing station, and Ray may have overheard the conversation because he was watching the door when David walked in. His chest was wrapped in bandages, and through them a tube extended to a receptacle at the side of his bed. The IV was still in his arm and an oxygen tube once again lay across his face. He looked at David and a faint smile touched his otherwise distant expression.

David pulled a chair over next to the bed and sat down.

"Good morning," he said. "How was your night?"

"Not bad, I guess," Ray answered in a faint, hoarse voice. "I really don't remember." He licked his dry lips and glanced in the direction of a water cup on the bedside table. David picked it up and held it where Ray could put his lips on the straw. After a couple of sips, he released the straw, turned his head slightly to signal enough, and caught his breath in short audible gasps.

"No marathon today."

"Not today," David agreed, and they sat in silence for a few moments.

"How was the traffic?"

"Not bad. Still backed up some at the bridge."

Even the closest of friends need small talk sometimes.

"Are you comfortable?"

Ray shrugged. "Got a sore chest."

"No shit."

Finally, Ray looked at David and said, "My quack was in this morning."

"Good. And what did he tell you?"

"He did his best 'Marcus Welby' impression, but that didn't change the message." Ray paused, whether to catch his breath or confront the facts David couldn't tell. Then he said simply, "There's nothing they can do."

David looked at Ray, struggling to find something to say, but it would have taken more wisdom or more distance than he felt at that moment, so he let the silence stand for thoughts they both understood.

"I keep watching the door," Ray said, "expecting him to come back, to tell me he made a mistake. It was the guy in the next room he should have been talking to."

David acknowledged the wish with a quiet grunt. As his friend lay in front of him trying to come to terms with the end of his existence, all he could say, finally, was, "I'm sorry, Ray."

"Yeah. Me, too. I still had some living to do." The words were matter-of-fact, but Ray was looking off in a daze toward the ceiling. "It's funny. When you get to be my age, the arithmetic starts to make dying more real, but it always seemed to be over a hill somewhere, you know? Out of sight, like there would always be time to do a thing or two we hadn't thought of yet." He turned his head and looked at David. "Guess what," he said. "It's not true."

David had tears in his eyes. He reached over the railing and put his hand on Ray's arm.

"Have you talked to my wife?" Ray asked.

"Yeah, last night."

"How is she?"

"Not too good, but she had a friend from the office go over and spend the night."

"Edith?"

"Yeah."

"Does Teresa know?"

"Uh huh. She asked me to come in this morning and she'll be along shortly."

"Being managed, am I?"

"I prefer 'supported'."

"You preachers are all the same."

David suspected it was he who was being managed, but he was glad for the levity. It seemed to provide some relief for Ray, too. As he relaxed, fatigue caught up with him, and when Teresa arrived about thirty minutes later Ray was sleeping.

"I told him you'd be in shortly," David said. "He's been asleep for a half hour or so."

"How is he?" she asked.

"Weak, but himself. And what about you?"

"About how you'd expect. Has the doctor been in?"

"Yes. Ray's still kind of in shock, but he talked to me about it."

They agreed that David would come back the next afternoon, and he left Ray and Teresa to begin the process of finding a no-fault path toward their pending separation.

When he returned the next afternoon, Ray was propped up in the bed and looking more like himself. He complained about the food, except that the pie wasn't bad. For the kind of money they were paying he thought the drinks should be stronger, but the linen was clean and the help was friendly, well, mostly.

As his nurse worked on his IV on the far side of the bed, he said, "There's this one woman who likes sticking needles in me and messing with my IV. Don't know what I ever did to her." He winked at David. "I told her if she kept it up, I wouldn't introduce her to my eligible bachelor friend."

David shifted uncomfortably and told him to stop picking on the poor woman.

"Oh, all right. Bonnie, say hi to my friend David."

They exchanged greetings and David said, "I think maybe you're doing too good a job with this guy. I thought we'd get at least a couple days off before he was back to his old self."

"This guy? What are you talking about? Dr. Baker's adorable." She reached over and pinched his cheek, firmly enough that he said ouch. "You just have to let him know who's boss."

The nurse left and things settled down.

"You seem a lot stronger today." David observed. "Is that just a short burst or are things much better?"

"Both. I feel stronger and I go longer between naps, but there's still no doubt that somebody stuck an axe in my chest."

They talked a little more about his recuperation, how much longer the doctor thought he'd be in hospital, but the subject of cancer didn't come up. There was nothing new to add, and Ray seemed relieved to have some time that wasn't dominated by his new reality. By unspoken agreement they would keep it that way for the time being. David wanted to know how his projects were being managed while he was out of the office. Ray was happy that daffodils had apparently poked through the leaf cover in the back yard in Arlington.

"They're bound to be early along the wall there," he said, "but it's nice to pretend that spring has arrived."

David couldn't shelve his own worries quite as well as Ray seemed to be doing. Thoughts of Jerry kept creeping into his mind. At one point, Ray said, "You seem preoccupied. Is everything all right on your end?"

He should have said fine and left it at that. Instead, he answered, "I've got a bit of a dilemma."

"Uh-oh," Ray said. "When a neurotic good guy says he's got a dilemma, there's trouble. What's going on?"

"Well," David said hesitantly, "Are you up for a story?"

"Sure, but if I fall asleep, don't take it personally."

David moved his chair a little closer to the bed, glanced around to make sure there was no one else in the room, and began.

"You know those attacks against National Guard facilities in Ohio last December?"

"Yeah."

"I think I know who's behind them."

"You're not going to tell me you belong to some latter-day version of the Weathermen, now, are you?"

"Funny. But, in fact, that's who the FBI thought might be behind the attacks, too."

"And now you've got an in with the Bureau, as well? You'd better start at the beginning."

David told Ray about his faculty colleague, Jack Stockton, about Stockton's involvement in the Ohio investigations, and the visits over coffee that had become part of their routine.

"I'm sure, with his background, he doesn't say more than is appropriate, but he's been telling me about this case and about the profile they're developing of the shooter." He told Ray how Stockton had reached the conclusion that the attacker had military experience and outdoor skills.

Ray wasn't impressed.

"Come on," he said. "Put an age limit of twenty to forty on that and you've narrowed your suspects down to only three or four million."

"Yeah, but remember the notes that were sent to the Guard with the names of the Kent State victims," David replied. "If you look for military and outdoor connections among the families and friends of the victims, the numbers become very manageable. That's what Jack did. As of this week he's found eight."

"Now that starts to get interesting," Ray admitted. "But I haven't seen any dilemma yet."

"OK, now for the weird part. While I was driving home the other day after talking with him, I was ticking off the characteristics Jack listed, and it dawned on me that I was picturing a guy in my high school class. They're a perfect fit. He grew up hiking and camping in the Park—hunting, too. He was drafted and served in Vietnam. While in the central highlands he did something many people thought he should have been decorated for. Instead, he was court-martialed and sent to Fort Leavenworth. Then, while he was in prison, his girlfriend was shot at Kent State."

"Those are the makings of an unhappy camper, that's for sure," Ray commented. "And to think that you're in the loop on this thing, between the investigator and someone who could be the attacker! That's cool."

"Yeah, small world story number twenty-seven, I know. I also know I should just pick up the phone and tell Jack where to find him, but I don't want to do that."

"Why not?"

"I don't know." David hesitated. "Yeah, OK. I'm worried that they could come down like a ton of bricks on him, and it would have nothing to do with what he might have done. There's a lot of unfinished business around that Kent State affair, and the FBI got its knuckles rapped on the Weatherman investigations, too. You walk somebody with the right profile into a situation like that and what chance has he got?"

"You're not doubting our legal system now, are you?"

"Yeah, I guess I am. But even if it worked, technically, would it consider the facts back far enough to treat him fairly?"

"Oh, my! A difference between legality and justice. Somebody's got his big boy pants on."

David ignored the remark.

"Nobody was hurt in those attacks. And he's had some heavy shit happen to him, and to people he cares for. The government evicted his family from the Blue Ridge mountains to make way for Shenandoah National Park. As far as he sees it, they lost their farm just so FDR could create employment for a bunch of lowlanders. Then, in Vietnam, he protected the people of his village, literally from rape and pillage, and got sent to prison for it. Ten years, he served! And on top of all that, the only woman he's ever cared for is part zombie today because some week-end warrior got pissed off at antiwar demonstrators. Jerry may have taken the law into his own hands, but you have to admire his loyalty, his courage."

David had been looking out the window as he spoke. Now he turned back to Ray.

"OK. Assuming it's him, the right thing to do would be to turn him in. But part of me wants him to get away. He may have broken the law, but I admire what he did."

"Blowing up propane tanks?"

"Well, not that specifically. But he saw a wrong that was not only going unpunished but was even unacknowledged—soldiers shooting unarmed students in a protest demonstration—and he brought the whole Ohio National Guard to its knees without hurting a soul."

They sat in silence for a few moments, Ray waiting, David wondering how to pull the whole thing together.

"OK. Bottom line. Do I tell Jack? Or do I help Jerry? I just can't figure it out."

"But hang on," Ray said. "That's not the question."

David was instantly annoyed. He had no interest in philosophical niceties at this point and was about to say so when Ray pointed out the obvious.

"If you don't tell Jack about your high school classmate, how long do you think it will be before he sees your pictures on the same page of the yearbook and begins to wonder about your sympathies?"

"Oh, shit!"

"It's not whether you tell him or not. It's who you decide to help after you tell him."

"That gets even trickier than I thought."

Ray let the conversation hang there for a moment.

"OK, you've been most eloquent on why you should help Jerry. Let's see if I can summarize the other half of your dilemma. It's fairly simple, really. If you don't tell your colleague about your friend, you're breaking the law."

David looked at Ray with a stunned expression, as though hearing him say it had made it real for the first time.

"And depending on how they decide to treat your curiosity during those friendly coffee breaks," Ray said, "and your encounters with Jerry since he got out of prison, you could be looking at a felony."

"You're kidding, right?"

"No, I'm not. With your background you'd probably get the benefit of the doubt and have your knuckles rapped. Then all you'd have to worry about is how the college and your friends at the co-op would feel about your conviction."

It was true. Whatever the formal sentence might be for aiding and abetting, trouble with the law would probably mean the end of the life he had begun to build in the Shenandoah Valley.

"Now, let me change the subject," Ray said.

David had a fleeting moment of relief until Ray introduced the new subject.

"How would you feel if you helped your boy escape and, when he went back to Ohio to finish the job, someone got killed?"

David felt sick. He knew immediately that this risk was a big part of the ambivalence that had hung over his decision.

"How am I doing so far?" Ray asked.

David had slumped forward in his chair and was looking at the floor.

"You can stop any time."

Ray was tired and the pain in his chest flared like the wandering edge of a grass fire. He needed the morphine, but he knew it would keep him from finishing this conversation. Something else needed saying, and now was as good a time as any.

"I love you, kid," Ray said.

David was caught off guard by the strength of the sentiment, but he was touched by it.

"I love you, too, you old fart. Thanks."

"No," Ray frowned. "I'm not finished. I love you, but you're an idiot."

"What?"

"You're an idiot. You've got a brain and a heart of gold and you're wasting them both trying to make everybody happy. Not just in this thing about propane tanks in Ohio. In everything. You act out some skit on the main stage of your life, based on what you think people expect you to be. Then you fritter away what remains of who you really are in a pathetic off-Broadway search for something that'll make you happy."

David couldn't believe what he was hearing. His immediate response was to be hurt and deny everything, but he sat in silence, looking at Ray.

"And guess what," Ray continued. "You're not doing anybody any favors. Do you think your high school sweetheart was better off marrying you just because you couldn't face the risk that she'd be hurt if you didn't? Do you think your old man is better off living with the hope you'll come back to the church just because you're afraid to tell him what you really think? Were there really no signs from Diane that she had a different agenda from yours, or was it only when she told you her view of your relationship that you realized you had no idea what you really wanted? How can you be so decisive in your work and such a shadow boxer when it comes to the people in your life?"

David was embarrassed by this litany of his weaknesses, but he couldn't deny the relief that grew as Ray spoke. At last, he didn't have to hide because he couldn't. Everything Ray had said was true.

"You know what really pisses me off?" Ray continued. "I'm lying here in front of you, proof that time is no joke. I'm going to be dead soon and you're living as though you've got all the time in the world. I thought you were headed in the right direction after you dried out, but you're back where you started. You act as though there's some way you can be all things to all men and still be happy, when you know goddamned well that at some point you have to make a choice. This whole thing with Jerry is a dilemma only because the choices won't let you play both parts. There's no way you can script them for different stages."

It was hard to tell if it was fatigue or frustration, but Ray had been pushing his words, insisting on them, and he was exhausted.

"So, what do I do?" David asked lamely and Ray looked at him in dismay.

"Have you not heard a thing I said? It's not important what I think you should do. Right now, I don't give a good goddamn what you do. You have to pick a path, that's all. One that has heart. Thank you, Mr. Castenada."

"Who?"

"Never mind. Call it your gut, your heart, I don't care. You have to go with what feels right. And if you don't know what feels right, then you'd better start learning."

Ray was done, spent. His ragged breathing was the only sound in the room as he pressed the nurse's call button.

David sat in a chair by the window, trying to make sense of what he had just heard. If Ray was right, he already knew what to do. He just had to learn how to listen to himself. After some time, when he thought Ray had fallen asleep, he stood and moved toward the door.

"Sorry to give you a hard time" his friend muttered. "But I think you needed it." Then he winked.

CHAPTER 23

Jerry had just pulled the cover off the differential of a 1970 Econoline when Katie called from the office doorway.

"Jerry, phone call."

"OK, there in a minute." He wiped his hands on a shop rag and headed toward the office. He was expecting NAPA to call about some parts he had ordered for another job, but normally they would just leave a message.

"Who is it?" he asked Katie as he reached for the phone.

"I don't know. Some woman."

"Hello."

"Jerry?"

"Yeah, who's this?"

"It's Joan, Jerry. How are you?"

"Oh. Hi, Joan. I'm fine. Is something wrong? Is Karen OK?"

"She's fine. Doing a little better, actually. That's not why I'm calling, though. Can you talk for a minute?"

"Yeah, sure. What's up? What's that noise in the background?"

"I'm calling from a booth in town. We had a visit from the FBI yesterday."

"Oh, shit!" Jerry said. "I guess I should have told you, but I had a visit, too."

"What's going on?" she asked.

"They're looking into the explosions at Ohio National Guard installations last December."

"What's that got to do with us?"

"Nothing. They seem to have a theory that it was someone connected to one of the Kent State victims and I figure they're working down the list."

"It was so weird," Joan said. "I didn't know what to say to the guy. I took him down to the packing room because he wanted to talk to Karen, but she got mad at him for coming around and I had to take him back to the house."

"That's all she needs," Jerry interjected.

"I explained her behavior," Joan continued, and gave him her doctor's name, so I think he understood. He asked to look around the house, but I told him Karen would explode so, if he needed to do a search, he should get a warrant and let me know when he's coming. Then I'd take Karen for a drive or something while they're here."

"Good thinking. That would upset her for sure." After a moment he continued, "Listen, Joan. They know about Karen and me and they know we went to Kent State last fall. That means they know about her breakdown, so there's nothing that you need to worry about."

Even as he spoke, he was thinking about the wall in her room. That would certainly trigger more intense interest by the FBI. But trying to hide it now would be too dangerous, so he didn't say anything. He'd just have to depend on the fact that the Guerstens knew nothing of his visits to Ohio or even his thoughts, beyond normal empathy with Karen.

"And I've seen a dark sedan parked down the road from our driveway a couple of times. Is that them, too?" Joan asked.

"Probably. I know it's upsetting to have them nosing around, Joan, but we're all just part of a broader investigation, so don't worry. Answer their questions and give them what they want and the whole thing will eventually go away. That's what my parents and I are doing, too."

"Well, OK, but it's adding insult to injury, you know? Karen is finally starting to come out of her shell and now this happens."

"So, she's getting over her visit to Kent, is she?"

"That's going too far, but I do see improvement. Why don't you drop by sometime and say hello?"

"Thanks. I might just do that."

As he walked back to his work bay, he was pleased with the fact that Karen was getting better. But he was also satisfied that the conversation with Joan couldn't have been scripted any better for the agents who were probably listening.

In the several days since the agent came to see him, Jerry had begun to take a realistic look at his situation. He was reasonably sure there would be no evidence tying him directly to the events in Ohio. But his skills, his military experience, his court martial conviction, his ties to Karen, their visit to Kent State—the circumstantial evidence—was entirely too compelling to not force at least a very thorough investigation. Special Agent Johnson would be back, with others no doubt, and who knew what the threshold might be for them to make an arrest purely on circumstantial evidence.

He eventually concluded that he had two choices: Wait to be arrested and then make the most of punishing and embarrassing the Ohio Guard during his trial. Or, make a run for it, knowing that probably meant leaving Virginia. Not a very attractive set of options.

The more he thought about it, the more doubtful he became of any benefit to a courthouse campaign. He might score a few headlines by dragging out the studies that faulted the Guard's performance. There'd be a few choice quotes from defense witnesses, but why should the eventual outcome be any different this time around? After a couple of months it would be business as usual among the good people of Ohio, and he'd be back in prison. To hell with that. If he could elude the FBI, he'd be better off finding something useful to do on the outside.

He had no idea how long it would be before they tightened the surveillance on him or even arrested him on suspicion. For the moment, the essential thing was to continue with his normal routines and assume that phone calls and vehicle movements were being tracked. Then, as soon as he was ready, he'd slip out quietly and be gone. He was left with two problems: where to go and how to say goodbye.

CHAPTER 24

David's conversation with Ray had made one thing clear. He'd been dealt a hand in the game between Jerry and the FBI, and he decided to play it. Over coffee, the next time their schedules coincided, he told Stockton how, driving home after their last visit, it had suddenly dawned on him that his former classmate fit the profile of the Ohio shooter.

"I hadn't seen him since high school," David explained, "but I recognized him at the gas station in Front Royal last fall and we had a visit. He came back to see my place and that was about it. So, I can't help you much, but I wanted you to know about him."

Stockton didn't seem particularly surprised to hear of the connection, but he thanked David for telling him and that was it.

*****

David spent more time than usual in Front Royal over the next several days. To the casual observer he was running errands, but a closer look would have revealed an anomaly. When he stopped for gas, he only bought a couple of dollars' worth. When he went to the grocery store, it was for a quart of milk one time, a dozen eggs another. He took to browsing the aisles at the NAPA parts store, each time picking up just enough items—some car wax or a tire pressure gauge—to make the stop seem legitimate.

He was watching for Jerry, and on the third day he came out of Martin's supermarket and spotted Jerry's van heading north on Route 522. Hoping the traffic light would cooperate, David jumped into his car and followed. Two minutes later he saw the van turning into the NAPA parking lot. He pulled in, made his way into the store, and went purposefully toward the windshield wiper display. As he leafed through the catalogue for the right model, he glanced around the store and spotted Jerry loading a couple of boxes of motor oil onto a store dolly.

When Jerry stood up, David made a show of recognizing him and called out, "Hey, Jerry."

"Oh, hey, Preacher. What are you up to?"

"Trying to find wiper blades. Can I get your advice?"

Jerry left the dolly at the end of the aisle and came over. "Are you still driving the '75 Nova?"

"Yeah. I've found a couple of options here, according to the size charts, but there's a big difference in price. I guess my question is whether it's worth it to pay more for these?"

He reached across in front of Jerry to point to the hook that held the more expensive model.

As he got close, he said quietly, "Listen to me carefully."

Jerry was startled and looked at him warily, then continued to scan the rack of wiper blades.

"There's no time for discussion," David continued, "so if any of what I say makes sense to you, take it at face value." In a louder voice he said, "What's the difference between the two brands? Is it the quality of the rubber or the cost of the advertising?"

"I think in this case, it's the quality of the rubber," Jerry replied, then added softly, "I'm listening."

Speaking quickly and quietly David said, "The office next to mine at the college is occupied by an FBI consultant. The profile they have for the Ohio National Guard attacks fits you like a glove."

With enormous effort, Jerry managed to control the alarms that went off as David spoke.

"We see a lot of these better blades coming into the shop that are more than a year old and still working well," he said. "You'll probably save with them in the long run." Then, quietly, "What do you plan to do about it?"

David looked at him as if he was offended by the question. "I'm doing it," he said, in a forced whisper. Then, speaking normally, he continued, "I guess I'll take these then," and pulled a set of the expensive blades off their hook.

Jerry mumbled, "I've already had a visit from your friends, but it sounds like they may be back." As they made their way toward the front of the store, he asked in a normal voice, "Got any plans for the summer?"

"No, not much. I expect to be busy with the cooperative." They reached the end of the aisle and he added softly, "Listen to WSVR weekdays at 12:10. When I learn anything more, or if I have any ideas, I'll find a way to work that into the program."

"OK. Thanks."

"And, Jerry," David murmured insistently, as Jerry reached for his dolly. "They know you and I are friends, and they know about Karen."

"OK." Then, in a normal voice, as they stood in line at the cash register, "I think you'll like those blades."

"Thanks. Maybe I'll see you over the summer."

CHAPTER 25

On the Friday afternoon following his conversation with Joan, Jerry put a knapsack and some camping gear in the van as usual and headed for the Park. As he pulled away, he saw that the dark sedan was still next door. Waiving to his father, who was with a customer on the sales lot, he shouted, "See you Sunday night."

When he reached Thornton Gap, he didn't turn into the Park but headed down the other side of the Ridge, coasting and braking through the switchbacks toward Luray. He was going to see Karen again, and it took some effort not to get too excited.

Ed and Joan came out to the van when he arrived. Joan gave him a generous hug before leading the way to the house with the men in tow, chatting about the weather and the egg business. He had no idea what to expect when he saw Karen, but as they entered the kitchen she looked up from the counter where she was preparing a lunch dish, looked directly at him, and smiled.

"Hi, Jerry."

It was a tentative smile, and God knows what effort it took for her to deliver it, but Joan was right. There had been a big improvement since their return from Kent last winter. At that moment he wanted nothing more than to take her in his arms, but the memory of the last time he did that, the sudden emptiness as her arms went limp around him, kept him at bay. Instead, he got close enough to put his hand on her arm and lean over to inspect the bowl in front of her.

"Mm, mmm! Macaroni salad. Someone must have told you I was coming."

"It's got eggs in it," she said, apprehensively. Was that because he might not like hard-boiled eggs in his macaroni salad, or because she needed to create space?

"It looks perfect," he said, giving her arm a gentle squeeze. He moved toward the table, where Ed was now seated, in time for Joan to set a fistful of utensils in front of him.

"Here, make yourself useful," she said, then, nodding in Ed's direction added, "He's hopeless. Let's see what you're made of."

"Only one fork? What kind of establishment is this?"

"Touché," she acknowledged.

Lunch was relaxed and easy. Karen withdrew into her own space from time to time, but only briefly. It seemed to take conscious effort, but she managed to return each time with a comment or a new topic, to stay in touch with those around her. The mood changed briefly when the subject of the FBI came up, but Jerry took a light approach to the whole investigation. After only a couple of comments and questions, they moved on to the next subject, the switch-out of old laying hens in House 3 that was planned for the following week.

Out of nowhere, Ed began to sing, improvising the words to a popular television jingle as he waived his fork in time with the tune, "Oscar-Meyer has a way with hens that can no longer lay…"

Jerry laughed and Joan managed to keep the smile off her face just long enough to fake disgust and say, "I swear, you are incorrigible."

It was lost on no one that Karen was also enjoying the moment.

After the meal, as the two women cleared the dishes from the table, Jerry put a small package at each of their places and winked at Ed.

"What's this?" Joan asked when she and Karen returned to their seats.

"Oh, just a little souvenir of my travels," Jerry said. "Hope you like it."

The turquoise and silver bracelet for Joan and the earrings for Karen were a hit.

*****

Late spring in the Shenandoah Valley is a magical time, with the colors, textures, and aromas of burgeoning plant life on all sides. Jerry and Ed relaxed in the Adirondack chairs on the back lawn, enjoying the view in silence until Jerry decided that he couldn't put off any longer telling Ed that things were about to change.

"It would probably put your FBI friends down the road in a panic if you said anything," he began, "but I'm going to have to go away for a while."

Ed looked worried, but only said, "Is it something you want to talk about?"

"Not at the moment. It's better if you just tell anyone who asks that we had a nice lunch today and then I said goodbye as usual."

"I understand," Ed said, "but we're all going to miss you."

"Yeah, me too."

The women appeared at the top of the back steps and started toward them.

"Karen seems to be getting her life back," Jerry said quietly. "I'm going to draw the flack for a while, so she won't have any more setbacks."

Joan and Karen were too close now for Ed to respond so he had to let the subject drop.

"Thank you for ordering this perfect day for my visit," Jerry said to Joan.

"You're welcome," she answered and, surveying their surroundings, added, "I do good work, don't I?"

"For sure," Jerry replied. Then he turned to Karen.

"How about taking a walk?"

"I guess so. Not too far, though."

"No, no. Just up through the back fields a bit."

As they started up the back lane, the overgrown space between the tire tracks took care of the issue of how closely they should walk together. After a couple hundred yards, they passed through a gate into one of the hay fields that defined the eastern boundary of the farm. Haying was more a matter of farm maintenance than serious production for the Guerstens, so wildflowers had crept back into the field in the years since it was last sown to fescue. Some, already in bloom, were tall enough to tease at fingers and palms as the two made their way toward a rail fence that had become their destination.

The walk was mostly in silence, but it was a good silence. Not that long ago words had made matters worse between them. Now they both seemed content to let the sound of their movements and the peripheral shadow of each other's presence nurture a comfort that words might once again put at risk. But as they leaned against the fence and looked toward the mountains, Karen finally spoke.

"The Ohio National Guard has had some trouble lately."

"So I understand," Jerry replied.

"I've collected some interesting newspaper clippings about that trouble."

"It couldn't happen to a nicer bunch," he said.

After a few moments, she asked, "Are you going away again?"

The question seemed to come out of nowhere, but he realized that she knew him well enough to sense what hadn't been said. In that moment he felt closer to her than he ever had.

"Yes," he said quietly. "If I stay it will only cause trouble for the people I care about."

Karen looked at him as if she was about to say something but then looked away again.

"I am sorry for what you've been through," he said. "I wish I could have protected you."

When she turned back to face him there was a struggle in her eyes between the fear of being close and the fear of losing him. Her arms were folded protectively in front of her but, tentatively, he reached for her, and she didn't flinch. He stepped toward her, and she didn't withdraw. Then her arms yielded the space between them, and they held each other closely for the first time in a very long time. Resting her head on his shoulder, she burrowed gently before looking up at him.

"I want to get well, Jerry," she said. "I really do."

"You're doing just fine."

"Maybe someday..." her voice faded.

He bent toward her and kissed her on the cheek.

"Karen," he said, "Maybe in your good times, maybe in your bad times, I don't know, but when you think of me, please know that I love you."

He used that word because there was no other word, and for the first time in his life he knew what it meant.

A short time later, he said his goodbyes to Ed and Joan on the porch and Karen walked him to the van.

"I'm going to miss you," she said.

"And I'm sorry to be leaving you." Then he added, "If you ever need a Jerry fix, I want you to look up an old friend of mine. His name is David Williams. I went to school with him. He works with the co-op that has that weekly market in Front Royal and he's often there on a Saturday. He's always good for a story or two."

"I'll remember that," she said as they reached the door of the van.

Jerry turned toward her and, with a determined expression, said, "Please do."

She didn't hesitate as he took her in his arms once again.

"You know what?" he said matter-of-factly. "We're going to be together someday."

*****

He reached the cave with enough light left to clear the cobwebs and get a fire started. He shone a light into the hole in the back wall to make sure the rifle and cartridges hadn't been disturbed and then, with housekeeping chores complete, he opened a can of Dinty Moore and set it at the edge of the fire to heat.

It was good to be here. Much of his life could be told from this cave, the history, the survival skills, the adventures, early brushes with the law—even the night with David Williams and his buggered-up ankle. To return here was to revisit that past and reaffirm who he was.

But since Vietnam and Leavenworth, those visits had not given him the full measure of comfort that he had once known. The space hadn't changed, but somehow it felt incomplete. It didn't need anything, but something was missing. Walking back to the trailhead after each visit, he had settled for the explanation that he had simply failed to leave his troubles in the lowlands where they belonged.

This evening, he became aware of the void even as he sat by the fire. He had been thinking of Karen and the explanation became awkwardly clear. Of course! She was beyond the realm of the cave. So was Tom Douglas. So was Y Nur Kpa. Important parts of who he had become were not among the memories that could be unearthed by returning here, tended lovingly like the remains of an ancestor, and then returned to the past for safe keeping.

Expecting the cave to take on these new memories had been a disservice to those that rightly belonged here. Restored to its proper role, this space would always contain important knowledge of who he was, but his life had grown beyond it. If he had a future, it too would be beyond the realm of the cave.

As he finished the last of the stew and put the can and utensils into a plastic bag, his mind returned to the question of what next? What was he going to do when he disappeared? He'd thought often about that since the FBI had come on the scene, but now it had become urgent.

He stepped outside the cave and sat by the entrance with his back against the rock wall. The oaks weren't fully leafed out yet and through their loose canopy the Big Dipper began to appear in the darkening northeastern sky.

With his knowledge of the Park, there was no doubt he could survive here and elude capture, at least until enough people were sent against him that sheer luck would be on their side. And then what? He had no interest in a messy fight, so the end would be the same as if he surrendered now, and that wasn't an option. So, the Park would be the first step in eluding the FBI, but then he'd have to move on. To New Mexico, maybe. Bigger territory. Better chance of avoiding capture. But he didn't know the area as well. He wasn't as attached to it, and finding something useful to do would be a challenge.

His thoughts circled back to the conversation with Paul Anderson about the Montagnards, about the guys around Fort Bragg who were helping them. That was useful work, taking up the slack where the policy types had failed to honor their commitment. Could he contribute to that effort?

By the time the sky was completely dark and the Little Dipper put in an appearance, he had settled on stage two of his escape. Back in the cave, he opened his wallet and found the folded piece of paper with Butch Walton's contact information.

There was still one important piece of the plan missing: how to dispose of the rifle and cartridges. He had never seen evidence that anyone knew about the cave, but he couldn't count on it remaining a secret in the years to come. A hiker, a poacher—someone would eventually happen across it. If the Garand was found, authorities might well make the connection to the Ohio attacks. He couldn't risk a link being made to the Fletcher family, even if he was long gone.

Putting the weapon in the gun show circuit wasn't an option because the FBI would probably be watching for Garands. He'd seen too many detective shows to have any confidence in the permanence of throwing it in a river or burying it. As he mulled over options and ruled them out, the idea began to form that, if the FBI wanted the gun, maybe they should have it. It was a short step from there to the plan for a final strike at the Ohio National Guard. *This time we'll make it personal,* he thought, *a parting gift for the Adjutant General.*

CHAPTER 26

David was sitting at his desk after class when Jack Stockton put his head in the doorway and said, "Coffee's on."

It was the first time their paths had crossed since David told him about his acquaintance with Jerry, and he was relieved at the sense of business as usual in Stockton's voice.

"Be right there," David replied, and took a few moments to complete his notes on the morning class before getting up and heading next door. "Here you go," he said, putting a sack with a couple of muffins in it next to the coffee pot. "Something from the bakery table at the market."

"Well done. I missed breakfast this morning."

"Good. I'll pretend I did, too."

As they fixed their coffees, Stockton said, "I've been meaning to ask you, how's your friend doing? The one you visited in the hospital."

"Not very well," David replied. "He went home for a little while, but his wife had to call for an ambulance the other night. He couldn't get enough air, and he's back in hospital now."

"I'm sorry to hear that. What's the prognosis?"

"Not good. Actually, I don't expect him to come out of the hospital."

David had always been good at compartmentalizing his life. It had been a relief not to have to do that since he moved to the Valley, but these days, with his concerns about Ray and about Jerry and his need to keep up the work on the college and co-op fronts, that ability had once again come into play. He invoked it now, to set thoughts of Ray aside for the moment.

Stockton saw that a change of subject was in order. "It's hard to believe we're in the home stretch of the semester already," he said. "Just a couple of weeks to go."

"Funny. I was thinking along those lines when you came to my door just now. We spend most of the time during the semester trying to get the material across, making sure the students can give it back correctly, and I guess that's the right place to start, but do you ever wonder if they'll be able to apply it?"

"All the time. We put it in there, but does it get wired up so that it becomes part of the equipment?"

"That's the question. I've been at this job for the grand total of two semesters now," David said, "And I think that checking how it's wired—testing how students might use the material under actual conditions—may be the most important part of what we do."

"You're probably right. On the other hand, I'd hate to be paid on that basis!"

"Scary thought!" David said.

After a few moments of comfortable silence, Stockton said, "This is a damned good muffin, by the way."

"Glad you like it. The bakery table is always popular on market day."

"So, the cooperative is doing all right these days, is it?"

"Yes, it is," David said, reflecting as he spoke. "Whether it's muffins or feeder calves, production is seldom a problem, but issues come up in organization and planning fairly often. I have to be careful because these people are used to working independently, doing things their own way."

"So, the lecture approach doesn't work, then, huh?"

"That would empty the seats faster than a fire alarm!" David took another sip of his coffee and then changed the subject. "I'm a bit apprehensive asking you about your FBI work. I don't want to make things awkward for you."

"Never mind, I can take care of that end. Anyhow, it's not likely to be an issue for you to worry about much longer. Things are moving along quite nicely."

"That's good. Congratulations."

"Well, that's premature, but it does look like we'll be making an arrest before long."

The first task for David was to avoid any appearance that what he had just heard was significant, so after taking the last bite of his muffin he said, "You're probably ready for a case a little closer to home anyhow."

"Yeah, and one with less exposure to old headlines, too."

So, the FBI was about to move on Jerry. On the drive back to Browntown that afternoon, David tried to pull together what he had to work with. At best, it was probably only a week or two before they arrested Jerry. Since the Park had been part of his normal movements during the time he was under surveillance, another visit there wouldn't concern Jerry's watchers. It was logical that he would use the Park as the first stage in his escape plan.

Getting out of the Park undetected, beyond the FBI net, would be the trick, and that's where David decided to concentrate. What he needed was an excuse to be in the Park to collect Jerry, a legitimate reason to travel, and a way to package those movements for his radio listeners. He shut down the small voice that asked, "What if he isn't listening?" and began to look for the pieces of a plan. His comments to Stockton about the co-op came to mind and an idea began to take shape.

When he reached Browntown, he headed for the Bruckman farm.

*****

A light rain had been falling all day, but Bruckman was outside when David arrived. He was a few yards up the back lane beyond the barn, tossing hay over the fence to his cattle. David swapped his loafers for the pair of boots he kept in the trunk and headed out the lane. The dozen or so cows seemed to be having trouble deciding whether to take the hay seriously. They looked back and forth, between Bruckman's offering and the open field where lush new grass was carpeting the hillside.

"Kind of mean to make them eat hay when there's that good-looking grass across the fence, isn't it?" David asked.

"It looks good from here, all right," Bruckman agreed, "And they're pissed they can't get to it, but the ground is still soft this time of year, so their hooves punch through the sod when it rains. I bring 'em in here in a rainy spell," he said, indicating the small paddock where the cattle stood. "That way I cut down on the damage they do to the pasture and I get to use up a few more bales of last year's hay."

"Always something," David said, taking a flake of hay from the bale that Bruckman had just broken open and tossing it over the fence.

The greeting routine continued, touching on weather, family, and how the tractor was running now with its new clutch plate. When the conversation came around to something about the coop, David was able to get to the purpose of his visit.

"You know, I've been thinking about the discussion at the last Board meeting," he began. "There are a couple of questions about where the business is headed that need some more thinking before we make any decisions. Looking for new produce buyers, for example, and getting some equipment that members could rent."

"Yeah," Bruckman said. "That kind of thing would need some careful consideration, all right." David recognized the Bruckmanese for 'I'm not sure myself whether those are good ideas'.

"The trouble is," David continued, "We're heading into the busy season for you all. The last thing you need is a bunch of meetings added to your load."

"That's for sure."

"I've got an idea I want to try on with you," David said. "First, the Executive Committee needs to do some background work and prepare proposals for a couple of the issues the Board has to consider fairly soon, right?" Bruckman nodded his agreement and David continued. "That would best be done with a bit of peace and quiet, away from the daily grind, but that is going to be harder and harder to arrange between now and next fall."

"Peace and quiet? What's that?" Bruckman asked, sardonically.

"A bit of a fantasy, I know. But I have an idea."

"You've got my attention, that's for sure."

"When's the last time you were at Skyland Lodge, up in the Park?" David asked.

"Oh, it's been years."

"I figured as much, but it's only about an hour's drive from here, right?"

"'Bout that. Nice place as I recall."

"Good views of the Valley from up there, too," David agreed. "Why don't you, Roger, and I head up there next weekend, sit on the deck of one of those nice little cabins and sort through a couple of ideas for the Board? I think we'd get more done in a day up there than we would in a summer's worth of meetings in the middle of everything that goes on around here."

"If you had a pipe, I'd ask what you were smokin'," Bruckman said. "I can't afford to take the missus to MacDonald's more than once every couple of weeks. How am I going to justify goin' to a fancy place like that?"

"No, no. I don't mean that. I would like to invite you and Roger. I think it would be a good investment in the co-op and I'd record the cost as unearned surplus on the coop's books."

"What's that, 'unearned surplus'?"

"Oh, it can be several things, but in this case it's the value of something somebody contributes to the organization. Remember those folding tables you gave to the co-op for the weekly market? That's how I recorded their value. It's like an investment, but it doesn't earn dividends, it doesn't vote, and it doesn't have to be repaid."

"Sounds like a no-win for you."

"On the contrary. I'd get to spend some time in a pleasant spot, talking with friends about something I care about. You all have included me in barbeques and lunches and such, so in a way it would just be a thank you—with a string attached, of course. You'd have to work while you're there!"

"I don't know," Bruckman said, although the idea had clearly caught his interest. "There's all this," he added, sweeping his hand to indicate the farm.

"Tell you what. Do the morning chores first thing on Saturday, leave the wife and kids to take care of things through the day and then have them join us for dinner Saturday evening. We can have a working breakfast Sunday morning and you'd still be home in time to check on things before church."

"That's a bit tight," Bruckman said, then added with a wink, "Maybe the church part would have to slide."

"You can blame me for that," David smiled. "It wouldn't even make a scratch on my rap sheet."

They agreed that David would stop by Roger Atkins' place on the way home and raise the idea with him. Then he'd check on availability at Skyland Lodge. Bruckman would talk with Roger that evening and with their wives. David would call them the next evening to see if it was a go.

*****

A couple of days later, David began his broadcast with the usual byline and an item of interest from Virginia Tech.

"Good day, folks. This is David Williams, with the Farm Notebook for April 20th. It's probably not a coincidence that, as we head into the busiest season of the year, Virginia Tech has just released the results of a recent study on improving efficiency in farming operations. Some of these academic exercises are a mix of the obvious and the useless, but our growers tell me that this study has come up with some good practical recommendations. The best way to combine field operations, for example, to reduce tractor hours and cut down on fuel consumption. There's also a section on how to rearrange your workshop so you spend less time on maintenance and repair jobs."

He described a couple of other recommendations from the study and concluded the segment with, "For your own copy of these recommendations, just send a request to the address we'll give you at the end of the program, and the Cooperative Extension folks will get one in the mail to you right away."

David went on to tell listeners about new research in the use of plastic tunnels to speed up strawberry development in the early spring. Then, hoping Jerry was listening, he turned to the next item in his script.

"And here's an item from what I'll call our Overheard-at-the-Co-op Department. A fellow in the next aisle was telling his friend about somebody just dropping in on him unannounced. It didn't matter that he had a lot going on this time of year. This guy just showed up and expected our friend to drop everything and spend time with him. As you can imagine, the FCC would never let me tell you exactly what he thought of the idea.

"Maybe it's just the price we pay for living here in the beautiful Shenandoah, but unexpected visitors can certainly put an added strain on our day.

"Here's a thought. Maybe we should ask Tech to compile a list of chores we can assign to unexpected visitors. I'm sure we could all make a few suggestions for a list like that."

Now he had to tell Jerry the plan.

"Finally, folks, a programming note. I'll be with the Executive Committee of the Small Farmers Cooperative at Skyland Lodge next weekend for a planning session. Then, on Sunday morning, I'll be headed to Blacksburg again to follow up on some important work that will be of interest to those of you with orchards."

As an added touch for credibility, he said, "While I'm away, The Notebook will continue to come to you, with a couple of segments we've prerecorded on new approaches to managing parasites in cattle."

He concluded with, "That's it for now, folks. Stay tuned for the address for that publication on farming efficiency and, 'til next time, happy growing!"

CHAPTER 27

Jerry finished a wheel alignment about ten o'clock on the morning after David's radio message and went into the office. His father and Katie were at their desks.

"Katie, there's nothing on my schedule for the next couple of hours, right?"

"Not for the moment."

"Good," he said, then turned to his father. "Hey, old man. How'd you like to take a drive with me to Front Royal?"

"Why, did you forget how to get there?" Gerald asked, slightly puzzled by the request.

Jerry glanced back at Katie.

"Always the smart-ass," he said, tossing his head in the direction of his father. She enjoyed the repartee between these two, and it was good to see them together again after so many years.

Jerry turned back to his father. "No, I just thought maybe we could talk shop while you help me with a couple of parts that I need to pick up at NAPA. If you're good, I'll even buy you a coffee. Katie can cover for you, right, Katie?"

"Sure."

The request was unusual enough that Gerald knew there was a good reason for it.

"OK, just give me a couple of minutes to finish these two calls." He gestured toward two sheets from a small message pad on the desk in front of him.

"Good. I'll be in the back," Jerry answered. "Shout when you're ready. By the way, bring the keys to that blue F250 you put on the lot yesterday. I want to see how it rides."

As they pulled out onto the street ten minutes later, Gerald surveyed the sales lot and nodded approvingly. He ignored the dark sedan under the oaks in the parking lot next door.

The silence in the cab as they started toward Front Royal had an unusual edge to it, so Gerald didn't wait too long before he said something he had been thinking about for several days.

"I'm guessing you may be planning to leave again sometime soon."

Jerry exhaled as though a weight had just been taken off his shoulders.

"Yeah. How'd you know?"

"Well, putting two and two together isn't all that difficult if you keep your eyes open. There's that Agent Johnson asking questions about Ohio. There's the guys in the black Ford next door every day. I just hope you haven't gone and got yourself into something you can't handle. Are you alright?"

"I'm fine, at least for now."

"When are you planning to leave?" Gerald asked reluctantly.

"I heard from a friend that the FBI plans to move on me soon, so probably this weekend."

"Well, no need to tell you, but I'm awful sorry to hear that. Anything I can help you with?"

"Yeah. Mom."

"I'm not going to tell her you're leaving, if that's what you mean."

"No, no. I have to do that, but it would be good if you could be around and maybe help her understand."

"I'd like to understand a bit better myself, first."

"I don't know, Dad. I haven't told you anything 'til now because I didn't want you to have to hide information or lie if you were questioned. That's still a factor."

"Look, that's all well and good, but unless you just plan to be gone for a few weeks, it would be a damned sight worse not knowing anything than having to lie about it." After a moment's silence he added, "You're not the first one in this family to ignore the law from time to time, by the way."

"Well, aren't you the sly one?" Jerry said with a chuckle. "You know, when I was growing up, I always thought the meat on our table tasted better after you'd been to the mountains."

"OK. Never mind all that. I don't figure we're talking about a little poaching this time around."

"No, that's right." Jerry looked at the road ahead and collected his thoughts for a few moments. Then, tentatively, he began to speak.

"Even when I was a kid going to the mountains on the weekends, I was never very good at playing by the rules, especially if they were rules made by some outfit that had done something wrong, like the government taking Grandpa Jake's land to make it a park."

"Can't imagine where you'd get an attitude like that," Gerald said.

"Of course not, but you were right to want me to know what the family went through. It's just that it was a wake-up call for me, and I've seen a lot of shit ever since that falls into the same category—people doing things in the name of the government that really aren't right. I don't know about parks. I guess there may be a reason to have them, but kicking people off their land, destroying their way of life and not giving a damn…that's where I get off."

Gerald nodded his agreement and Jerry continued, "Then I get to Vietnam and see the 'Yards going through the same thing—losing everything to the government. One day the taking gets personal. This motherfucker helps himself to Y Bam's daughter, telling me he can take what he wants because he's the government. But you know that story. Anyhow, while I spend ten years behind bars to learn how to be a good little pawn, the same outfit that sent me over there to defend some corrupt generals turns around and shoots a bunch of students back home for daring to object to the war. My girlfriend gets part of her skull blown away for exercising her right to free speech, and the bastards who did it get praised for their defense of the American way of life."

As Jerry recounted the pieces of his story, Gerald sat in silence, shocked once more by the stark reality of events in his son's life.

"Today, after the best part of ten years, she can get twelve eggs in every dozen she packs. She can even balance the farm books. But she still can't trust anyone. She can't love anyone, and a trip to town terrifies her."

Nothing Gerald could have said would have amounted to more than noise.

"It's funny," Jerry continued, a half mile further up the mountain. "The official line between when it's OK to kill and when it isn't is so damned arbitrary. If you're in uniform it's OK to shoot a guy running from a village, even if he's just in the wrong place at the wrong time. But it's a crime to shoot some bastard who's raping a girl in front of her parents."

Gerald turned to look at his son, intending to commiserate, but his face set grimly as he realized where Jerry might be going with these comments.

"But somewhere along the way I guess I developed a line of my own. That's probably your fault, too—you and Y Nur Kpa. Anyhow, I couldn't do what I really wanted to do in Ohio. I wanted some of those bastards dead for what they did to Karen. Instead, I pussy-footed around, wrecked a few pieces of equipment, and burned some buildings. Big fucking deal."

Gerald was so relieved he exhaled and shifted in his seat. "The news coverage made some of it look pretty spectacular," he said in a lame attempt to counter Jerry's dismissal of what he had done.

At that moment a squirrel darted into the road and froze when it saw the oncoming truck. Jerry glanced in the rearview mirror and touched the brakes as he crossed the center line to steer the frightened animal back in the direction it had come from.

With the encounter safely behind them, Gerald said, "Doesn't handle too badly for a heavy-duty truck."

"No, it's very good. Suspension's harder than I like but we knew that."

"Are you thinking about trading up from the van?"

"No, no. I just wanted to make sure nobody would be listening to our conversation."

"You mean you think the van's bugged?"

"Why not? It makes sense, doesn't it?"

"I don't know. This is all new to me."

As they topped the rise at Chester Gap and started down the far side of the ridge, Jerry picked up his train of thought.

"The trouble is, I've got nothing to show for my efforts but a pack of hounds on my trail. OK, I brought the goddamned Ohio National Guard to a halt for a while and made people think back on Kent State, but in the end nothing's changed."

Gerald didn't want to belittle his son's concern with some inane comment, but he did have one practical worry.

"It would be ridiculous for me to tell you what you should be doing," he said, "but it seems to me you need to shake that pack of hounds before you try to do anything else."

"Yeah, my options would be fairly limited back in prison all right. I've got an idea on that, but you don't need to know about it."

For a moment, Gerald felt left out, but he knew his son was right. There was no way he could be smooth enough under pressure to avoid revealing that he knew more than he was saying. That would mean trouble for everyone.

"But getting away isn't enough," Jerry continued. "It would be sad if the high point of my life turned out to be avoiding capture, don't you think? I mean it's all well and good to get upset by the kind of shit we're talking about, but I need to be able to do something about it."

Gerald admired the sentiment, but it was unrealistic.

"I appreciate your sense of what's right," he said, "but I think you're being a bit hard on yourself. I mean the war's over, and the Park's forty years old. Besides, continuing to fight might just make matters worse for people who are trying to adjust to what they lost."

Jerry remembered Paul Anderson's comment about how the guerilla efforts of some of the Montagnards had meant trouble for the whole community under the new government in Vietnam.

"Yeah, you're probably right about that, but I've come across something that may work. I can't get the place in Fletcher Hollow back for Grandpa Jake. I guess I can't get even with the bastards who hurt Karen. But I think there's something I can do for Y Nur Kpa and his people."

"The guy who wrote the letter, right?"

"Yeah, that's him. On my way to New Mexico, I stopped in North Carolina to see the guy who sent you that letter. It seems there are some former Special Forces guys putting their money where the government's mouth used to be. The flag wavers are all busy trying to forget their promises to the 'Yards. They'd rather focus on business with the new government in Nam, but these guys are helping the people who were our real allies during the war."

"Good for them. What are they doing?"

"I don't know much, but it seems a lot of Montagnards are making it across Cambodia these days to camps in Thailand. Conditions there are pretty rough, and I guess maybe these guys are putting together money, blankets, food—the usual stuff—for them."

"Sounds good but, whatever they're doing, it wouldn't help much to have a fox run through their camp with a pack of hounds on his tail."

"No, I'll need to fix that first. That's the part I'm working on now."

The idea that there was something productive that Jerry could do with his anger, his sense of injustice, had a settling effect on the conversation. Both men were pleased with the idea that the story could have a happy ending. But it took only a moment before the reality of that outcome seeped back into their thoughts. Jerry was leaving.

"One more thing," he said as they pulled into the NAPA parking lot. "Tell anyone who asks next week that I'm spending a few days in the Park."

CHAPTER 28

David was working late at his desk in the front room, pushing to get the last of his students' grades together. With the meetings at Skyland Lodge to plan for and Jerry's escape to worry about, he couldn't afford any loose ends on the academic front.

The telephone startled him when it rang. He reached apprehensively for the receiver, knowing it couldn't be a routine call at this hour.

"David, it's Teresa."

He looked away from the phone momentarily to prepare himself.

"Hi. Please tell me you're calling with good news."

Silence on the line, and then, "No. It's not good."

Was it resolve in her voice, or shock?

"I just got home from the hospital," she said. "Ray's headaches have been getting worse the last few days and today they said the cancer has spread to his brain."

"Oh, damn. Are they sure?"

"Yes. He had one of those new CT scans and there's no doubt."

"The poor bastard. That's just too much. What's the plan?"

"There isn't one. The doctor says there's nothing they can do. There are tumors everywhere. All they can do is keep him comfortable."

It was his turn to break the silence and all he could think of to say was, "How are you?"

"It's no fun, but I'm not the one who's sick. Sometimes I wish I was. I wouldn't have to watch him suffer. I wouldn't have to think about life without him."

David had asked, but he had no idea how to respond to the gut-wrenching answer. After a few moments of silence, he ventured a distraction. "Are they able to control his pain?"

"They could, but he won't let them."

"What do you mean? That's crazy."

"He says the morphine puts him in La-La Land, so he only takes it when the pain is too much. When he thinks I'm not watching, his face twists and his fists are clenched so tightly his knuckles are white. But he still won't call the nurse."

"I can't imagine what it must be like. For him or for you."

"And that's not the worst. Sometimes he'll use the wrong word for something or the sounds that come out are garbled. At first, he doesn't seem to notice but then he'll realize what's happening. The sadness in his eyes at that moment is the worst thing I've ever seen."

David was at a loss to imagine what Ray must be experiencing or to know what to say to Teresa. Was it Ray's speech that was the problem, or the thought process that had always worked so quickly, so sharply, for him? Which would be worse?

He didn't know how long it had been since either of them had spoken, but eventually the sound of crying on the line brought him back to the present. This time he didn't ask.

"Leave the front light on," he said. "I'll be there in a couple of hours."

When he arrived at the house in Arlington, he found Teresa in her bathrobe curled up on the sofa. He sat beside her and she put her arms around his neck and cried. Comforting her gave him a measure of peace as well. She eventually fell asleep with her head on his chest and, managing to work one of the throw pillows behind his head, he also slept.

The sun was up when her stirring woke them both. There was no awkwardness as they smiled at one another and stayed close for a few moments, letting the events of yesterday and the comfort of last night find the balance that would start their day.

Then, pushing herself to a sitting position, Teresa said, "I'm hungry."

It was a good sign and, as the reality of why they were together seeped back into their thoughts, David knew that he had been right to be there for her. Over toast, marmalade, and pressed coffee, they talked about what the doctor had said—even how long Ray might have left. Weeks, maybe. They agreed that David would go to the hospital alone that morning and Teresa would come in later. She wanted to put a few things together so she could stay overnight, depending on how things would go.

The first time Ray had a spell of gibberish that morning, David started to ask him to repeat what he'd said. Realizing what had happened, he stopped mid-sentence, mortified, and watched as Ray's expression morphed from embarrassment through frustration to anger that threatened to overtake him. Instead, he closed his eyes, and breathed heavily until the anger passed.

"It's a nasty business, kid," he said. "Sometimes I can't think. Sometimes there's no connection between what I want to say and what comes out."

"I wish there was something I could do, Ray. Something they could do."

"They? Huh. They're as useless as marionettes in a wrestling match."

David grunted.

"Hey, how about that?" Ray said. "I managed to put a four-syllable word in that sentence."

David smiled because his only other choice would have been to cry. It wasn't that long ago that this Ohio State professor could hold graduate students spellbound on the intricacies of monetary policy. Now he struggled with the rudiments of thought and speech as if they were the tiles of a game of Scrabble, tossed randomly about at any moment.

The episodes of incoherence came and went as the morning passed, but both men were learning to take them in stride. In reality, they were no more disruptive than his cough, and no more ominous.

*****

Back in Browntown that afternoon, David took a walk up the dirt road toward the Park and turned into the back fields. The cool spring air and the afternoon sun played on his face and the backs of his hands as he made his way through the winter-beaten stalks of sunflower and Queen Anne's lace. Their days of swallowtails and honeybees were a distant memory. New growth cushioned his steps and hinted at next year's memories.

He had been taught from an early age the importance of caring for others, but somehow that kind of caring had insulated him from the vulnerability of true compassion. It had taken years of mistakes and carelessness to lead his spirit to the place where it could know a full measure of either tears or laughter. Ray had been part of that journey. Ray had witnessed some of those mistakes. He was the unassuming friend who had steered him in a different direction.

Now the mentor was himself becoming the lesson. As his friend struggled at the edge of life, David realized the sorrow of imminent loss and the honor of accompanying him as far as he could. And he wept.

CHAPTER 29

Jerry made a point of striking up a conversation with the ranger at the Park entrance. He asked about conditions on several trails and said he was planning to hike toward the south and camp for a few days. He parked as usual at the Meadow Spring trailhead, took his gear from the van and headed east instead, toward Fletcher Hollow.

It would be as much as a week now before the FBI suspected anything unusual in his absence. If he understood the message in David's broadcast, he had six days before catching his ride. But he had a lot of work to do in that time, not to mention the little matter of an undercover trip to Ohio.

At the cave, he checked as usual for whatever species might have taken up residence since his last visit and built a fire to drive off the damp chill. He watched as the smoke drifted back through the hole at the rear of the cave, drawn by an unknown web of cracks and caverns. Eventually it would emerge, untraceable, somewhere on the mountain.

Spreading the ground sheet from his bedroll near the fire, he emptied the contents of his backpack neatly to one side. Then he retrieved the Garand and the cartridge box and proceeded to disassemble the weapon. Dipping the corner of a soft cloth into water from his canteen and then into ash from the firepit, he proceeded to work the resulting slurry over the metal surfaces of the rifle. He paid particular attention to the scope, the bolt, the trigger, and guard—anywhere he was likely to have left a print. Clean, damp cloths eventually removed the last of the ash film and he completed the job with a quick rub of gun oil.

It was a damned shame, but alcohol was the solvent of choice to remove fingerprints from the walnut stock and handguard. A ceremonial swig of the moonshine before he soaked the rag, and again when the job was done, eased his guilt for condemning good whiskey to such a lowly chore.

The smaller components went into his backpack along with the cartridge box. The barrel and stock, both too long to fit in the pack, were wrapped tightly in the bedroll blanket and put in a one-man tent bag brought specifically for the purpose. Finally, he tied the tent bag to the outside of the pack and sat back to examine the result. It looked enough like a typical thru-hiker's kit that a casual observer wouldn't take a second look.

It was a long haul from the cave to Swift Run Gap and the road to Harrisonburg, but if he was going to preserve the illusion of a routine hiking trip, he couldn't risk moving the van. He'd have to travel on foot although, with any luck, he'd be able to hitch a ride before dark for part of the trip. He'd just tell the driver that he was meeting a friend at one of the campgrounds to continue their hike.

To avoid being seen leaving the Park, Jerry would drop down into Hensley Hollow about five miles before the Gap and pick up one of the back roads. Thru-hikers often took a break from the Appalachian Trail to restock their supplies or buy a hamburger, and the locals were good about giving them a lift.

The plan was to be at the car rental office when it opened the next morning. Allowing a couple hours for sleep along the way, and a stop he'd have to make at the Lewis Mountain campground, he figured he would need to leave the cave about four o'clock that afternoon. A check of his watch confirmed that he had a couple of hours to spare, time to kick back and have a meal. He poked a couple of holes in the lid of his usual Dinty Moore stew and set the can in the coals at the edge of the fire.

As he rested against the backpack, his thoughts returned all too quickly to the kitchen in Flint Hill, to his mother, standing with her hands at her breast as silent tears found their way down her cheeks. Had it not been for Gerald's large hands at her shoulders and the nod from his resolute face in the shadows behind her, Jerry could never have turned and walked away. As it was, he had assured her he was leaving in pursuit of something that would make him happy, but the brief smile she conceded was scarcely enough to see him down the back steps, into the van, and away. He swore to himself that one day she would know that he was happy. That was the least he could do.

Broth from the stew bubbled over the side of the can and sizzled in the hot coals. Pinching the can between two sticks, he removed it from the fire. When it had cooled sufficiently, he steadied it with one hand, flipped his hunting knife over and cut the rest of the top open.

*****

There was no moon that night, so Jerry felt safe covering most of his hike along the shoulder of Skyline Drive, ducking quickly out of sight for the occasional passing vehicle. At about two o'clock he cut through the woods and approached the Lewis Mountain campgrounds. The only sounds were of June bugs in search of a mate, and the occasional snore from a nearby tent.

If he was going to rent a car for the trip to Ohio, he'd have to 'borrow' a driver's license and a credit card. Ten years in Leavenworth may have taken the edge off his stealth skills, but they were still up to the job, and he arrived undetected among the cars in the extended parking area. He began prying gently at doors and weather stripping, looking for those that would offer the least resistance to a shim or the hook he had fashioned from a coat hanger. Each time he found a likely candidate, he'd wait for a dispute to break out among the courting insects, to cover the metal click as he opened the door. After a quick search of the glove compartment and under the seats, he'd relock the door. Most owners would never notice anything awry.

The fourth car he broke into was a '65 Ford wagon with Tennessee tags. A man's wallet, complete with driver's license and American Express card, was waiting for him under a sheaf of paper in the glove compartment.

*****

Jerry was the first customer through the door of the Avis office in Harrisonburg the next morning. It didn't take much effort to look like the bedraggled hiker he was pretending to be.

"Yeah," he said to the agent. "My father's birthday is a good excuse. I'm ready for a break and a hot meal."

"I can imagine," the agent said. "Where are you headed?"

He had anticipated this kind of exchange and was ready with information like destinations and directions to plant in case the hounds should ever pick up this part of his trail.

"My folks are in Nashville," he answered.

"That's a long way to go just for a day."

"Yes, it is," Jerry admitted, "But if I'm going to make Maine by October, I can't take too much time off the trail." Mention of the Appalachian Trail earned him an admiring glance.

With those pieces of false trail laid down, he headed south on Route 11 for a few miles before picking up the interstate and setting out for Ohio.

Jerry stopped for gas and a bathroom break outside Charleston and asked an attendant wearing an NRA cap if there was a gun shop nearby. There was, and he picked up the one remaining item he needed for his project. A used canvas rifle case.

Careful to avoid being stopped for speeding, he made it to Columbus before the four o'clock quitting time at the Ohio National Guard headquarters. He found a spot among several other cars parked down the road from the Beighler Armory, where he could watch the main entrance and the officers' parking area.

Scrolling through the microfiche reader at the library back home, Jerry had turned up enough pictures of the Adjutant General to recognize him when he emerged at the end of the day and made his way to a late-model Impala in a designated parking space near the entrance.

Tailing a vehicle without being obvious was a whole lot trickier in real life than it seemed in the movies, but eventually he saw the Impala turn into the driveway of a brick home in an up-scale subdivision. From the curb, two houses away, he watched as the AG got out of the car, briefcase in hand, and entered a side door without knocking.

OK, this is where he lives, Jerry thought. After a few moments he pulled out and drove slowly past the house. It had no flood lights in the eaves, no streetlamp nearby, and no fencing in the yard to suggest a dog. He also noticed a garden shed in one corner of the back yard. Its padlock hung open on the latch.

Satisfied that the variables were stacking up in his favor, he made several reconnaissance sweeps of the neighborhood and memorized two different entrances to the interstate. Returning to a commercial district he'd noticed earlier, Jerry parked among the cars in a K-Mart parking lot. Now, all he had to do for the next eight hours was reassemble the Garand.

"Hurry up and wait," he said to himself. "Heard that somewhere before." But the wait also gave him the chance to think through a contingency plan that had been forming in his mind since seeing the residence. He had planned to hide the weapon and ammunition behind the rear seat of the AG's car, and he had the wire and the know-how to deal with a car door if it was locked, but the garden shed could be a better solution. Putting them in there would be quicker and simpler, provided there were items inside that he could use to conceal them.

When the K-Mart closed at ten pm, he left with the last of the customers as the parking lot cleared and drove past the house again to make sure there hadn't been any changes that would affect his plan. Then, he found an all-night drugstore, parked a couple of rows back from the entrance, and waited until it was time to begin the operation.

A little after two am he pulled to the curb two streets over from the AG's address. There was no sign of residents being awake in any of the nearby houses, so he put on the cotton gloves from a side pocket of his backpack, took the rifle case and the cartridge box from the back seat, wrapped the case loosely in the blanket from his bedroll and began to walk casually along the sidewalk.

When he came to an overgrown vacant lot he ducked quickly into the brush and began to make his way toward the next street. From that point, he was in recon mode, using whatever structures and shadows were available to remain out of sight as he made his way silently through several properties. There was a brief standoff with a possum near a trash can until the animal gave up trying to play dead and shuffled off. Otherwise, the trip was uneventful, and he arrived at the back corner of the AG's yard without being seen.

He was just a few steps from the garden shed so he decided to check it out first. Lifting on the door as he opened it, to reduce the risk of squeaking, he stepped inside and closed the door behind him. With a small penlight he surveyed the contents of the shed and saw what he was looking for. Several canvas bags—camping equipment probably—were piled on top of a stack of lumber to one side of the floor. It would be easy to move the storage bags, create a space among the boards for the gun case and cartridge box, and put the camping equipment back the way he found it.

"Too easy," he whispered with a smile. Twenty minutes later Jerry and his travel blanket were back in the car. He stopped briefly at a mailbox on the main street and deposited a letter addressed to the FBI Regional Headquarters in Cincinnati. On the back of the envelope, instead of a return address, he had scribbled the address where the Garand could be found. Then he merged onto I-70 and joined the steady flow of eastbound trucks and overnight travelers.

CHAPTER 30

Sitting in his study late in the afternoon, following his visit with Ray, David didn't recognize the car that pulled into the driveway. Nor did he recognize the driver at first. But when she got out, retrieved a shopping bag from the back seat, and started toward the front door, it was Linda who looked in his direction and smiled. He had the door open before she reached the top step, and he stood speechless as she walked toward him.

"Meals on Wheels," she announced.

"It's you," was all he could say.

"Last time I checked it was. Is this OK?"

"It's very OK," he answered, leaning toward her for what he expected would be a kiss on the cheek, but she didn't turn her head and their lips touched in a moment he would always remember.

"I'm so glad to see you," he said as he took the bag from her and held the door open. "What brings you to these parts?"

"Oh, I heard there was some guy around here who could use help with his garden."

"Hey, always!"

"Actually, I was visiting a couple of clients at the Inland Port and decided that it was going to be too nice an evening to spend in traffic. Then I remembered what a good time we had over lunch a couple of weeks ago and decided to take my chances."

"Well, I never thought I'd say it, but thank you, traffic!"

"And how was your day," she asked as she moved down the hall toward the kitchen.

"Good, but even better now," he replied.

"That's good to know. What were you working on when I arrived?"

"Oh, I'm trying to get the final grades in for my students."

"Well, why don't you continue with that?" she said, "and I'll put something together for dinner."

"I'd sooner visit with you. Can't I help?" he asked as he set the bag on the counter.

"No. I can manage fine, and we'll visit later."

There was something very appealing in the notion that it was normal for her to be here, that "putting something together for dinner" was said as if it was an everyday occurrence.

She put her hand on his chest to move him back toward the hall without any idea how much more difficult her touch made it for him to leave.

A couple of minutes later she came into the office and set a glass of red wine on the desk, along with a small wedge of brie and some crackers.

"Here," she said. "This will tide you over. Dinner will be ready in about an hour."

"How am I supposed to work when you're here? It's not fair."

"Try," she said. "Pretend you have a deadline."

"I do, of course."

"Then it should be easy." She dismissed his protest with a shrug and a wink and disappeared back down the hall.

"How'd it go with your clients?" he called after her.

"Don't change the subject. I'll tell you later."

The tantalizing aromas that came from the kitchen over the next hour were confusing: bacon one minute, garlic the next...

Rosemary? Did he even have rosemary in the cupboard? And the sounds were no more revealing; the chopping of vegetables, the searing of meat, the hiss of liquid being added to a hot pan.

"What are you doing out there?" he called at one point.

"Never mind. You've got work to do."

Linda finally called from the kitchen, "Dinner's ready," and he followed the mysterious fragrances down the hall.

She had arranged the table the way it had been for their lunch together, but now at each place steam rose from plates that held pieces of chicken in a rich dark sauce. They were accompanied by a mound of buttered noodles, and side plates with a mixed green salad. Wine glasses and an open bottle of pinot noir completed the presentation.

"This is incredible," David said, "and I love chicken."

"Julia calls it coq au vin," she corrected with a superior air.

"Julia who?" he asked, but when she glanced at him in surprise, he winked.

"Cretin," she growled. "Let's eat."

He held the chair for her, then took his own place.

"This smells absolutely wonderful."

"Well, let's see how it tastes," she cautioned, then added, pointing to the pinot noir, "Perhaps the sommelier would do the honors?"

At the end of the meal, David raised his glass to Linda. "A resounding success," he said.

"Thank you, kind sir."

"I bet that's the best meal a banker has put together in a long time."

They collaborated on cleaning up the kitchen and then adjourned to the parlor. It had hosted the occasional co-op committee meeting and, once in a while, he struggled with the old TV in the corner to try to pick up the news or put himself to sleep with a rerun sitcom. But the sofa was comfortable, and the coffee table was just right for their wine glasses and the last of the pinot noir.

Linda sat facing him, her feet tucked under her, as they sipped their wine and savored the space they had begun to create for their relationship.

"How is your friend doing?" Linda asked eventually. "Dr. Baker, is it?"

There was a peculiar sense of relief in hearing the question. Linda's arrival had been a welcome break from the constant undercurrent of concern about Ray. But his illness was the most important issue in David's life at that moment and he wanted to share it with her.

"Ray's in bad shape," he began. "I was in to see him at GW this morning."

Linda looked at him sympathetically, inviting him to continue.

"I don't know what's worse. To see him in pain or to watch his mind deteriorate. How can anyone who had an active and inquiring existence bear to lie there and watch that happen to themselves?"

She shook her head as if to wonder at the same question.

"And knowing it will only get worse?" he said with despair. "What a way to live, I mean die. And there's nothing I can do, nothing anyone can do."

"That feeling of helplessness may be the worst part for Ray, too," Linda offered. "Tell me about him."

David told her stories of Ray as they came to mind and a picture formed of the humorist and the quintessential professional, of his wit and his insight.

"...right there in the middle of the staff meeting, do you believe it?" he said, and they laughed.

He was glad to see Linda warming to someone so important to him. But the story of Ray wasn't complete without the role he had played in David's life. Dragging him, dead drunk, out of a bar.

Being part nurse, part therapist during his recovery. Then reinventing their relationship when David was back on his feet—that was the man he wanted her to know. The trouble was that a revelation like that about himself would be sure to send her running for the door.

He wanted Linda in his life, but he couldn't let himself fall back into the old trap of managing a relationship by managing what someone learned about him. What had Ray called it? "Some skit based on what he thought people expected." He didn't want any skit with Linda.

David picked up his wine glass. "You know, this is the first alcohol I've had in more than a year."

Her eyes widened. "I'm sorry," she said. "You should have told me. We could have had something else."

"No," David said purposefully. "I'd like to be able to enjoy the taste of a drink from time to time without abusing it. Tonight was a test."

"How's the wine?" she asked, pretending to introduce a new subject.

"Just fine. A good red wine, good company. A perfect evening."

A wisp of something more than friendship drifted through the moment.

"I appreciate you telling me about the wine," Linda said lightly, "but it's coming up as you're talking about Ray. I suspect there's an interesting story to connect the dots."

She was taking this new information in stride. Reassured, he told her about his life at the Bank, and how bourbon became important in coping.

"Ray was my sounding board, my touchstone. He was careful about what he said, but he knew, for example, that Sherry and I were in trouble—so did you for that matter."

Linda nodded.

"He smelled trouble with Diane long before I did," he continued. "And he was my punching bag when I had problems with Bank management. But he didn't see the problem coming with the bourbon. I was good at hiding it. We often had a drink together, but I was usually able to pace myself until I got home."

He stopped to assess the impact his story was having.

"With all this crap I'm telling you, I'm amazed you're still here."

"I know where the car keys are if I need them," she said. "I want to see where this comes out."

David smiled appreciatively.

"It wasn't until Diane walked away that I lost it completely," he admitted. "Ray came to my rescue."

"You were stuck on Diane, weren't you?"

He felt awkward talking with Linda about his feelings for another woman. But he was in the thick of the story now, and he wasn't going to revert to a managed script.

"Yeah, I fell ass-over-tea-kettle for her," he admitted. "She seemed to be everything Sherry wasn't. But I've realized that she was my white rabbit. She took me to Wonderland, and I didn't see that it was an illusion until it came crashing down around me.

"Ray said she had an agenda. He meant it as a criticism in her case, but what he said next was the real clincher, that I did *not* have an agenda. I didn't know what I wanted from the relationship. He was wrong, of course. I did. My agenda was as clear as it was ridiculous. I wanted to have someone else fix things for me, to help me escape my life, and if I did my best to please her, she'd make it happen."

Linda respected the silence as David paused.

"It suited her to help me do that for a few hours a week," he continued. "For the rest of the time, I kept up the fantasy of some ideal life with her. But I was the problem. I wanted someone else to give me something that in fact I could only give myself."

"So, what's your agenda these days?"

"It sounds stupid, I'm sure, but I'm trying to be myself, to know who that is. That's really hard to do if you've been raised to think that someone or something else is the repository of right and wrong. Your job is just to follow the rules. Ray really chewed me out for not being able to know what my own heart was telling me.

"It's terrifying to think that there isn't anyone in a better position than me to know what I should do. The textbooks call it self-determination but, whatever you call it, it's scary as hell for a recovering Baptist."

"It sounds radical, the way you put it," Linda said, "but the idea's straightforward. I guess girls catch on quicker than boys. Some knowledge seems to come with the training bra."

"But what kind of a late bloomer only catches on at thirty?"

"Someone who cares for others at the expense of himself, maybe?"

"No, that's too easy. It's true, I think. I do care for other people. But needing to please them so they'll like me can make for some cold charity. I think maybe I'm just slow on the uptake."

Linda chuckled. "You may be a lot of things, but you're not slow on the uptake."

David smiled. "Would you like more wine?"

"No, thanks. That will do me."

"I'm sorry I talked so much," he said.

"Not at all," she replied, "and I appreciate how honest you were. Your life's been an interesting trip so far, but at heart you're still the man I knew in graduate school." Then she added, "In case you were wondering, that's a good thing."

He reached to rest his hand on her arm. She took it in hers and intertwined their fingers. They found their way into each other's arms, and when they kissed there was a new closeness between them.

"Stay with me tonight," David said.

She kissed him again. "I'd like that."

CHAPTER 31

Jerry had no idea what time it was when he opened his eyes and saw light streaming into the cave. With little sleep during the night in Ohio, and only a couple of hours napping beside the trail on his way back to the cave last night, he was exhausted. He had crashed without starting a fire, without eating anything or even undressing, other than kicking his boots off.

He fumbled in the grub box for a bottle of apple juice and guzzled it, as much to mask the foul taste in his mouth as to quench his thirst. Staggering outside to relieve himself, he went over his to do list. Happily, there was nothing urgent this morning. Back inside, he barely managed to pull the travel blanket over his shoulder before he fell back to sleep.

He awoke the second time several hours later feeling rested and stretched casually before reaching for his boots. *Strange place to find a boot*, he chuckled to himself, as he retrieved one of them from the fire pit.

A few minutes later, as he built a small fire to heat a meal, Jerry pictured the boot again, lying where he was now arranging the kindling. Nobody would ever think to look for a boot there. Nobody would ever think to look for anything there. And the pieces fell into place for another of his windup tasks.

After a meal of beans and Spam, he took an old envelope, a pad, and a pen from his backpack, moved to the cave entrance for better light and wrote a note to Karen.

It was probably a fantasy, but he refused to rule out the idea that she might want to be with him someday, that someday she might be able to make such a decision. When he had finished writing, he folded the note and put it in the envelope with the letters from Paul Anderson and Y Nur Kpa. Then, he wrapped them tightly in several layers of Saran wrap from a roll in the grub box and set the package to one side. Before he left the cave for good, he would clear the ashes from the fire pit, bury the letters a few inches below the surface and redistribute the ashes. A small kindling fire to cover the site with a layer of undisturbed ash would be the finishing touch.

The note to Karen was ready. The Garand and the cartridges were safely gone. The wallet of one Thomas Andrews of Knoxville Tennessee would by now have been found by the duty officer checking the drop box at the Lewis Mountain Park Service office. The hundred-dollar bill folded into it would cover the Avis charges.

There was only one important job left: getting the van back to his father. He had a plan to do that without putting his father in a compromising position, but he'd wait another day for that, in case his luck changed and he needed wheels in a hurry. He relaxed with a sigh. The rest of the day was free.

Maybe it was a good time to say goodbye to the old family place. He would put the cave in order and then hike over to Fletcher Hollow.

He filled his canteen at the spring and spent a couple of hours sitting on the stone hearth. The surrounding trees and weeds yielded to scenes of family life that Gerald had recounted to him so many years before. This place would always be part of him, and its memories would always be with him.

When the sun began to settle noticeably toward the ridge, he scuffed the ground in Jake's old garden patch with the toe of his boot, took a final look around and headed back to the cave.

*****

Before dawn the next morning, a dark form materialized at the Meadow Spring trailhead and crossed the road quickly to disappear under the van in the parking area. Arranging the travel blanket around him to block the light, Jerry switched on his penlight and located the copper brake line that ran along the frame of the vehicle.

With the light in his mouth, he held the sharp edge of a quartzite rock against the line with one hand and struck that hand as firmly as he could with the other. The second strike produced the rough gash he was looking for. Brake fluid dripped onto a rag beneath the cut until he pushed a small peg he'd shaved from an alder branch into the opening.

Less than ten minutes after it had first appeared, the form crossed the road again, carrying the blanket and the old rag, and disappeared down the trail.

Later that morning, Jerry greeted several hikers as he made his way back to the trailhead. He waved as a car passed on Skyline Drive, towing a camper, then crossed the road to the van. As he backed out of the parking space, he was relieved to see that the sapling peg had held; there was no tell-tale stain of brake fluid where he had been parked. Now he had to hope that it wasn't wedged in too tightly; if it was, the plan to coast into the Panorama parking lot with damaged brakes would be a write-off.

Heading north along the Drive, he used the brakes very lightly at first and the wedge held. Then, as he covered a larger share of the distance back to Thornton Gap and increasing use of the brakes had not forced them to fail, his concern shifted from losing the brakes prematurely to not being able to force the peg out at all.

He would have to hit the pedal hard to eject it. When there were no other vehicles in sight, he punched the brakes as if to avoid an animal and felt relief and fear at the same time as the brakes grabbed momentarily before the pedal went soft beneath his foot and settled toward the floorboards.

Gearing down, he kept the van from accelerating as it went through the tunnel at Mary's Rock and down the last grade to Panorama, leaving a dark wet streak of brake fluid on the pavement. He swerved into the parking area and coasted to a stop in a vacant part of the lot. Then, in first gear, he crept to a parking space and got out to inspect the damaged brake line. Several other visitors who had witnessed his erratic arrival walked up to see if all was well.

"I remember hearing the stone hit underneath me," Jerry offered as they all looked on. "But what are the chances of it cutting a brake line? It's crazy."

The curiosity of his arrival faded quickly and visitors to Panorama returned to their own activities in a matter of minutes. Jerry locked the van and walked to a payphone outside the visitors' center.

"Hi, Katie. It's Jerry. Is the old man around?"

"No, he's not here at the moment," Katie replied. "He should be back in half an hour or so."

Jerry didn't know whether to be disappointed not to hear his father's voice one more time or relieved that he didn't have to go through the difficulty of another goodbye.

"OK. Would you give him a message for me?" he asked.

"Sure. What do you want me to tell him?"

"Well, I feel kind of stupid, but I took the van on a rough stretch of road this morning and a rock cut my brake line. It must have flipped up against the frame when it was pinched by the front tire, I guess. Anyhow, there's a cut where the line runs along the frame on the right side."

"Playing tiddlywinks with rocks, huh? So that's what you do when you go to the Park."

"You're spending too much time around my old man," he chuckled. "Anyhow, I managed to get it to the Panorama parking lot, and I guess he'll have to send Bobby and the tow truck for it."

"Will you be around?"

"No, there's no hurry. It's not in anybody's way, so he can come anytime. It's open and I left the key under the floor mat on the driver's side. I thought I'd continue on north—maybe take the Trail as far as Front Royal."

"OK. I'll give him the message."

There was a finality to the call that Jerry couldn't shake as he placed the receiver back on the cradle. It took a conscious effort to let go of the phone and walk away. He bought a candy bar and sat on a stone retaining wall, watching people come and go until those who might connect him with the van or have overheard his phone conversation had all gone their way. Then, he strapped on the backpack, picked up the Appalachian Trail and headed south.

CHAPTER 32

David had told the Skyland reservations clerk that he and the others would like to have some of their discussions on the porch if the weather was good, so it would be great if she could give them cabins somewhere away from the main Lodge.

That had apparently worked. When Jerry scanned the area with his binoculars Saturday afternoon from an outcrop on Stony Man Mountain, he saw David's '75 Nova parked near the south end of the compound, next to a grove of trees. *Perfect,* Jerry thought. He'd be able to approach the car undetected before dawn the next morning.

*****

"It may be time you got yourself a pickup," Bruckman said to David as the men made their way back toward the cabins Sunday morning, after breakfast at the lodge.

"What makes you think so?" David asked.

"I walked by your car on my way to breakfast this morning, and that's a hell of a load you've got in the back seat."

David's gut suddenly twisted. What had Bruckman seen?

"Sort of the way it looked with all my 'maters in there last summer!" Bruckman laughed. "What you got in there this time?"

A quick swallow to regain control and David said, "Oh, that's a bunch of stuff I'm taking home from the college now that the semester's nearly over." He made a guess and added, "I just threw the blanket over it so it wouldn't look too messy. Maybe a bonfire would have been better than taking it home, but you never know. Sure as I throw a document away, I'll need it."

Talking helped him start breathing again. He had no idea how Jerry had arranged himself in the car, but he must have made good use of the blanket David had left on the seat. *Thank God he was lying still when Dan walked by,* he thought. *The sooner I get this venture underway the better.*

When they reached the cabins, David waited while the other two collected their overnight bags and returned to the parking area.

"Well, I think it was a productive exercise, don't you?" he asked. Both men agreed. They had, in fact, accomplished a great deal. David's notebook was full of the raw material for position papers on half a dozen issues for the Board, and the three men had agreed on the recommendations they would make.

"Not a bad place to work, either," Bruckman added. David recognized that that was as close to a thank you as he was likely to hear. Gratitude could imply indebtedness, and rural society had long ago adopted appreciation as a safer proxy.

"The wife and kids had a good time last night, too," Atkins said. "You can bet the whole church knows about it by now."

When the others left, David retrieved his own overnight bag from his cabin, tossed it on the passenger's seat and got into the car. Without looking back, he asked, "Are you dead or alive back there?"

"Alive, barely," Jerry growled from beneath the blanket. "Why couldn't you drive something with a decent size, like a Galaxie? I'm bent like a fucking pretzel back here."

Looking down so an observer wouldn't see him talking, David said, "Just hang tight. We'll be out of the parking lot in a minute and then you can at least lie on the seat and stretch out."

Pulling onto Skyline Drive, he said, "OK. You can move now. Just stay down. Hello, by the way. I guess this means you got my message."

"Yeah, but this isn't a good time to be looking for a thank you."

David laughed. "Never mind, you can sit up after we clear the Park. I'm just glad it all came together."

"Me, too. Don't quote me, but this was actually a pretty good idea. Are all preachers this devious?"

"I'm not a preacher."

Jerry grunted. "That may not be your profession, but it's in your blood." He wondered how David and Paul Anderson would get along. For a guy who had never darkened the door of a church, he'd had good luck with the preachers in his life.

They reached Swift Run Gap about forty minutes later and headed for Harrisonburg. David had been checking the rearview mirror and, after a few miles on the open road, he was fairly sure no one was following them.

"You're probably OK to sit up now," he said, and Jerry's form slowly emerged from beneath the blanket.

"Don't think I'll ever be able to stand straight again," he moaned, twisting from side to side to loosen his torso as he rose to a sitting position.

It was only as they descended toward the Valley and left the Park behind that David realized how tense he had become in the days leading up to Jerry's escape. Breathing was getting easier now. His shoulders loosened and he felt strangely tired.

"I think I'll need to stop for a coffee before we go too much further," he said.

"That sounds like a good idea. I was squirreled away in some guy's car this morning when I should have been back in the cave with my own coffee."

They had not discussed Jerry's plans, so David had no idea what direction he intended to travel. He didn't need to know any specifics, but it would be good to at least agree on the plan for today.

"I'm in no hurry to get to Blacksburg," he told Jerry. "I don't have any meetings at Tech 'til tomorrow morning. I thought maybe, just to be safe, we'd stay on the normal route in that direction, at least to Staunton, but then I can take you wherever suits you. I just need to make it to Blacksburg tonight in time to check into the hotel."

"I thought catching a Greyhound would be my best bet," Jerry replied, "You know, inconspicuous."

"Right, but it needs to be far enough away that your friends aren't likely to have posted surveillance at the depot."

"Yeah, I was thinking Charlottesville."

"That would probably work, but it's a bit close. Why don't we go to Richmond? I-95's a busier corridor, too, so there'll be bigger crowds to work with."

"That's quite a detour for you. Are you up to it?"

"Ah, what's a hundred miles between friends?"

"All right, man. You're on."

They stopped outside Staunton to pick up coffee, and then headed east. David stayed on the old highway for a while instead of I-64, just to break up their trail. At Afton, they picked up the interstate and set off for Richmond.

*****

Conversation was easy for the first hour or so, but as they travelled away from the Park, the reality of what was happening began to settle over Jerry. This was goodbye. Goodbye to the Blue Ridge, goodbye to his parents and, at least for now, goodbye to Karen.

Could it have been different? Did he have to leave everything behind like this? Maybe this was just a radical version of what every man had to do: grow up and leave home. But it felt selfish. Did he have to hurt his mother? Was there something more he could have done for Karen? Would they ever be together? He withdrew with his thoughts and watched the passing countryside.

David had an idea what might be going on, so he didn't say anything, except to ask if the radio station that he had tuned in to was OK.

Somewhere east of Charlottesville, Jerry drifted off. He spent the next hour slumped back against the doorpost, stirring only when they entered a construction area in the Richmond suburbs. He took a moment to get his bearings and then sat up. "Guess I dozed off," he said, feeling a little foolish.

"No sweat. You probably had a short night last night."

"Yeah, and there's been a lot going on."

A couple of minutes later, he spoke again. "I know it's crazy after all you've done for me, but I need to ask for your help on something else."

"Sure. What can I do?" David was already hung out a fair way and he wasn't excited about taking on anything more, but what else could he say?

"Do you remember we talked about the girl over in Page County?"

"Yes, of course."

"I guess I never told you much about her. She was badly messed up in that shooting in Ohio but she's gradually getting better."

"That's great. Does she know you have to leave?"

"Yeah, we talked about it the other day. She wasn't too happy, but I think she understood. Anyhow, she's important to me. Her name's Karen, by the way. I know she's in good hands with her brother and his wife, but she worries about me, and I'd like to be able to put her mind at ease."

"How can I help with that?"

"Well, I told her about you, that we were friends. I told her you could let her know how I was doing."

"Yeah, but how?" David asked. "Can we stay in touch safely?"

"No. Of course not. That's the thing. I told her if she ever wanted an update on me, she could find you at the weekly market in Front Royal on Saturday mornings. If she does get in touch with you, it may just be to see how I'm doing. In that case, make up some story that I'm safe and that I'm doing something useful, will you?"

"Like what?"

"I don't know. Use your imagination. No, don't do that. Tell her you hear I've found a way to help the people I used to live with in Vietnam."

"OK. By the way, if that's true, it's really cool."

"Yeah, well, we'll see. It's also possible she will ask you if you know where I am. You won't, of course, but if you get the idea that she's really serious, that maybe she wants to find me, there's a way."

"You mean that she might want to join you?"

"Yeah."

"Is that safe?"

"Nothing's ever safe, son. Haven't you learned that by now?"

"Yeah, I guess you're right."

"Anyhow, if you think that's what she really wants, then I've left a package for her in the cave. I'd be grateful if you would retrieve it for her."

"Come on, Jerry. It's more than a decade since I was at the cave. I could never find it."

"Yes, you could. I know you're no Daniel Boone, but I'm going to tell you how to get there. You remember the old Fletcher homestead, right, with the chimney?"

"Yeah, I've sat there a few times. I can find that all right."

"OK. From there you take the trail that goes southwest. Go about nine-tenths of a mile. For you that's about half an hour taking it easy or twenty minutes if you push it."

"Right. So now I'm on the side of a mountain in a bunch of trees that all look the same. Now what?"

"Relax. Just watch for a big gnarly oak tree on the downhill side of the trail that has an old trumpet vine growing on it. You hardly ever see those vines that far up the mountain, so you can't miss it."

"Sounds like something Bob Hope would say to Bing Crosby. 'You can't miss it.'"

Jerry looked out the window for a moment and then turned to face David. "Look, I know I'm asking a lot, but this is important."

"OK. I'm sorry. If you think I can find it, then I'll certainly give it my best shot."

"Good. Thanks. So, you go about twenty-five feet past that tree and watch the ground on the right side of the trail. If you're careful, you'll be able to see the track that leads through the undergrowth up the side of the hill. About a yard off the trail I hid a Snicker's bar wrapper under some ferns, just to let you know you have the right spot. If it smells like soap, it's 'cause I made sure the 'coons or the deer wouldn't run off with it. Anyhow, the entrance to the cave is a couple hundred feet straight up that hill."

"Piece of cake," David said, and then, more seriously, "I'll do my best."

"There's a package with a couple of letters in it, buried about four inches down in the fire pit. That's for Karen."

"In the fire pit?"

"Yeah. You'll be able to dig it out with a stick. I suggest you don't open it, so you won't have any trouble pleading ignorance if you're questioned. Hell, never mind. That's up to you now."

"OK. Just remember, if I do find it, you owe me a coonskin cap!"

"You're on. And one more thing. Try not to let anyone see you passing the letters to her."

"Come on. I may not be Daniel Boone but I'm not Alfred E. Newman, either."

Jerry's list was complete. He had done what he could to tie up the loose ends of his life in Virginia. But it wasn't satisfaction he felt; it was an uneasy sense of being cut adrift. Even as he spoke, he felt foolish, but he needed contact, no matter how fleeting.

"By the way, the coonskin hat? That was Fess Parker. Boone wouldn't have been caught dead in anything but beaver."

"Where'd you ever come up with a bit of trivia like that?"

"Oh, even a mountain man can get interested in the library if he has ten years to kill."

It took them a couple of loops around the downtown area to find the bus depot. When they saw it, David pulled into the unloading area and got out to stand by the curb while Jerry retrieved his backpack.

"I guess this is it," Jerry said. "I sure appreciate all you've done."

"It's no big deal, my friend. If I don't have your strength, I'm glad I can at least help out."

Jerry looked away awkwardly, then changed the subject.

"The first time we said goodbye you were standing on a crutch and one leg, about to hitch a ride. Now you've got two good legs and your own wheels. Things are looking up!"

"And you have a plan and a woman who loves you. Not bad all 'round."

"Yeah. Maybe the good guys will win some day after all."

They shook hands and David said, "If I can ever help, you know where I am."

He smiled, got back into the car, and watched as Jerry disappeared among the people in the depot.

CHAPTER 33

The bus pulled into the Greyhound depot in Fayetteville late Sunday evening. Tired and dazed after the long ride, Jerry waited in the muggy night air as the driver set passengers' baggage beside the bus. Finally, his backpack appeared. He swung it over his shoulder and left the depot, walking along Person Street until he eventually saw what he was looking for. A small sign that read 'Whitfield Hotel, Rooms Daily or Weekly' hung above a doorway leading to the second floor over a row of shops.

If he was right, this was the kind of place that didn't charge a lot of money and didn't ask a lot of questions. The entrance was lit, and the door was still open. At the top of the stairs, he presented himself to a sleepy clerk at the reception counter and ten minutes later closed the door of a small but clean room that looked out on the rear of the building.

There were screens on the two windows and a box fan on the little table by the door but, even with the fan on high, the room's stifling air barely moved. Jerry stripped to his shorts, tossed the blanket off the bed, and lay spread-eagle on the sheets. It wasn't the cave, but it would have to do for now. After an hour or so, fatigue prevailed over discomfort, and he fell asleep. Other than a trip down the hall to the bathroom sometime before dawn and struggling with the tangled sheets when he got back into bed, he slept well. He awoke the next morning with his 'to do' list ticking over in his mind.

In thirty minutes he was showered and ready to go. Grabbing a copy of the *Fayetteville Observer-Times* at the reception desk, he added a quarter to those already in the little dish and left to find a nearby diner where he could have breakfast and organize his day.

Office workers and shopkeepers milled around the front counter, placing and picking up take-out orders. A few regulars sat on stools or in booths, lost in their own worlds of newspapers, coffee, and rugged porcelain plates of griddle fare. Jerry headed for a booth near the back of the room and a waitress was at his table with the coffee pot by the time he was seated.

"Just put it there," he said, pressing his index finger against the vein in his arm.

"Don't you worry, hon. This stuff is strong enough to get where it needs to go in a hurry."

"Sounds good."

"And what'll you have this morning?" she asked as she poured the coffee.

"How about a couple of eggs over easy and some sausage?"

"And grits?"

"Of course, and give me a couple slices of toast, too."

"Comin' up."

While he waited for his meal he went through the classifieds and circled several ads for used cars. It looked like he'd be able to find something basic for about five hundred dollars. But before he called the sellers he needed to get in touch with Butch Walton. There was no use starting to settle into the area if there was no place for him in Walton's operation. He'd never been much on having a Plan B, but the secret to surviving without one was mobility—the ability to disappear in a hurry. Things like car titles would leave a trail.

"Here you are, hon," the waitress said, setting his breakfast in front of him. "Anything else I can get you? More coffee?"

"No, this is great, thanks," Jerry said, and proceeded to enjoy his first hot meal in two days.

There was a phone on the wall at the back of the room, and he planned to make that call to Butch as soon as he finished his breakfast. But, as he ate, he became increasingly apprehensive. Maybe Butch wouldn't want to take the chance of letting a fugitive into his operation. Maybe there was nothing useful he could do with the group; or, maybe he'd be welcomed in only to find that the Feds had been able to track him. There was no knowing what corners Butch had to cut to help people the government no longer cared about. The last thing he needed was to have Feds nosing around his operation.

It was easier to accept the worry about being followed than the possibility that he wouldn't be welcomed but, either way, Jerry decided to lay low for a couple of days and he left the restaurant without making the call.

*****

Shortly after Gerald Fletcher opened the shop that morning back in Flint Hill, Special Agent Johnson entered the office, accompanied by another agent.

"Good morning Mr. Fletcher," Johnson said.

"Good morning, gentlemen. What can I do for you?"

"Do you know where your son is, Mr. Fletcher? We'd like to talk to him."

"He's up in the mountains. He took a few days off last week to spend some time around the old family place."

"Is it normal for him to be gone this long?"

Gerald decided not to comment on the fact that Johnson seemed to know how long he'd been gone. Apparently, the Agency was no longer trying to conceal its surveillance.

"Well, normal isn't a concept that comes to mind for my son, but I did kind of expect him to be back over the weekend," Gerald said. He turned to Katie. "What did he tell you when he called on Friday, Katie?"

Now the agents turned toward Katie and she hesitated briefly, glancing at Gerald. When he nodded his OK, she said, "He told me he was going to hike north, toward Front Royal."

"He had trouble with the van," Gerald volunteered. "Lost the brakes, so he left it at Panorama. I'm sending the tow truck up there this morning to bring it back."

Johnson did not tell him that the Agency already had the van under surveillance.

"How long does it take to hike from Thornton Gap to Front Royal?" he asked.

"Well, it's a little over thirty miles," Gerald said, "and not very difficult, so a serious hiker would do it easily in a couple days."

Turning back to Katie, Johnson asked, "Did he say he'd call again?"

"No," she answered but again Gerald volunteered, "I won't be surprised if he calls for a lift when he's ready to come back."

Johnson realized he wasn't going to get any further with this approach, so he squared to face Gerald and said, "Mr. Fletcher, we have a warrant for your son's arrest."

Katie gasped involuntarily and Gerald blurted out, "What the hell for?"

"Destruction of government property," Johnson answered flatly.

"That's the most absurd thing I've ever heard," Gerald said angrily. "What did he do, knock over a stop sign?"

"I'm not at liberty to tell you, Mr. Fletcher, but this is a serious charge. If he's convicted, he's looking at up to ten years in prison."

It was all Gerald Fletcher could do to control his temper before he spoke. "Weren't the ten years you took from him in Leavenworth enough for your masters?"

"Furthermore, Mr. Fletcher," Johnson continued, ignoring Gerald's comment, "we have reason to believe that your son may have left the area to avoid being arrested. I'm obliged to tell you this now because, if you are withholding information about his whereabouts, that would be considered aiding and abetting a fugitive and obstruction of justice."

Gerald had to make a special effort to remain calm.

"Agent Johnson," he began, in a measured tone. "So far you have conducted your inquiries around here in a courteous manner so I'm going to respond to that comment in the same way. I find your charge against my son completely absurd. I have told you that, as far as my wife and I know, our son is hiking in the Blue Ridge Mountains, as he often does, and we expect him to return when he's ready. That is the simple truth."

Johnson decided that Gerald was probably telling the truth. He wasn't going to learn anything more here because Gerald in fact knew nothing.

"Nevertheless," he concluded, "I must ask you to contact the Agency if you hear from your son or learn of his whereabouts." With that, he nodded to his colleague, and they turned to leave. At the door, he paused and looked back at Gerald.

"Oh, by the way. The van in the Panorama parking lot is now part of a criminal investigation. You will be contacted when it's released."

CHAPTER 34

Almost a week had passed since David last visited the hospital, and he was anxious to see how Ray was doing. As he passed the nurses' station on Ray's floor, one of them recognized him and called out, "Mr. Williams."

"Yes?"

"Dr. Baker isn't there. He's been moved to a different room."

"Oh? Has there been a change in his condition?"

"Well, his doctor and his wife can fill you in, but he took a turn for the worse last evening, and they moved him to Intensive Care. It's just one flight up if you'd like to take those stairs." She pointed to a set of doors behind David.

Only moments earlier he had been hoping for some improvement since his last visit. In the stairwell, he had the sudden urge to head down instead of up, to flee the building, as if not going to the intensive care unit could change the script, keep Ray from being there. But the fantasy vanished with the cold touch of the stair railing, and he dutifully began the climb.

Emerging from the stairwell on the next floor he stood in a large open space with a nursing station at its center and individual glass-fronted rooms around the perimeter. People and machines were going methodically about their work, sharing a language of acronyms, blinking control panels, and coded chimes. He was getting his bearings when a woman spoke to him from behind a counter at the nursing station.

"May I help you, sir?"

"Good morning. I'm looking for Dr. Baker's room. I understand he's…"

"Yes, of course. Dr. Baker's in Room D, around that way," she said, pointing to his left. "Mrs. Baker is with him now."

The curtains of Ray's room were partially drawn. Between them he could see Teresa standing by the bed, her back to the window. She was wiping Ray's forehead with a facecloth. His eyes were closed, and he appeared to be asleep. But something was different and, as he entered the room, David realized what it was: there was no oxygen mask over Ray's face, no cannula or breathing tube. The IV pole had been moved back from the bed, and there were none of the tubes or wires that had been attached to Ray since he was admitted. He wasn't connected to anything.

Teresa looked up and smiled as David came into the room.

"David's here, Ray," she said, as normally as if she was standing at the front door in Arlington.

"What's happened?" David asked anxiously.

She continued in a calm voice, "Well, while he was sitting up last night picking at his dinner, he got one of his nasty headaches. Then he just slumped over, and he's been in a coma ever since."

David went over to Teresa and wrapped his arms around her. She seemed to welcome the comfort, but there was something different about her, too.

"Tell me about this," he said, nodding in the direction of the discarded equipment.

She turned to Ray, put her hand on his arm, and said, "David and I will be back in a minute, my sweet." Then she led the way out of the room and closed the door behind them. "There's nothing more they can do, so I decided to make him comfortable." She looked back through the window. "He looks pretty good, don't you think?"

It was either the strangest question ever, or the most natural.

"Yes, he does," David answered. "Peaceful."

It struck David as he stared back through the curtain that he should have been here yesterday instead of in Blacksburg. He'd have been with Ray before he collapsed, talked with him, laughed with him, visited with him. To help one friend, he had abandoned the other.

"According to the CT scan it was a hemorrhage near the base of his brain that made him pass out," Teresa explained. "It's also gradually shutting down his diaphragm and his heart. They will stop working soon. He has always been clear about not wanting to be on life support… I have to let him go, David," she said as tears filled her eyes. She turned to look through the glass at her husband. "It's what he wants."

David put his arm around her again. The reality of her loss would catch up to her soon enough but, for the moment, she was finding strength in doing what she knew Ray would want.

"You're right, of course. Just another reason he loves you."

"Go in and talk to him, David," she said. "They say people in comas can hear. I don't know, but I want to think so. He was talking about you last night before he collapsed, so I know he'd be glad you're here."

When they went back into the room, David took the chair closest to the bed and leaned over to put his hand on Ray's arm. "Hey, you old codger."

He caught himself waiting for a response, then pushed on with the one-sided conversation.

"I gather the food disagreed with you at dinner last night. We'll speak to the management about the menu."

Imagining Ray's smile took the awkwardness out of the situation. He was just talking to his friend.

"You've been a good friend, Ray. Thank you. I'm going to miss our time together. I can imagine that you shook your head a few times at my foolishness, but thanks for sticking with me. You showed me that you can't take credit without taking the blame, too. That was maybe the toughest lesson. But mostly, thank you for being you. I know I got the best part of the deal. All I had to do was rake a few leaves and listen to a few stories. And the stories weren't all that bad, either."

A few moments went by in silence before he added, "You showed me what friendship is all about. If it's all the same with you, I'm just going to sit here for a few minutes and soak up some more of it."

About half an hour later, as he and Teresa sat quietly by his bed, a gurgling noise began to come from Ray's throat and his body tensed slightly under the covers. With tears streaming silently down her face, Teresa stood over him and put her hand on his cheek as David left to summon a nurse. She came into the room followed by a doctor, who asked Teresa to step aside as he began to monitor Ray's heartbeat. After several minutes, he looked at his watch, then turned to her and said, "He's gone."

*****

Teresa's friend Edith arrived an hour later to accompany her home and David left the hospital. He made his way across the street to the park in the center of Washington Circle and sat on one of the benches. He was exhausted, and the tangle of events and feelings of the morning would be slow to unwind. But Ray was gone, Teresa was in good hands, and he was alone. Now it was OK to mourn, and his mind began to serve up the packets of memory that would shape his loss in the days and weeks to come. When he remembered Ray's hand on his shoulder during the early days of his alcohol recovery the year before, the tears returned. *I guess that's something I need to get used to,* he thought.

He decided to walk for a while and made his way along K Street toward Rock Creek. There were a few joggers on the footpath, and women with strollers, but everyone was in their own world. It was peaceful in the dappled sunlight beneath the oaks and poplars. He crossed the little bridge where Rock Creek empties into the Potomac, bought a sandwich at Thompson's Boathouse and found a bench near the edge of the water.

A mallard swam upstream toward him, leading her brood. Others, that didn't have the worry of a family, waddled across the lawn announcing as they came that he was expected to contribute to their lunch, and he tossed a few small pieces of bread in their direction. David couldn't tell whether their response was gratitude or complaint, but there was comfort in the simple sketch of life playing itself out around his feet.

The ducks lost interest when the sandwich was gone and wandered off. David walked back to a payphone at the boathouse, picked up the receiver, and dialed a number from his wallet.

"Hi, Linda. It's me." He had no plan for the conversation, just the need to hear her voice. "This is a purely selfish call," he announced. "Will you accept the charges?"

"Yes, operator. I'll take a chance on that," she said, playing along. "Where are you?"

"Down at the boathouse by Rock Creek."

"What are you doing there?"

"Ray died this morning. I've just been walking around."

"I'm so sorry, David. Can you stay in town 'til I get off work?"

"I was hoping you'd say that."

"Good. My apartment is just up Virginia Avenue, at Columbia Plaza. That's about a ten-minute walk from where you are. I'll call the front desk and tell them you're coming. Make yourself at home and I'll see you around six."

CHAPTER 35

On his third morning in Fayetteville, Jerry decided it was time to call Butch Walton. It would be too easy for someone to listen in if he used the phone in the diner so, finishing his breakfast, he paid his check and found a phone booth by the curb in Market Square. He took the small piece of paper from his wallet, put a quarter in the coin slot, and dialed the number. After half a dozen rings, as he was about to give up, someone came on the line.

"Walton's," the voice said.

"Yeah. Hi," Jerry said. "I'd like to speak to Mr. Walton, please."

"Hang on a minute."

He could hear the high-pitched whine of machinery in the background—a saw, maybe—and after ten or fifteen seconds someone picked up the phone.

"This is Butch Walton," said a familiar voice. "Can I help you?"

"Hi, Butch. This is, ah, Jerry Fletcher."

Walton recognized the voice instantly. "Jerry, it's great to hear your voice. Paul Anderson told me you might call someday, and I've been hoping to hear from you."

Any apprehension about the reception Jerry might receive vanished with the tone of Butch's voice.

"Where are you?" Walton asked, before Jerry said anything more.

"I'm in Fayetteville," he replied. "I thought maybe we could have a visit."

"Of course. Are you mobile?"

"No, but that's not a problem. Just let me know where you're located or where you want to meet, and I'll get there."

"Nonsense. I'll pick you up."

About an hour later, a brown van with a sign on the side that read 'A. Walton, Cabinet Maker' pulled up to the curb in Market Square. Butch Walton got out and came around the hood to take Jerry's hand.

"I wasn't sure I'd ever get to see you again," he said. "You left Gong Krek in kind of a hurry that day."

They both laughed and Jerry said, "Yes, thanks to you. Otherwise, I might have left in a body bag."

Walton's expression changed and, more quietly, he said, "You've had a rough few years since that."

"Yeah, well, I guess the Army had a point to make with the Vietnamese."

"I hope you've got the time to stick around for a while," he said as they pulled away from the curb. "I'd like to hear what you've been up to since you got out, what your plans are."

"Yeah, of course, and Paul told me that you and some of the guys are helping the 'Yards. I'd like to hear about that, too."

They headed north on Bragg Boulevard. With the growth of troop numbers in the late sixties and early seventies, it had become one of the main axes of commercial and residential expansion. Then, with the troop draw-down and the end of the Vietnam war, the strip became just another example of the shifting fortunes of small business in a free enterprise economy. "Grand Opening" and "Going Out of Business" signs rubbed shoulders with those proclaiming lowest prices and best buys—the business cycle in paint and neon. Fast-food chains and one-offs vied for the traveler's food dollars. Car and truck dealers promised no money down and easy payment plans, hoping to tap into the thousands of government-backed pay checks that arrived every month just up the road.

"You were from the Midwest somewhere, weren't you?" Jerry asked.

"That's right. Indiana. A little town outside Lafayette."

"Did you go back when you got out?"

"Briefly."

Jerry guessed he knew what was coming, but he waited for Walton to continue.

"Things had changed. Even people who supported the war didn't know what to say when we met. Jobs were hard to find." Then he added, "And the country was so goddamned flat! I don't know, I just didn't fit in. So, I came back here one day to look up some of the old Airborne buddies and just stayed."

"I get it. And I see you're in the woodworking business."

"Yeah. That's what I did before I was drafted, so it kind of came easy to me.

"What's the 'A' stand for?"

"Never mind."

"It's that bad, is it? Anton, maybe?"

"It's Albert," he grumbled. "Any wonder I go by Butch?"

"No, that was probably a good choice once you decided not to be an English prince!"

"Smartass. Anyhow, it's taken a while, but we've built up a good little volume in the business. The sign says cabinetry and we do some custom work—built-ins and the like—but my bread-and-butter is actually components for the furniture business over in High Point. I keep a couple of guys busy full-time making chair legs and arms for a big outfit there."

"Excellent. And why Cameron?" Jerry asked, remembering the address on the van's sign.

"I hate this kind of suburban chaos," Walton said, indicating the sprawl they were driving through. "Cameron is quiet. It's close enough to the guys who've settled around here and it's on the way to High Point."

"Makes sense," Jerry said. "It sounds like a good fit."

"In case you hadn't guessed," Walton continued, "that's where we're headed now."

"Good. It'll be great to see your set-up."

About five miles beyond the edge of the suburban sprawl they turned west and headed across typical Carolina farm country, with fields of cotton and tobacco punctuating the ever-present corn and soybean.

They traveled in silence for several minutes and then Jerry spoke. "There's something I think you should know before you introduce me to anyone."

Walton glanced over at him. "OK," he said, "but that's up to you."

Jerry hesitated a moment, gathering his thoughts.

"As you can imagine," he began, "I wasn't too happy with the way things turned out at the court martial."

"No shit," Walton growled in disgust.

"But I had a lot of time to look back on it. I was pissed with the whole thing, but I could see how it happened. I mean there were reasons why things went the way they did. I was a pawn, but at least there was a game."

"That's mighty understanding of you," Walton said, his voice laced with sarcasm. "A whole lot of people thought you should have been thanked, not punished."

Jerry appreciated hearing that but didn't respond. "Then, while I was inside," he continued, "something happened that really threw me off."

Walton was expecting to hear about an assault by other prisoners and was already preparing something supportive to say in response.

"My girlfriend was shot at Kent State."

Walton pulled off the road onto the first wide shoulder he could find, turned the key off, and turned to stare at Jerry. "You've got to be fucking kidding me," he exhaled.

Jerry filled him in on the whole story—Karen's injuries, her long, slow recovery and the trip they had made to Kent. Then he said, "I don't want to put you in an awkward position by telling you more than that, but I had to leave Virginia because the FBI is looking into some trouble the Ohio National Guard has had. They figure I may have had something to do with it."

Walton knew better than to ask. Instead, he said, "What do you suppose would ever give them an idea like that?"

"What I'm trying to get at is that I don't want to make trouble for you by being around if somebody brings it up, or if the FBI gets wind of me being here and comes calling. I was careful not to leave a trail, but you never know."

Walton waited a moment out of respect for what Jerry had just told him. Then he said, "I appreciate what you're saying but you need to understand something, too. You're among friends down here. The guys who know your story think you were shafted. They're not going to be inclined to talk to anybody snooping around. And you haven't told me anything that would be awkward for me if I was questioned. Officially, let's just leave it at that."

"I appreciate that," Jerry said. "It means a lot."

"Now, unofficially," Walton continued, "the very fact that people know your story creates another problem. The risk is that someone will get excited about you being in the area and tell the wrong people. Nothing malicious, but just as dangerous."

"It seems strange that people know about me, but I'll have to take your word on that."

"Are you kidding? Trust me. In the right circles you wouldn't have to pay for your drinks for a month around here."

"That would be sure to make somebody curious," Jerry said. "Maybe coming here wasn't such a good idea after all."

"No, no. Just a minute. The only problem is the 'Jerry Fletcher' part. There are lots of guys drifting in and out of the area. Love-hate with the Army, failure to launch when they were discharged or, for some, just the draw of being around others who understand what they've been through. Whatever the reason, Airborne automatically makes you part of a community around here. These guys don't do a lot of prying into your business but they're ready to do some listening if you want it."

"That sounds kind of nice but, if you're right, my name screws that up."

"Have you ever read the telephone book?" Walton asked.

Jerry was baffled by the question. "Uh, no. What do you mean by read the phone book?"

"It's very interesting," Walton said with a wink. "It's full of names."

Fifteen minutes later Butch Walton was introducing his friend Chris Adams to the crew in the workshop.

"Chris and I served together in the highlands back in '68," he said as they moved through the operation.

"Recon?" someone asked.

"Those were some heavy times," another commented.

"Left that in the A Shau Valley in '69," the lathe operator said, holding up the stump where his left forearm used to be.

The bearded guy at the drill press chimed in, "Makes the equipment in here only half as dangerous for him as it is for the rest on us," and there was a good laugh all round.

Walton was obviously doing something right. He had combined his knowledge of the woodworking business and his instinctive concern for fellow veterans to create a space where they could be part of something useful again as they reclaimed themselves from the heap of Army surplus.

Two members of the crew in particular caught Jerry's attention. One, working with a wooden mallet and a set of chisels, was carving scrollwork into chair backs; the other was gluing, assembling, and clamping cabinet components. But it wasn't what they were doing, it was their appearance: they were Montagnards. There were four million Montagnards in the world, but he suddenly had the urge to rush up to these two and ask about Kpa. Instead, he smiled when they were introduced and bowed awkwardly.

"I have many friends among the people," was all he could manage to say.

When they had finished looking around the shop they headed back to Butch's office at the front of the building.

"I felt stupid when we met the last two guys," Jerry said. "They're the first 'Yards I've seen since Kpa."

"They were scouts with a Ranger unit right up to the end," Walton said, "and they were choppered out to a ship with their teams when they were withdrawn. It seems both their families were lucky enough to make it to Thailand since then and we've been able to get some help to them—you know, like clothes and a few bucks in local currency."

"That's good. I gather a couple dozen came out with their units like that."

"Yeah, and most of them came to North Carolina. The biggest concentration is around Greensboro. The land and the climate on that side are more like what they're used to, and they can do the kind of small mixed farming they know about.

"Must be tough, though. New language, new surroundings, new culture."

"For sure. You gotta hand it to them," Butch said admiringly. "But one thing really does hang them up."

"What's that?"

"They're not used to anything with a motor. The slightest thing goes wrong with a tractor or a pickup and it might as well be a blown engine. I guess they'll eventually catch on but, in the meantime, they lose a hell of a lot of time with dead equipment."

Jerry's eyes lit up. "Maybe I could help with that," he said. "I grew up under the hood of anything with a motor. Other than the Army, the only job I've ever had was as a mechanic."

"I like the sound of that," Walton replied. "There may be a future for you in North Carolina, Mr. Adams."

Finding something useful he could do to be part of Walton's network was a big relief, and Jerry was visibly more at ease as they explored the idea. They agreed that he would accompany Butch to the Greensboro area the following week when he delivered the next load of furniture components. They'd touch base with some of the Montagnards in the area and Jerry would get an idea of the equipment that needed his skills. He'd also have a chance to get a feel for the country.

"...Just to see if you could hack it over there," Walton said. "It's not the Blue Ridge, but it's the piedmont country you're used to, and on a clear day you can see the Smokies."

Walton decided it wouldn't hurt to add one more reason for Jerry to make the trip.

"And there's a fellow over that way that I'd like you to meet," he said. "Clyde McPherson has a farm machinery business a few miles west of High Point. His mechanic is a friend of mine who's decided to go back to Wisconsin to get married. Great time of year for a wedding, but in the farm machinery business, it's not a good time to be without a mechanic."

"This is sounding better all the time," Jerry said, making an effort to control his enthusiasm.

"But first, Mr. Adams, we've got to do something about your existence."

"My what?"

"Your existence," Walton said. "You've got a name, but that doesn't mean squat without things like a driver's license and a social security card."

"Oh shit," Jerry said. "I wasn't thinking about that. Are all your visitors this naive?"

"Never mind that. I have a friend in Fayetteville who's a real artist with government documents. He could even make you a passport that would pass muster, but he'll fix you up just fine with everything you need. And, by the way, use this as your address for now. There's a room upstairs that new guys use 'til they get settled."

Later that week Jerry returned to Cameron driving the ten-year-old Ford pickup he'd found through the local classifieds. Adjusting the carburetor had made a big difference in how it ran and, overall, it was in good shape. The Airborne and Fort Bragg decals he'd put in the rear window had already earned a few nods from passing drivers. His backpack was on the seat beside him. In his wallet were a North Carolina driver's license and a well-worn social security card, both in the name of Christopher Adams.

CHAPTER 36

Sometime during the night, a cold breeze had swept into the Browntown Valley from the northwest, rattling late-summer leaves, whispering in the window screens and ruffling curtains that had hung limp for weeks in the August heat. No one was under any illusion that this marked the end of hot weather, but the brisk morning air held the promise of autumn.

The end of the Dog Days was one reason for David's bright spirits this morning. The other was the woman in his bed. He had spent more time with Linda in the weeks since Ray's death. They had worked together in the gardens, hiked several of the trails in the Park and picnicked on scenic outcroppings. They had also spent several incredible nights together. She moved comfortably about the house now and kept a few clothes and personal items there to make stayovers easier. They were becoming a presence in each other's lives, and it pleased him.

As he returned to the bedroom with two cups of coffee, Linda opened one eye just above the covers, and smiled at him.

"Good morning, sleepyhead," he said.

"Good morning," she murmured. "It's cold in here. What happened?"

"Pshaw. That's fresh air, city girl." He set the cups on the bedside table and sat on the bed beside her.

"It wasn't too bad until my bed warmer got up and left," she complained.

He bent toward her, kissed her lightly on the lips and whispered, "Maybe he needs more practice."

"I was thinking more along the lines of an electric blanket," she said, forcing herself not to smile.

David pouted and shifted to leave, but she reached from under the covers and caught his arm. "Well, maybe a little practice would be OK."

He shed his slippers and climbed in next to her.

"Hey, you're freezing!" she exclaimed, pushing him away and rolling over to face the other direction.

"OK. OK. Just give me a minute."

He rubbed his hands briskly together and waited a few moments until his body had begun to warm the space around him. Then he reached and pulled her to him until she was tucked snuggly into the curve of his body.

She wriggled appreciatively and murmured, "Mmmm, that's better."

Making love with Linda had been different from the beginning. It wasn't a matter of suggesting or accepting, of giving or taking. Whether it was in a passionate rush or, like this morning, in the gentle cradling of their bodies as they became one, it was something they created together.

Sometime later, as they lay spent in each other's arms, Linda whispered, "I'm not cold anymore."

"That's good," David replied, "I couldn't do anything about it if you were."

She touched his cheek gently and slid out from under the covers. Pulling a shawl around her shoulders, she took the two untouched cups of coffee back to the kitchen and returned with them refreshed a couple of minutes later.

"Here you go," she said, "Let's drink it while it's hot this time."

David pulled himself up to sit with his back against the head of the bed and took the cups as Linda climbed in beside him.

"What's the plan this morning?" he asked.

"Nothing too strenuous. It is Saturday after all. But I do want to drive over to the Inland Port and check on progress at a couple of clients' construction sites. Do you want to come?"

"I would like to see how things are going over there," David answered, "but not this morning. I should spend some time at the market in town. We have a couple of new members participating for the first time this morning."

He hadn't told Linda about his agreement to keep an eye out for Karen in case she decided to come to the market to ask about Jerry, but that was another reason he made a point of spending time there every Saturday.

"OK, that's good." Linda said, as she shifted to get out of bed. "I'll just come back here when I'm done and work in the garden for a while. We can put something together for lunch when you get back."

"Sounds great. I'll bring something from the bake table for dessert." Then he added, "But I have a different idea for next week. Let's plan on meeting in town for lunch. There's a little café on Main Street that I think you'll like.

*****

With the hint of autumn in the air there was a different feel to the market. In the spring there had been the excitement of the first produce to arrive. In summer that had given way to indulgence in the rich variety of fruits and vegetables. But now customers moved about as though the chill in the air had triggered a greater sense of purpose. They were more intent on stocking their pantries and cellars than creating decorative salads. Sacks of potatoes and baskets of apples had replaced the zucchinis, beans, and berries of earlier markets. Jars of preserves were on display everywhere.

David felt a sense of pride in how the idea to supplement his neighbors' income had evolved into such a fixture in the community. More subtle and more rewarding was the feeling that his neighbors had changed, too. In the early days, they had seemed awkward, ill at ease, as they interacted with visitors. But they had become more confident in their ability to contribute to these exchanges, to share experience and points of view. Their faces were more expressive, their manor more inviting, and the space between "Mornin' Ma'am" and "Come back and see us" was filled with an ever-increasing sense of ease.

He cared for these people, and he played a part in their well-being. On one occasion, reflections like these had kicked up the word congregation, and he had chuckled at the indignation he knew his father would feel toward such an analogy. But he wondered if there wasn't some small part of the man that might be willing to acknowledge common ground, where the spiritual and the temporal were expressions of each other, instead of separate realms that vied for the soul in a zero-sum game.

David was manning a stall while one of the co-op members helped Dan Bruckman with a load of apples. Nearby, another member was having a conversation with a woman David didn't recognize. The man pointed in David's direction and she began walking toward him. An attractive woman with prematurely graying hair pinned in a bun at the back of her head, she moved with a slight limp, carefully but steadily. Her jeans and plaid jacket were the practical choice of someone at ease in this part of the world, but they were fitted well and did not hide the woman beneath.

"Are you David Williams?" she asked as she reached the stall where he was standing.

"Yes, I am," he replied. "Can I help you?"

"My name is Karen Guersten," she said. "Perhaps someone mentioned that I might…"

"Yes, yes, of course. I'm very happy to meet you, Miss Guersten. I've been wondering if you might drop by."

"Well, there were some things I needed to take care of first," she said. "Is there somewhere we could talk?"

"Of course, but if you don't mind a suggestion," David said, lowering his voice, "it might be better to stay here and look over some produce while we're talking. It would draw less attention, and I don't think anyone will overhear us."

Karen seemed unsure for a moment, then reached toward a basket of apples and turned a couple over as if considering them.

"How's Jerry?" she asked, without looking directly at David.

"I gather he's doing fine."

She glanced at him as if she didn't know what to make of his answer.

"I don't have everyday contact with him," David explained, using his compulsion for the truth to create a deception. The fact was he hadn't heard from Jerry since he dropped him off at the Richmond bus depot. "But I know he's with friends and doing something he wants to do."

"That's good," she replied, and again seemed slightly disoriented, as though not sure how to proceed.

"Do you know where he is?"

"No, I don't," David answered, looking around as he spoke to make sure no one was paying attention to them. "But I know he wants it that way."

"I need to find him," Karen said.

"This may sound strange, Miss Guersten, but may I ask why?"

Karen looked directly at him now and quietly but firmly said, "Because I want to be with him."

David smiled.

"Those are the magic words," he said. "Our friend told me that, if you said that, I was to give you something."

Karen struggled to contain a surge of excitement. She fidgeted with her purse and looked at David in anticipation but, instead of elaborating, he renewed the pretext of their visit.

"Shall I put some of these galas in a bag for you?"

"Yes, sure. This basket will be fine," she replied, pointing impatiently at the one closest to her.

As he began to transfer the apples from the basket to a paper bag, he said, "It will take me several days to get the letters he left for you, so why don't you plan on coming back next Saturday? I'll have them for you then."

She was briefly crestfallen at having to wait but nodded and paid for the apples.

"Thank you very much, David," she said. "I'll see you next week."

One morning toward the end of the following week, David left his car at the Meadow Springs trailhead and set off for the cave. He had forgotten how far it was from the parking area, and how steep the trail was, but eventually he found the big oak with the trumpet vine. A few yards further on, he saw the slight indentation in the ground at the side of the trail. Parting the ground cover with his hands he followed the hint of a path for several feet and was relieved to find the Snickers wrapper. He felt foolish raising it to his nose, but it did indeed smell of soap.

The rest of the search was straightforward and three hours later he was back in his car, headed for Browntown, with a dirty Saran-wrapped packet of letters lying on the seat next to him.

CHAPTER 37

Jerry stood in a doorway next to the work bays at McPherson Farm Machinery Services. He held a work order in one hand.

"Hey, Dhong."

"Yes, boss?"

"How about you and Korem pulling the front wheels off that Massey Ferguson when you're done?" He gestured toward a weathered old tractor that waited in the yard. "We need to replace the bearings on both sides."

Clyde MacPherson had agreed to take on the two Montagnard men at Jerry's request and in the ensuing couple of months they had certainly been earning their keep.

"OK. We finish tire job. Then we pull wheels off Massey Ferguson."

"And be sure those jack stands are set right before you loosen the lug nuts."

The little shop was having a good year. The local area had had better rainfall than the North Carolina coastal plain, so crop yields were up but prices were holding. One consequence was a steady demand for repair and replacement work to keep the farm fleet operating.

Another factor was also at play in the shop's performance. Clyde's son had been its only licensed mechanic, and when he was drafted in 1971, it had been difficult to find a competent replacement for him. Then, when he was killed at An Loc in '72, Clyde took it hard, and for several years the business didn't get the attention it needed. By the time Butch Walton's delivery van limped into Salisbury in the fall of '75 with a bad alternator, MacPherson's Equipment had been reduced to a low-tech general repair shop that was struggling to survive.

As Butch put it, "It was a case of two and two making four." The mechanic he sent to Salisbury from among the vets he had been helping happened to be the same age as MacPherson's son, and his presence had triggered renewed interest in the business on Clyde's part. The following years had seen everything from new paint and bigger parts inventories to new customers. Some of the old-timers thought it was a bit much when Clyde planted flowers around his street sign, but the final straw was when he took a day off in the middle of the week to put his bass boat in the water for the first time since '72.

Just a month before Jerry arrived on Butch Walton's doorstep, Clyde's mechanic decided to move back to Wisconsin and get married. So, Clyde was, as they say, an eager buyer when Butch introduced him to Chris Adams.

Jerry had hit the deck running. What's more, he was able to leverage his knowledge by having Dhong and Korem do the routine work on a lot of the jobs. John Deere and Massey Ferguson machines both had a few design quirks that kept him busy with the manuals over lunch and in the evenings, but that took care of time that might otherwise have been spent thinking about Virginia.

The other end of Jerry's daily commute was a two-bedroom bungalow about fifteen miles west of town, near Lake Norman State Park. It wasn't the house that had first appealed to him as much as the setting. There were miles of trails in the park and the house's ten-acre property would provide plenty of fuel for his wood stove. The clincher was a good view of the Great Smokies from his front porch. To him they were just an extension of the Blue Ridge, but he was careful not to put it that way when he complimented any locals on their piece of the Appalachians—locals like the woman who ran the little corner grocery where he often did his shopping.

"I think you must live alone, Mr. Adams," she said one day as she was ringing up his purchases.

"Yes, I do, actually," Jerry admitted, although he was afraid, he was being set up for a blind date. "How could you tell?"

"Well, if truth be known, you go through a lot of Spam and Dinty Moore stew!"

It had taken longer than he had expected to change the wheel bearings on the tractor that afternoon. That made for a long day at the end of a long week, and he was tired and dirty when he finally reached home. He stood in a hot shower for a few minutes and then pulled on a t-shirt and sweatpants before taking a beer out onto the front porch. Settling into one of the Adirondack chairs, he let the last of the day's strain drift off in the evening air.

*****

Back in Virginia the next morning, Karen returned to the market to meet David. She made a valiant effort to conceal her excitement by chatting with him as she picked a few decorative squash for a table arrangement and a half-dozen apples.

"These should be good for a pie, shouldn't they?" she asked.

"I believe so," David replied, thinking back to conversations he'd heard among those who knew about such things.

When he opened the shopping bag to pack her purchases, he held it low behind the counter at first and made sure she was watching as he placed the packet of letters in the bottom. When the packing was complete and she had paid for her purchases, he took the Snickers wrapper from his pocket and folded it with her receipt.

"Tell our friend that I won't be needing this anymore either," he said with a wink.

*****

Karen was too anxious to see what Jerry had written to wait until she reached home. She pulled into the parking lot at Martin's supermarket and struggled to reach down through the produce to retrieve the letters. Setting the old envelope aside, she opened the folded note.

> *Dear Karen,*
> *If you are reading this note, it means that you have decided to try to be with me. That means more to me than you can imagine, but before you go any further, I think you should know something about what happened in Vietnam. I know I did the right thing, but you need to hear that from someone else before you walk away from the life you've built with Ed and Joan.*
> *There are two letters in the enclosed envelope, one from an American missionary who became a good friend while I was in the highlands, and one from the chief of the Montagnard people I worked with. If, after you've read them, you still want to join me, I've put Paul Anderson's address at the bottom of the page. He'll be able to help you find me.*
> *One more thing: I'm sorry to have to ask you this, but it is important that you keep everything in this packet completely confidential. A lot more may depend on that than just our freedom.*
> *Be careful and be safe.*
> *I love you, Jerry.*

*****

At the Guersten farm that evening, Joan called to Ed from the kitchen.

"What's up?" he asked, coming into the room.

Without saying anything, she pointed out the window. Karen was standing by the incinerator in the back yard, feeding a fire from a sheaf of papers in her arm. From time to time her gaze followed sparks in the thin ribbon of smoke that drifted upward. Then she would return to staring at the flame in the barrel, its light reflecting on her face, as the ceremonial dismantling of her wall of clippings came to a close.

As the flame died down, Karen looked at the one piece of paper remaining in her hand, a recent clipping from the *Columbus Dispatch*.

The headline read:

GOVERNOR ACCEPTS RESIGNATION OF GUARD COMMANDER

The article went on to describe how the Adjutant General of the Ohio National Guard had become the subject of an FBI investigation following the discovery of a weapon and ammunition at a residence in suburban Columbus. During the inquiry, investigators also learned that the Adjutant General was a frequent visitor to that residence. The pattern of those visits, occurring as they did during the absence of the homeowner, raised questions of impropriety in relations between the Adjutant General and the wife of one of his senior officers. The general was not available for comment.

Folding the clipping, Karen put it in her pocket. "This one's for Jerry," she said, and headed back toward the house.

CHAPTER 38

Gingham curtains and matching tablecloths were a nice touch for the little restaurant near the park on Main Street where David took Linda for lunch the following Saturday. Its modest but credible German menu had earned it a steady clientele, a mix of local regulars and visitors who made the trip to Front Royal from somewhere around the Beltway. At times the favorable review in the *Washington Post* felt like a mixed blessing to the owner, but she had learned to take the appreciative and the pretentious in stride and keep her focus on the quality of her offerings.

Since David first approached Mrs. Bauer about sourcing some of her produce with the cooperative, the relationship had grown steadily and happily for everyone. She was pleased when she looked up to see him coming into the restaurant with Linda.

"Good afternoon, David," she said. "Welcome."

"Thank you, Hanna, and I'd like you to meet Miss Allen," he said, turning toward Linda.

"Hello, Miss Allen. So nice to meet you."

"Call me Linda, please. It's a pleasure to meet you, too, Mrs. Bauer. You have a charming place here."

"Thank you and, may I say, you're much better looking than the people David usually comes in here with."

"Well, I'm glad to hear that," Linda said, and they all laughed.

"I have a table I think you'll like," Hanna said, and smiled discreetly at David as she led the way to a table for two on the far side of the room.

When Hanna had seated them and returned to the reception area, Linda said, "You really have become part of this community, haven't you?"

"Yeah, I guess so," David answered. "There's something good about feeling like I belong. Not to get carried away, but it's like people care."

When they had met in the parking lot a few minutes earlier, he detected a hint of unease in her manner. Now that they were alone it surfaced again. A slight hesitation making eye contact, an awkwardness opening the menu, pages turned too quickly.

"How did you find things at the Inland Port?" he asked.

"About like the clients had reported. One company overstated its progress a bit, but nothing serious." There was a brief pause. "I'll have to take it up with them Monday morning." She seemed to be studying the menu. "Nothing serious."

David reached across the table and rested his hand on hers until she looked up at him.

"Is there something we need to talk about?" he asked.

To her credit, she didn't try to avoid the question. In fact, she seemed relieved as she began to speak.

"Yes, I... I guess there is."

Their waitress chose that moment to come to the table.

"You go ahead," Linda said, reopening the menu, "I haven't decided yet."

When the waitress left with their orders, silence returned as Linda collected her thoughts. Then she began, "I wonder sometimes if I crowd you when I come to the Valley."

"What do you mean?" he asked, suddenly worried about what might be coming. "I love it when you're here. Have I done something to upset you?"

"No, not at all. On the contrary, you're very sensitive and thoughtful. Maybe too much so."

"Now I'm lost," he said.

"I'm sorry. Let me see if I can explain. When we had lunch together last spring you talked about life being easier alone, and I can understand that. Hell, I've basically been alone, too, and I know what you mean. It's just that, now, when you are so attentive to me, I wonder if you're setting aside other parts of your life, putting me ahead of other things that are at least as much a part of who you are as I am—maybe more. You have a good life here—your friends, your work, the farm–and I don't want to take you away from that. I don't want you abandoning that and racing off to fight some fire in Linda Land every time you think you hear an alarm."

Even as he opened his mouth to launch a vehement denial, he knew she had put her finger on an issue.

Linda shook her head. "Please don't say anything. Just listen. We haven't used the word yet, but I know we love each other."

"Oh, yes, Linda. I do love you," he exclaimed, his smile celebrating the arrival of that word in their vocabulary.

Her eyes acknowledged what he had said without breaking her train of thought.

"And that's a wonderful place for us to be," she continued, "but only if it's not at the expense of the rest of you. That would be a fatal flaw in anything we ever tried to build together. I guess the question is whether you can take care of your own interests when I'm around. Can you pursue those interests, or do you get preoccupied with me and with us?"

David was glad their table was off to one side. She had raised something he had scarcely been willing to admit to himself, and he blinked to catch the tear that was trying to escape from each eye.

"Right now," he said, "I can't imagine life without you. But the fact is that I have learned that life alone is possible and, what's more, it would be a good life." He paused as she nodded her acknowledgement. "But I've also discovered these last few months that it's a different world when I share it with you. Color, harmony, pleasure—things come alive. If you give me the choice, I'll choose life with you every time."

Now it was Linda who touched her napkin to her eyes. Then she giggled.

"I remember thinking to myself, the day you walked into the student union at UVA, 'Here comes trouble.'"

"That obvious, huh?"

"Not really, but I knew even then that someday we'd be more than teaching assistants together."

"That's amazing. I was just intimidated. Here's this beautiful woman a semester ahead of me in the program, an experienced TA who walked on water as far as Dr. Dreifus was concerned. I probably stuttered."

"No, silly, you didn't. Your shyness was charming."

The waitress approached with their food, and they drifted happily in their own space until she had arranged the plates and left. Then, when the mustard had been passed and the first approving bites of their lunch were behind them, David spoke again.

"But you're right to ask that question about me. There's always the risk that I'll put other things in my life aside to get approval. I guess it's a reflex from church days. Let me tell you a secret. Scenes of the Garden of Eden don't show it, but there's a big scoreboard just off-camera, where you can always check and see how you're doing with the Big Guy."

Linda chuckled at the image.

"Just follow the rules," David continued, "and you're in. But in a world of values instead of rules, there's no scoreboard, and some of us are late learning how to operate that way."

Linda was intent on his words, but now she interrupted.

"I don't think I've ever met anyone who understands themselves as well as you do."

"Well, getting even this far has not been easy," David said. "Ray lit into me that I tried to be all things to all men. He was only wrong on one point. The biggest issue wasn't with men, it was with a woman."

"Diane, right?"

"Well, she was the subject at the time, but really it has been any woman who became important in my life."

"Speaking of your mother, I'd love to meet her sometime."

"Cute," David said, "but of course you're not wrong. It's embarrassing to be such a textbook case but, hey, at least it's out there where I can look at it now."

"I appreciate you putting this all in the past tense," Linda said, "but is it something that ever really goes away?"

"No. It will always be a risk with me, but I've seen the harm it can do, and I've seen how good life can be when I keep it in check. If we both keep an eye on it, there may be hope."

"I'm glad to hear that," Linda said, "because I have another question for you."

David furrowed his brow.

"There's more?"

"Do you think you could handle a little more of me in your world?"

"You mean without exploding with happiness?" he answered. "I don't know."

"Come on. Please be serious."

"OK, tell me what's going on."

"What would you think about me working full-time in the Valley?"

"That would be perfect," he said, "for me. But what would you do? I mean there aren't a lot of exciting jobs in banking around here."

"Well, Riggs has asked me to manage a new joint-venture branch in Winchester and that would include our clients in the Inland Port."

"That's fantastic! Congratulations. How long have you known?"

"They made me the offer yesterday."

"How come you didn't tell me last night?"

"I wanted to have this conversation first."

He looked at her in silence for a moment and then said, simply,

"I'm a very lucky man." Then he added, "And I know how you could make a little farmhouse in Browntown very happy, too."

"How's that?"

"By making it your home."

That moment was complete in itself. Neither of them noticed Hanna smiling at them from across the room.

CHAPTER 39

Weeks of clear days and cool evenings with their soft yellow light are the hallmark of autumn in the Piedmont. For millennia they have drawn men back from their seasonal wanderings to consolidate their gains and take shelter from the vagaries of the coming winter. In the quiet moments of this season the soul draws near to conscious thought and, given half a chance, will offer peace and fulfillment to even the most challenged existence.

The pieces of Jerry's life in North Carolina had begun to come together nicely. The wages he earned with MacPherson were nothing to write home about (even if he could) but they were more than enough for his needs. He took pride in the changes he could see from his work with Dhong and Korem, and his extra time and income had quietly begun to find their way into Butch Walton's projects with the Montagnards. It wasn't a formula he could ever have imagined, yet friendships and purpose had begun to dovetail nicely for him in the lee of the Smoky Mountains.

Reflections like that had only one drawback; they invariably left him longing for Karen, longing to share his day with her, to hold her and talk with her far into the night.

Sitting on the porch one evening, in what had become an important part of his day, he heard a sound that didn't fit into the usual chorus of the setting. A vehicle had turned off the road and was coming up the lane—a light truck, he guessed. As it emerged from the trees, he recognized Butch Walton's van with Butch at the wheel. It stopped at the gate, the passenger door swung open, and a woman got down. Leaning forward in his chair, he watched as she made her way up the path.

He would never be sure of how the process of recognizing Karen played out. He knew only that one moment she was the missing piece in his life and the next they were in each other's arms.

Walton waited several minutes before he approached to put Karen's suitcase on the porch. Then, as he turned to leave, he called over his shoulder, "By the way, I told Clyde you'd be late in the morning."

*****

When Jerry awoke the next morning, Karen was not in the bed beside him. More curious than concerned, he got up and found her sitting at the kitchen table. Her purse was open, the contents of her wallet spread out in front of her.

"Good morning," he said with a yawn. "Missing something?"

"No," she smiled, reaching for his hand. "I've found everything I want."

Their lips touched in a gentle, lingering kiss. Then, nodding in the direction of her purse she said, "Butch talked with me about changing my name. I'm pulling out everything with my old name on it."

"And tell me, then... who did I have the pleasure of sleeping with last night?"

With a scolding smile she replied, "My name is Andrea Keeler."

"Well, Miss Keeler, it was a very special pleasure to meet you."

"I was nervous," she said seriously. "It's so long since I've been close to anyone."

Jerry could tell this had been a real concern, so he replied more seriously. "Me, too. But I think we were great."

Her eyes were warm and smiling. He set about making coffee while she finished going through the items in her wallet.

"Butch took my driver's license and social security card," she said. "Somehow, he gets them turned into new ones in a few days."

"His connection in Fayetteville is a real artist," Jerry said. "My social security card looks like I've had it forever."

"What about how you feel?" she asked, and he could see that the idea of pretending to be someone else was troubling her.

"At first it's weird when somebody introduces you by that name," he answered, "or speaks to you, and you have to be paying attention to actually make the connection. But I decided it was like a nickname someone tagged me with, so once I learned to hear it, I didn't have any trouble relating to it."

"That's a good idea. I think that might work for me, too. Andrea Keeler beats The Egg Lady all to hell, anyhow."

Jerry chuckled. It was strange to see her confronting issues that had so recently been part of his own transition. Setting their coffee on the table, he concluded, "Just be careful for a while not to let the new name trip you up and, before you know it, it'll be as comfortable as an old pair of jeans."

An easy silence settled over the kitchen as they took the first sips of their coffee. Then he asked, "How did you handle things with Ed and Joan?"

"Not very well, I'm afraid, but after all they've done for me, I don't think there was any way to handle it well."

"Yeah, that's probably right."

"Thanks. You were supposed to say something reassuring, like 'I'm sure you handled it just fine.'"

"That, too. It's just that they love you and they'll miss you, not to mention all you did around the farm."

"That was the easy part to take care of. I made sure my helper was up to speed and I left the records and the schedules up to date." After a moment she laughed and added, "Poor Dennis, the driver for Krug's. When we'd finished loading their eggs, I threw my suitcase in his truck and climbed aboard. He was so nervous I thought he was going to have a stroke."

They had a good laugh, but Jerry was, all of a sudden, thinking about the FBI.

"How did you travel?" he asked.

"I caught a cab from Krug's warehouse in Harrisonburg to the Trailways depot, bought a ticket on the first bus going anywhere but south. To DC, as it turned out. Then I got off in Manassas instead and caught the next bus to Greensboro."

"That was some good thinking," Jerry said.

"Yeah, maybe, but the damned thing stopped at every town on Route 29. It took ten hours to go, what, three hundred miles? Then I called Paul Anderson. He put me up the night before last and then drove me to Butch's place yesterday."

"It's unlikely anybody would be able to trace that route."

"You mean your friends in the black sedan at the end of the driveway, right?"

"That's them."

"As we left the yard, I bent down and pretended to look for something in my suitcase. I'm sure Dennis must have thought I was nuts, but I don't think the boys in the sedan even knew I was gone for a while."

"Picking up all sorts of new skills, aren't you? That's what you get for keeping bad company." He hoped making light of her effort would help put her mind at ease as she began to adjust to life with him, but he was also relieved with what he had heard.

"Oh, I brought something I thought you might like to see," she said, reaching into her purse. She pulled out the clipping from the *Columbus Dispatch* and passed it across the table to Jerry.

"What's this," he asked.

"I don't know. I thought you might be able to tell me about it."

He read the article with no outward sign that he knew anything about the events it reported. After a few moments, he folded the paper again and passed it back to Karen. With a smile, he said simply, "It couldn't have happened to a nicer guy."

Karen knew not to ask him anything more about what he had just read. He wasn't going to reveal anything that she might later have to conceal. She took the paper from him, and he watched as she crumpled it and tossed it in the wood box next to the stove.

"I love you," she said.

After another sip of their coffee, Jerry said, "How about traveling with me today? I have to put in a few hours at the shop, and I'd like you to meet the guys I work with. Then I need to do some shopping for a 'do' this weekend."

"I'd love to. No time like the present to get into the routine."

"Come to think of it," Jerry said, "I've got a job for you."

"Oh. It's like that, is it?"

"The thing this weekend is with the Montagnards," he said, ignoring her quip. "It's their harvest festival."

"A little early to be having a harvest festival, isn't it?"

"Not in Vietnam, it isn't. That's just one of the changes they have to get used to here. Anyhow, they've invited the guys who've been working with them, too."

"You mean you, Butch, and his friends?"

"Yeah, and Paul Anderson and a few wives and girlfriends."

"That sounds really good. I want to meet everyone, especially the Montagnards."

"The trouble is, most of them escaped directly with the units they were attached to," he said, "so there are almost no wives or family members here with them, at least not yet."

"That's got to be tough."

"Yeah, in lots of ways, including the food department. The men aren't usually the cooks in a Montagnard family and, what's more, around here it's hard to find some of the ingredients they like. So, this party will be a sort of potluck. That's where you come in, if you're up to it."

"I make a mean macaroni salad, if that will help."

"I remember," Jerry said, pleased that a plan was taking shape to draw Karen into his new life. "That would be perfect."

The festival was short on traditional food and clothing but long on the sense of community that Jerry remembered from his days in the highlands. The mix of dishes included enough rice, exotic herbs, and fish sauce to say Southeast Asia if not central highlands. Some of the older men had even managed to produce quite a credible version of moom, their traditional brew. The source of the five-gallon buckets it was served from might have given pause to some, but Dhong and Korem were determined that their new friend Andrea would try the drink.

"It's not all that bad," she murmured to Jerry after a swallow of the cloudy substance, but then she made straight for the food table and helped herself to a serving of bitter melon.

She missed her new name a few times in conversation, but no one seemed to give it any thought. By the time afternoon had turned to evening she was part of the group, mixing and chatting easily. Jerry and Paul Anderson were talking about final arrangements for a shipment of clothing to a refugee camp in Thailand when they heard Karen's voice rise in laughter over the group she was with. Anderson nodded in her direction.

"You've got a real winner there, my friend."

As they were about to leave later that night, Dhong called out to Karen, "Remember, Andrea, you promised to come and look at my hens."

"OK, maybe I'll come with Chris tomorrow when he checks that pump."

"What was that about?" Jerry asked as they drove away into the darkness.

"Oh, he's got a small flock of layers and they aren't doing very well. I don't know what else I'll find, but it sounds to me like they need better ventilation. He's got them crowded between two sheds and there's apparently no shade."

"So, Andrea. Making yourself useful, huh?"

"Oh, Jerry, they're wonderful. If those guys are any indication of the people you knew in the highlands, it's no wonder you liked them."

In the weeks that followed, she began to help several of the Montagnards get better performance from their poultry. That soon led to a growing list of requests for her know-how in bookkeeping and management. In the evenings she was full of stories about the events of her day, and Jerry was delighted to see her old vitality returning. She had gradually added her own touch to the little house near Lake Norman. She was finding pleasure in her life with him, and her happiness stirred a sense of well-being in Jerry that he had never experienced.

One evening after their usual conversation over dinner, he set the dishes by the sink and looked around the room. She saw the smile in his eyes and waited for his thoughts to become words.

"Having you here makes this feel like home," he said.

She came over and wrapped her arms around him.

"Welcome home," she said, "wherever home is," and raised her face to meet his in a gentle kiss.

*****

The next afternoon they made a shopping run to Greensboro. Arriving in their regular shopping area, Jerry dropped Karen at the Lowes grocery store and headed for Sears and Roebuck to pick up some extra sockets for his tool chest. After a quick stop at the NAPA outlet, he was back in the lot at Lowes before she came out of the store.

When he saw her, he pulled over to the loading area and got out to help her with the bags. Coming around the rear of the truck, he came face to face with the headline in that evening's *Daily Record*, staring at him from a newspaper dispenser by the store entrance:

LOCAL POLICE JOIN SEARCH
FOR OHIO NATIONAL GUARD ATTACKER

It had been a long time since he had to manage sudden stress. The throbbing in his ears was strange. So, too, were the muffled sounds as he dropped the tailgate and pulled the shopping cart toward him. His own voice sounded distant as he said, "Go ahead and climb in. I've got this."

"Gladly," she replied. She hadn't noticed the headline.

He tried to keep things as normal as possible on the drive home, but his mind ricocheted among loose ends and contingency plans. He couldn't marshal his thoughts, and when Karen spoke to him, it seemed like he wasn't listening.

By the time they got the groceries put away, the adrenaline had burned off. Exhausted, he slumped into a chair at the kitchen table.

"What's wrong?" she asked, as she popped the top off a beer and set it in front of him. "You've been out of it since we started home. Are we OK?"

He looked up at her, disturbed by the question. "Yes," he said. "I'm sorry. We're fine. We're perfect. It's just that something's come up at the shop."

"Something we can talk about?"

"Yeah, maybe, but let me do some homework before I bother you with it."

That night, when he was sure Karen was sleeping soundly, he took the phone out onto the porch, closed the door carefully over the cord, and placed a call. After a half dozen rings, a sleepy voice answered.

"Butch," Jerry said, "it's me. I need to see you, man, first thing in the morning." Then he carefully set the receiver back on its cradle.

A passing breeze rustled the nearby oaks as he stared into the darkness, toward the distant mountains that, unseen, still defined this land. Two owls were having an insistent exchange over territory. The first drops of a welcome rain announced themselves on the porch roof.

He thought of other nights, other mountains; a water buffalo calling to her calf, the creak of a village handpump. The sounds were different, but they touched the same place in his heart. What was it Kpa had said?

"If we understand the mountains when we make our plans, our path will be good."

As he returned to their bed, Jerry knew the path Chris and Andrea would take.

EPILOGUE

NOVEMBER 2010

Linda came up the front steps of the house in Browntown with a bag of groceries and the afternoon mail. She didn't move as quickly as she once had, but the sense of purpose still showed in her gait. Walking past the study she called out, "Hi. I'm home."

"Good. What'd you bring me?" David replied, pushing his keyboard back and reaching for his cane to follow her toward the kitchen.

"You're incorrigible," she chuckled. "Just a couple of things we need for dinner." Then, putting the grocery bag on the counter, she asked, "Who do you know in Cambodia?"

"Nobody that I can think of."

"Well, you have a letter from the US Embassy in Phnom Penh," she said, holding an envelope out toward him. Then she turned back to the counter. "I'm going to go ahead and start dinner."

David looked at the envelope for a moment and then wandered out onto the back porch as he began to open it. Linda called after him,

"Remember, your granddaughter will want those stamps."

```
The Peace Corps, Office of the Director
#1, Street 96
Sangkat Wat Phnom,
Khan Daun Penh, Phnom Penh
```

November 14, 2010

Dr. David Williams
PO Box 423
Browntown, VA 22610

Dear Uncle David,

Greetings from Phnom Penh. I don't know whether Dad has mentioned it to you, but I was recently assigned here as Country Director, the latest move in a career I guess I can blame you for! After all, it was your stories of working with people in other countries that got this gangly kid thinking beyond borders and benefit packages when it was time for me to find a job. Now I have a story that I think you will enjoy.

Last week I went with a couple of our volunteers to Ratanakiri Province in the northeast of the country. Here the area is known as the eastern highlands but it's part of the same region that, in Vietnam, is called the central highlands. Our volunteers will be spending the next two years in the town of Banlung and I wanted to see for myself the conditions they'll be facing.

At least half the population is made up of Kmer Loeu, or what the French used to call Montagnards. Conditions are still rough, but there are signs that local leaders are starting to take the future of their communities seriously. I must say, I was very pleased with the reception our volunteers received.

Now here's the part I thought you'd find interesting:

While I was making the rounds with the volunteers, we were introduced to two Americans who have been living in Banlung for the last ten years. Chris Adams describes himself as a Vietnam veteran who decided not to return stateside after the war. The details are fuzzy on his first ten or fifteen years after the war, but he worked in the refugee camps in Thailand for a long time, helping Montagnards who had fled Vietnam. His partner, Andrea, was also a volunteer in the camps. I guess that's where they met.

David was puzzled briefly by the names, but when he recognized them as part of the plan Jerry and Karen must have adopted to cover their trail, he smiled warmly and continued to read:

As the camps closed in Thailand and things began to stabilize in Cambodia, they decided to move to Ratanakiri to work with the Kmer Leou. Many of them are Jarai, the same Montagnard people Chris had lived with in Vietnam during the war.

This is an amazing couple, Uncle David, and they are as happy as clams in their thatched roof bungalow on the edge of town. They are fluent in Kmer and Jarai, and there's a steady stream of friends and neighbors at their door. Chris has a workshop behind the house, where he repairs vehicles and small farm equipment and does some training. Andrea has a flock of good quality chickens that she says she uses to produce eggs for sale in the local market. I heard later, though, that she gives most of the eggs to families in the area to hatch and rear.

Anyhow, it caught Chris's attention that I was from Virginia, and when he found out my family was from Rappahannock County his eyes lit up.

"Maybe you know an old friend of mine," he said, and when I told him you were my uncle he was delighted. Apparently, you guys went to school together. He went off on a round of reminiscing that continued on and off for the rest of my time in Banlung.

The night before I left, the commune council hosted a meal for us, and Chris and Andrea were treated just like other senior members of the community. He sat at the table with the council and she moved back and forth with the other women between the reception area and the kitchen of the longhouse, keeping the food flowing.

Speaking in Jarai, Chris told a couple of stories about the two of you. One involved a bear and a ghost in the mountains, I think—something was lost in the translation. Then he held up a ladle of the local brew and proposed a toast to you.

I can tell you one thing for sure: if you ever visit Banlung you will be welcomed with open arms! As we were saying our goodbyes the next morning, Chris and Andrea asked me to give you their very best regards.

It was a pleasure to have that unexpected glimpse into your life as a young man, Uncle David. Perhaps the next time I'm transferred to DC you'll tell me more. I hope you and Aunt Linda are well and enjoying your retirement

With fondest regards,

Jacob

David smiled as he looked up from the letter. Evening shadows had crept over the fields near the house, but the mountains still glowed in the remains of an autumn sun.

THANK YOU FOR READING
THE PURPOSE BREAKS

If you enjoy the Two Roads Home books by
James G. Brown please post a review & tell a friend.

ALSO WRITTEN BY
JAMES G. BROWN

Two Roads Home

From the shadow of the Blue Ridge Mountains to Vietnam and the front lines of the American experience in the 1960s and 70s, *Two Roads Home* is a historical fiction series of standalone novels, intertwined tales of personal struggle told with grit and sensitivity.

The Morning Side

Fletcher's War

Out of Eden

The Purpose Breaks

#TwoRoadsHome #BairInkBooks
#JamesGBrown

ABOUT THE AUTHOR

James G. Brown was raised in the Ottawa Valley of Eastern Canada. He studied at McGill and the University of British Columbia before moving to the Washington D.C. area with his young family in 1971 to join the World Bank. His career in economic development, particularly agriculture and rural finance, over the ensuing 45 years took him to developing countries around the world.

In the late 1990s Jim and his wife Camilla settled on a small farm at the foot of the Blue Ridge Mountains. He continued to work in international development but living in this rural setting became an important counterpoint to the hectic world of air travel, head offices and crowded marketplaces.

Currently an adjunct professor of international development policy at the George Washington University, Jim has published books in the field of agroindustry and rural development and articles on life in rural Virginia.

The Purpose Breaks is the fourth and concluding novel in James G. Brown's *Two Roads Home Series*.

Made in the USA
Las Vegas, NV
23 February 2024